HOPE'S SUNRISE

JOHN GARY LONG

Dedication

This book belongs, first and foremost, to my wife Lisa — my best friend, my constant champion, and my 'good thing'. Her steady, unwavering encouragement was the vital force behind this manuscript, urging me forward to pursue my dreams even when the path seemed uncertain. She is, quite simply, my dream come true.

To my children, Sarah and John 2.0. You are the best parts of my 'here and now,' and you remind me daily of the wonders and possibilities in this world. Your bright, illuminating lights inspire every word I put to page and every ambitious path I follow.

To my parents, Johnnie and Jewelene, who gave me my first lessons in what matters: the importance of family above all else, and the dignity of hard, consistent effort. I dedicate this book to the foundation you built.

And finally, to the only One who is able to keep us from falling—for the grace, strength, and grounding faith throughout this entire journey.

HOPE'S SUNRISE

Chapter 1
Warning Dream

Hope sat bolt upright, the piercing scream dying in her throat. The bonnet that had protected her silk press was now cold and damp against her scalp from sweat, as the phantom taste of pills and the sickening memory of Caleb's confession still haunted her. Seven years ago, in the dim light of her hospital room, weakened from a week of treatment, he had delivered the venomous words: "It's over," followed by a second poison, "I'm with Rachel now." Her world had imploded. Later that night, after being discharged to go home alone to her apartment, she swallowed every pill she could find.

But tonight, the dream she had been having every night for the past month was different. The pills were in Rachel's hand, her face twisted in anguish. Hope saw the same desperation she had felt seven years ago mirrored in her sister's eyes. The nightmare replayed her suicide attempt, only now Rachel was in her place. It was a horrifying premonition that Caleb would destroy her sister's world as he had hers. This was no longer just a memory of betrayal; it was a warning—a deep, bone-chilling fear that Rachel's life was a ticking time bomb.

Hope felt around for her phone on the nightstand, the bright screen a jolt in the pitch-black darkness. The power had gone out again, a familiar occurrence during Houston's stormy season. She looked out the window as the cloudy sky blocked the moon and stars, creating a void of nothingness.

"Of course, another power outage," she muttered. The Texas grid strikes again."

She squinted, confirming the time: 3:15 a.m. The thought that she had at least an hour of restless, heart-pounding wakefulness ahead of her was a heavy burden. She didn't just want the fear to diminish; she yearned for simple, quiet peace—the kind that comes with sharing a bed and the safety of knowing someone won't leave.

A new, more pressing anxiety settled over her as the initial terror of the nightmare began to fade. It was Sunday. And today, she would see Caleb and Rachel for the first time in years. Initially, her resolve to go was rooted in defiance—they would not force her to leave her spiritual home. But now, it was about Rachel. Hope was no longer going to be a coward. She was going to save her sister's life.

Chapter 2
Inciting Announcement

"*Y*ou better get right before you get left!" Pastor Caleb Moore exhorted, his voice thundering through the Sea of Galilee Church.

The cavernous sanctuary buzzed with near-capacity attendance, a testament to its new leader. Parishioners raised their hands in affirmation, and deacons rose to their feet, echoing the fervor. No Black church in America can resist a well-executed "Take Them to the Cross" sermon finale.

With Big Preach's retirement, the church transitioned to the youthful and charismatic Pastor Caleb Moore. His background as a former NFL player and sports icon contributed to his widespread appeal. Pastor Caleb's contemporary sermons, blending video clips with powerful oratory, drew large crowds at his previous church in Dallas and resulted in explosive growth in both membership and financial contributions. He now commanded the pulpit of the storied Sea of Galilee Church in the heart of Houston. The sanctuary, with its vaulted ceilings and ornate stained-glass windows, easily accommodated the devoted crowd of 2,200. Richly carved pews and a grand pulpit bathed in warm, golden light gave the space an air of reverence and timeless dignity.

Hope, seated near the front with arms folded and eyes heavenward, couldn't fathom how Caleb's performance could sway anyone. Her patience had reached its limit. As he delivered his impassioned sermon, she internally quipped, *When will this fiery ordeal end? Even Meshach, Shadrach, and Abednego would be reduced to cinders.* She silently prayed, *Please, someone rescue them and me!*

Drawing his sermon to a close, Caleb prepared for his customary, energetic finale. The first lady, watching from the second row of the lower bowl of seats, knew the announcement was imminent. His sermon ended with a mighty, gospel-infused flourish.

Hope, who was the team leader for the church's sign language ministry, replaced the previous signer and took her position on the front stage, far left of the pulpit. Dressed in the sign language ministry's required black attire, she faced the small gathering of hearing-impaired parishioners in the corner pews, grateful she'd been spared signing Caleb's drawn-out message. She was even more grateful that the stage was large enough so Caleb was over thirty-five feet away from her. It wasn't until she was in the same room with him that she remembered how much she loathed that man.

"My entire life, I believed I was defined by the game," Caleb said, passionately addressing the congregation. "My identity was forged in touchdowns, tackles, and the roar of the crowd. But then, an injury took it all away. I was broken, lying in a hospital bed, watching the clock tick on a life I thought was over. But in the silence of that room, I learned something important. The years of pain, the long nights of practice, the sweat and struggle—they weren't about making me a champion on the field. They were about making me a man of God. That suffering didn't define who I was in that moment; it was preparing me for the man I was meant to become."

Hope commanded her eyes not to roll and kept a blank face as she signed his words. The congregation drank in his words like a man lost in the desert for days, finally consuming a cold drink of water.

Caleb called for silence. "Brothers and sisters, I have joyous news," he announced. "We are expecting a blessed addition to our family. Our first lady is pregnant."

A thunderous roar of victory echoed through the congregation. Hope stood frozen, her mind blank, unable to process the announcement, let alone sign it. The words struck her with the force of a physical blow, leaving her breathless. A wave of intense nausea welled up in her throat, and she pressed a trembling, cold hand against it, desperately trying to contain the rising tide of emotion. This was a different scenario from her nightmare, even more than she had feared. Emotional whiplash seized her. The terror of Caleb's baby growing inside Rachel was instantly compounded by a deep, hollow hurt and blinding, familiar anger.

Caleb, wearing a suit tailored to the millimeter, reveled in the congregation's worship, soaking up their love like a parasite. He scanned the crowd, his eyes finding Hope's piercing glare. He offered a fleeting smirk before returning his attention to the adoring masses. He avoided her gaze, knowing she saw through his pious persona. She saw the real Caleb, the manipulator destined to shatter Rachel.

The sight of Hope brought Rachel to Caleb's mind, and he signaled for her to stand. Rachel's heart hammered against her ribs. Rachel needed Caleb to solidify this reality, to confirm that this public victory was truly hers. The baby was supposed to be her ticket out of Hope's shadow and a guarantee of status, but a flicker of doubt gnawed at her: *Is this going to solve anything, or just multiply the lies?*

Rachel rose, her pageant-style wave a practiced motion. With her dark brown skin, high cheekbones, perfectly crafted braids in an intricate updo, and tall, statuesque frame, she exuded the air of a Nubian queen. She appreciated the crowd's attention but didn't share Caleb's insatiable appetite for it. The intensity of being the first lady was still something she was adjusting to.

Rachel's gaze fell upon Hope's grimacing face on the stage. The timing of their announcement struck her with sudden, sharp clarity; she could almost feel her sister's trembling hands and the overwhelming weight of her sorrow. Rachel's rehearsed smile, a mask of composure, concealed a flood of dreadful thoughts: *No, this can't be happening. I've done it to her again.*

"Yes, this is truly wonderful. We will be registered at Nordstrom's for all of you who want to show your love toward the first family," Pastor declared.

The taste of bile burned in Hope's mouth, a stark reminder of her trapped feeling. She seethed at the pastor's exploitation of his flock and her sister. Knowing she was moments from being physically ill, she motioned for someone to replace her as the ASL signer. She used the distraction of the standing ovation to flee quickly via the stage wings.

* * *

After emptying her stomach, Hope rushed from the stall to the sink, desperate to escape the church. As she vigorously lathered her hands, a lone figure entered the ladies' room.

"Isn't the baby news just marvelous?" a woman cackled, her voice a cruel caricature of delight.

Hope's eyes narrowed in the mirror, her body going on high alert. There was only one person whose voice could have that effect on her. Refusing to turn around, she watched her mother, Gina, through the reflection—a well-toned figure in a form-fitting pastel dress, adorned with pearls and diamonds.

"Honestly, I was taken aback myself. Me, a grandmother? I never imagined it," Gina remarked, her eyes searching Hope's reflection, not her face.

Hope turned from the sink, drying her hands, and advanced swiftly toward Gina. The older woman instinctively braced herself for a confrontation, but Hope veered away at the last second, slipping past her and out the door. Gina's fake smile dissolved into a venomous snarl, her mind already conjuring ways to make Hope pay for the slight.

Chapter 3
Digital Sleuth

Sunday night was always the quietest time, a sanctuary of stillness Hope had perfected since the world went dark. But tonight, the stillness felt suffocating. The announcement from the pulpit—Caleb's joyful declaration that Rachel was pregnant—replayed in her mind like a broken record.

On the wall opposite her desk hung a print of the striking painting "The Ascending Woman" by an acclaimed African American social activist. The subject, a woman with wings made of light, rose from a field of thorns. It was Hope's professional north star, a constant reminder of her own mission to help young women rise above their struggles.

Hope looked at Nelson, her faithful border collie, who sat patiently at her feet, his head tilted in question.

"A baby, Nelson," she murmured, the words feeling bitter on her tongue. "He's going to hurt her, and now he's going to hurt an innocent child, too. I cannot and will not allow that."

She had built a fortress around her heart, convinced

that to love was a weakness Caleb had already exploited once. Her relationships with men were strictly transactional, designed to fulfill her carnal desires or acquire gifts, but nothing more. Yet, she silently admitted to herself that these indulgences always left her craving something meaningful. She was afraid to trust another person, but the gnawing emptiness proved that the fortress was only a shell, and deep down, she longed for the simple peace she'd lost.

Sliding her glasses up the bridge of her nose, Hope's fingers danced over her laptop's keyboard in a familiar, furious rhythm. She was a master of back channels and public records, now using her skills for a personal crusade. She started with the basics: scrolling through Caleb's social media, which consisted of a gallery of perfect smiles, curated sermons, and flawless selfies. His polished appearance only fueled her frustration; he was so skilled at seeming perfect.

Hours melted away as the screen's harsh light illuminated the files. A single emerald-eyed woman's face kept appearing in the background of Caleb's posts whenever he traveled away from Dallas. Hope managed to put a name to the face: Twila Gooden.

The investigation narrowed. Twila's social media check-ins perfectly mimicked Caleb's travel schedule to the city. Hope's pulse quickened. Her certainty grew when she saw a comment on a recent post: *So great seeing you today, Pastor.*

The sickening wave of confirmation washed over her as the puzzle pieces clicked into place, leaving her hands so cold the keyboard felt hot. Twila was not just a fan; the digital breadcrumbs were too perfectly aligned. Hope was convinced they were having an affair.

It was nearly three o'clock in the morning. Hope stared at the screen; the evidence was a cold, hard fact. She had to tell Rachel. But how? Their relationship was a brittle thing, broken by years of silence and hurt. Rachel would never believe her, not with a baby on the way. The task seemed impossible, but the alternative—letting Caleb ruin Rachel's life, too—was a nightmare she couldn't bear to live through again.

Chapter 4
Nelson to the Rescue

Hope didn't fall asleep until well past 4:00 a.m. She struggled to get up, but Nelson, as always, was insistent on his morning walk. Hope pulled herself out of bed, got them ready for their walk, and they headed out the door. However, their usually peaceful stroll was shattered by a desperate cry.

"Deuce, STOP!"

The shout was sincere, but the roar of a muscle car's engine swallowed the alarmed father's cries.

Hope saw the car first—a blur of reckless speed on a quiet park road. Then she noticed the little boy, no older than four, running toward the street, his head turned back as he laughed at a small Chihuahua. Her heart seized in her chest. She watched the father sprint toward his son, his face a mask of raw, agonizing terror. She knew he wouldn't make it in time. The boy was just steps from a fatal collision.

It was instinct. Hope dropped Nelson's leash, gestured toward the child with her hand, and gave the command, "Nelson, go get!"

In a flash of black fur and muscle, Nelson was a blur, intercepting the boy just shy of the curb. Her loyal companion, doing what he was bred to do, gently but firmly herded the child away from the danger. The boy tumbled onto his rear, startled but safe. The muscle car's tires screeched as the driver slammed on his brakes. The boy was okay.

As the commotion settled, Justin, the boy's father, clutched his precious son tightly against his chest, then turned to look at Hope. His eyes were filled with relief and deep gratitude. Hope gave Nelson a well-earned treat and a gentle pat on the head.

Justin approached her, his voice thick with emotion. "Thank you...and him," he said, "for saving my son's life. I don't want to think about what would have happened if you hadn't been here."

A warm, dimpled smile appeared on Hope's face as she replied, "No need to thank him. He's just doing what he's bred to do. His telepathy in knowing what I want is innate, but it still surprises me."

Justin nodded affirmatively toward Nelson before turning to his son. "This little daredevil's name is Justin, just like mine. I'm his dad." Justin offered his hand. "I call him Justin 2.0, as he's the upgrade. Deuce for short."

Hope shook his hand. "It's nice to meet both of you, Justin and Deuce, the upgrade."

Hope's attention was drawn to Justin's hands when their palms met. They were strong and calloused, a testament to physical labor, yet his fingernails were meticulously manicured. She looked up at the 6'3" walnut-skinned man and met his warm, light brown eyes. His smile was sparkling perfection, and for a moment, her curiosity overshadowed her caution. She sensed his palpable relief, a warmth that seemed to promise safety and kindness.

"Do you visit the park often?" he asked, bringing her back to the present.

She gently pulled her hand away.

"Yes, I walk Nelson here every morning," she said, a faint smile on her face. "It's a lovely park. Border collies need at least an hour of walking a day, so circling this pond is a beautiful way to burn his energy."

"I've been here several times, but usually in the evening with Deuce. Is there any way I can show you how grateful I am?" Justin pleaded, his hand over his heart.

That's when Hope noticed the wedding ring on his finger, and her growing curiosity turned into cold familiarity. The possibility of a pure connection imploded. She was standing in front of a married man, a line she would not cross.

"No, I can't think of anything," Hope replied, her voice devoid of emotion.

Justin's attention returned to his son. "Alright then, I'd better get him home. Thanks again."

Justin walked away while whispering to his son, his words filled with a love that made Hope ache for a world she couldn't have. He then looked up at the sky, his eyes briefly meeting hers before speaking to what seemed to be an invisible presence.

"Thank you, God, for saving my son, but don't think this makes us even, not by a long shot."

The words were a quiet, defiant confession, and Hope was left to wonder about the secrets behind his perfect smile.

Chapter 5
Unanswered Call

A blend of dread and fragile hope kept Rachel's gaze glued to her phone. She wished for this call to start a reconciliation, a bridge spanning the deep chasm of abandonment she'd never understood.

She pressed the call button, resolving to hang up if it went to voicemail. To her dismay, the call was sent to voicemail after only two rings. It was a clear, deliberate forwarding—a silent rejection. She had anticipated a few more rings and a longer pause before hearing the prompt to leave a message.

Rachel squeezed the phone, the cold plastic reflecting the familiar ache in her chest. Every birthday, every holiday, every pageant—she was forever the daughter waiting by the phone. She longed for his proud voice, the simple reassurance that Hope always seemed to receive without effort.

The "leave a message" announcement was curt, and the beep followed almost immediately.

"Hi, Dad. It's me," she began, her voice a strained

whisper. "Umm, Rachel, your youngest daughter."

She cringed inwardly at the stilted, awkward phrasing. Of course, he knew who was calling.

"I hope Alejandra and the boys are doing well," she continued, her voice tinged with nervous energy. "It's been quite a while since we last spoke, and I have some news I thought you should know." She paused, then, unable to contain her growing excitement any longer, she blurted out, "I'm pregnant! Yes, Dad, you're going to be a grandpa!"

With her heart pounding, she reflexively waited for a moment of joyful affirmation. Still, the cold, empty silence of the voicemail served as a stark and painful reminder of their strained relationship.

"Uh, yeah, Dad," she mumbled, her voice losing its earlier enthusiasm, "I just thought you should know. Call me if you like. Alright, bye." Her voice trailed off, each word fading into a hollow, defeated whisper—a futile invitation, as she knew deep down that he wouldn't return her call.

Chapter 6
Give a Dog a Bone

Webb Park provided the perfect setting for Hope and Nelson's daily stroll. The morning was idyllic. As they entered the park, she spotted a familiar, handsome figure. The low cut, tight-faded head and powerful physique belonged to Justin, who stood by a picnic table with a bag in hand. He gave a subtle wave, and a pleasant jolt of surprise traveled through her. Changing course, she headed straight toward him.

"Mr. Justin," Hope teased, a smile playing on her lips, "are you following me?" She added playfully, "You should know Nelson is quite the protector and a fierce one at that."

Nelson trotted over to Justin as if on cue, sniffing and enthusiastically licking his hand. Justin knelt, petting him with both hands around his face and head.

"I see. I better be careful. Killer here might lick me to death," Justin joked, looking up at Hope.

She observed that his eyes, which were previously a solid brown, now held a mesmerizing hazel hue with glints of green. She felt an almost hypnotic pull, as if she was being drawn into their depths.

"And to address your question, no, I'm not stalking you," Justin responded, breaking the spell. "You mentioned your daily walks with your heroic companion. I wanted to give him a small token of my appreciation for his actions yesterday."

"Oh, that's not necessary," Hope replied, her habitual suspicion kicking in. She was always cautious of people's motives.

"Please, I'd really like to give him this," Justin insisted, pulling a clear plastic container with a red lid from his bag. Inside, a cooked roast beef bone, still generously covered with meat and fat. "Leftovers from last night's dinner. It was so delicious I almost ate it all myself. But I saved some for your heroic companion. I must warn you, though, it will unleash the inner wolf in any dog."

As he spoke, his left thumb instinctively rubbed the smooth gold on his ring finger, a quiet, almost invisible tick.

Hope was momentarily taken aback, rendered speechless by the sheer thoughtfulness of the gift. As she reached for the container, the glint of his wedding ring snapped her back to reality. She mentally scolded herself for engaging in such a lengthy conversation.

Meanwhile, Nelson, drawn by the irresistible aroma of the meat, looked at Justin with his tail held high and wagging eagerly. Hope's instincts were in a state of genuine conflict—her heart wanting to accept the kindness, her mind demanding caution.

"Thank you," she managed, a warm smile spreading across her face as she accepted the gift. "Nelson will certainly enjoy this breakfast. I, on the other hand, have a terrible habit of skipping it on workdays."

Justin's gaze was drawn to her dimples. He felt a surge of boldness, a desire to ask for her phone number. But then, Hope, unwilling to let her suspicion lie, let her voice sharpen into a knowing smirk.

"So," she inquired, her voice laced with playful sarcasm, "who should I be thanking for the roast beef? You or your wife?"

Justin took a slight step back, his breath catching in his throat. His right hand instinctively twisted the wedding ring on his left finger. It took a moment for the realization to sink in: Hope was keeping her distance because of the ring he still wore. He exhaled slowly, a tinge of vulnerability in his voice, and his eyes dropped briefly, a flicker of grief passing before his focus returned to the present.

"Actually, my mother made the roast beef. She lives with my son and me. My wife passed away just over two years ago. I apologize. I know the ring can be misleading. I wear it out of habit, I guess." He lowered his head, his gaze falling to his shoes.

Hope's heart plummeted, and a chill spread through her. Her smirk evaporated, leaving a face contorted with embarrassment. "I'm terribly sorry. I didn't mean to be so insensitive."

"Please, it's not your fault at all. I didn't intend to cause any confusion. Really, there's no need to apologize."

An awkward silence descended upon them, the air thick with unspoken words. Justin searched desperately for a smooth way to change the subject. Mercifully, Nelson broke the spell. The dog, his focus fixed on the delicious bones, jumped up and placed his paws on Hope's chest.

"Alright, down you go," Hope said, a grateful laugh in her voice as she gave Nelson's leash a gentle tug. "We'd better get going. If we don't leave now, he might turn into a full-fledged wolf. Thank you again for the treat."

As Hope and Nelson turned to leave, Justin tried to salvage the moment, but his mind went frustratingly blank. All he could muster was a weak, "You're welcome. Have a good day."

They parted ways, each feeling the regret of a missed opportunity, like a fumbled winning lottery ticket slipping through their fingers.

Chapter 7
Little Sister #2

Hope's gaze was fixed on Esther's hands, her mind working to interpret the flurry of signs. Although Hope was proficient in ASL, Esther's animated delivery was challenging to keep up with. Amira, having lived her entire twelve years in a deaf environment, followed with ease.

Sensing Hope's struggle, Amira translated, "Mom is overjoyed for Rachel. A baby is such wonderful news, and you'll be an aunt! What do you think it will be, a boy or a girl? You must be so excited for your sister."

Esther paused, her face filled with anticipation. Hope's instinct was to conceal her revulsion.

With a practiced smile, she signed and said, "A baby is always a blessing from God."

She fought in her usual mental battle, hiding her true feelings—she would rather Rachel have a child with a warthog than with Caleb.

Esther signed, "Indeed, it is a blessing from God."

Hope's proficiency in sign language was the key to her connection with Amira through the Big Sisters program. Amira's family resided in a beautifully decorated duplex, its walls a gallery showcasing Amira's life from her first moments to her many junior theatre productions. The tangible love within the household and the adoration they showered upon Amira always filled Hope with a sense of wonder. Amira seemed to receive more affection in a single day than Hope had ever experienced from her mother or father in an entire year.

As soon as Hope arrived, Amira was eager to leave.

"We need to go," Amira said, her voice full of anticipation. "The movie's starting in thirty minutes!"

Hope and Amira were excited to see the latest dystopian film. They were both captivated by stories of survival and resilience, where characters fought to overcome adversity—a theme that mirrored their lives.

"You're going to scream again when the Mutts attack," Amira teased, her smile widening with mischief.

Hope laughed and gave Amira a playful nudge. "I will not! But you have to admit, they are scary. They look exactly like the people they killed! That's just wrong." Hope then turned her attention to Esther and, using both verbal and sign language, said, "I'll have her home by ten o'clock."

Esther, a skilled lip reader, appreciated the effort and practice. "You can keep her," Esther signed, attempting a lighthearted joke despite her well-known struggles with humor.

Hope and Amira left, heading to the cinema. Hope always enjoyed her time with Amira, a highlight of her week. She often reflected on the ease of their relationship—a pure, uncomplicated sisterhood compared to the fractured, high-maintenance communication she had with her blood sister, Rachel.

Chapter 8
Justin's Business Troubles

"I'm not expecting any breakthroughs today," Ms. Kym said, her tone characteristically straightforward.

Justin often felt like he was being lectured. Though petite, Ms. Kym had a commanding presence, and Justin always felt compelled to sit to avoid the impression of looming over her.

"I'm confident we have a solid argument," Justin countered, leaning back in his creaking chair. "I'd be surprised if the commission denied the easement extension." He sat behind his vintage metal desk, a relic of the 70s, acquired cheaply from a corporate moving sale.

"It's a complete waste of my time to have to deal with this," Ms. Kym declared. "The previous owners operated a repair shop here for twenty years. Now, the county is systematically eliminating all 'mixed' zoned areas, and our space is a target."

"Perhaps you should consult with an attorney?" Hank suggested from his corner, a voice of unexpected concern.

"Do you have a spare lawyer lying around that you could lend me?" Ms. Kym retorted.

"If the commission rules against you, I'll be forced to relocate my business, and you'll lose my rental income," Justin reminded her, stating the obvious.

"This hasn't been a residential garage for three decades! It's a fully operational business," Ms. Kym countered, detailing every point she intended to present to the commission.

With her arguments rehearsed, Ms. Kym departed.

"Are you worried about Ms. Kym's case?" Justin asked, following up on Hank's unusual comment, his half-smile attempting to mask his anxiety.

"I don't worry, just concerned. I enjoy working here," Hank stated.

Justin's heart had been pounding since Ms. Kym informed him of the county's letter. He knew relocating would triple his rent, forcing him to close. Closing meant destroying a future he wanted to build for his son—a future where his son could be proud of his father.

"If you go out of business, I'll have to put in more hours driving for Uber," Hank added. "An old man like me can't sit in a driver's seat for eight to twelve hours a day."

Hank always referred to himself as an old man when talking in the shop. He worked for twenty-three years as an electrician at the now-closed engine plant. In his three years working for Justin, he had been Justin's best and most reliable employee. Justin always wondered why Hank hadn't opened his own shop, but he never asked, fearing Hank might do it.

"Hey, have you heard from Akil?" Justin asked him.

"Yeah, he texted me and said he had to go by Owens'

Supplies and get a belt for McDuff's air conditioner. It was just last year I replaced that belt for McDuff," Hank responded, a bit frustrated.

"I know we've been using some of the cheaper replacement parts. When the cash flow improves, so will the quality of our parts," Justin said with a shrug.

"You already know what I think. Quality parts now will pay off in the long run," Hank said in senior counselor mode.

Justin responded curtly, "And you know I agree, but if we don't save money now, there will be no long run."

Hank, one never to go back and forth, returned to his motor. Then, without looking up from his work, he added, "By the way, I think the kid is going to be all right."

Justin couldn't help but smile. He knew those simple words were a glowing endorsement from Hank. When he first interviewed Akil, Hank was concerned by his long braids and tattoos. Hank couldn't picture a man with long, braided hair working hard. Justin was a bit concerned, too. But Akil was eager and willing to work for a few dollars above minimum wage, a price Justin couldn't afford to refuse. Justin was happy that his investment in Akil was paying off because he had little room for error in his fledgling business.

Justin's smile faded as his mind shifted to Ms. Kym's hearing that day. She just had to get the easement extended. If she didn't, Justin would lose the business he'd built—a business that was his chance for his son to be proud of him and believe his dad was a good man. He considered saying a quick prayer, but then thought, *Why waste my time praying? God hates me.*

Chapter 9
Forbidden Fruit

The hot shower washed away the grime and mental haze from the flight. Long, cleansing showers were Caleb's post-travel ritual. He turned off the water, ready for the next task on his agenda.

While toweling off in the hotel bathroom, Caleb paused to admire his physique in the mirror. Maintaining a body fat percentage below 7% was a point of pride, a symbol of the self-mastery he preached. He viewed his physical discipline as essential to his ministry how could he lead thousands if he couldn't even control his own body? His surgically repaired knee was no obstacle; he planned a 5:30 a.m. workout even on this Denver trip for a church convention.

As Caleb stepped into the suite, clad only in a towel, he halted suddenly. Emerald eyes met his, belonging to a stunning, nude woman holding a bright red apple. He felt an immediate, undeniable attraction to her.

She smiled slyly and asked, "Do you want to take a bite?"

"Don't you think you could be a little subtler than using an apple?" Caleb asked, taking a step towards her.

Tilting her head back, she placed her left hand on her thigh, extended the apple with her right hand, and repeated, "Do you want a bite?"

Caleb moved forward, taking the apple into his hand. "Twila, I would love to take a bite."

He looked at her, and a simple, narcissistic justification crossed his mind: *I am focused on my mission. A leader this committed deserves to be refueled.* He believed his indulgence was the reward for carrying the burdens of the church.

He dropped his towel and took a bite of the forbidden fruit.

Chapter 10
Breakfast for the Park

*J*ustin peered into the shopping bag again, a small ritual to reassure himself that the contents were still there. Sitting at the picnic table, his mind was a whirlwind of scripted lines and possible conversations, each one rehearsed and then discarded. He had a restless night, his thoughts a tangled knot of her face, her laugh, her dog. Today, he was determined to make it right, to erase the fumbled ending of yesterday's conversation.

"I thought you assured me you weren't stalking me," Hope said, catching Justin off guard.

She had approached from behind, using a different path. Justin's carefully rehearsed opening lines were rendered useless.

"Well, any self-respecting stalker would say, 'No, I'm not stalking you. I just happen to be where you are all the time,'" he replied, flashing a charming smile.

"Oh, I'm a complete novice when it comes to being stalked," Hope said, her tone playful. "Shouldn't there be roses delivered to my office? Or perhaps some extravagant gifts?"

Their playful exchange had successfully broken the ice.

"Yes, ma'am. Coincidentally, I have a rather extravagant gift right here for you." Justin gestured towards the nearby bench.

Hope raised an eyebrow as she took a seat. "By all means, lavish away."

Without a word, Justin reached into the shopping bag and pulled out a large, reversible placemat, placing the solid blue side up. Next, he offered Hope a small bottle of hand sanitizer. She watched as he arranged a paper plate, plastic utensils, and a bright red apple.

"An apple a day keeps the doctor away," he quipped, then added a bran muffin.

Hope couldn't suppress a quick, involuntary laugh. She watched him work, a small, professional assessment forming in her mind: his movements were confident, his actions organized, and his motives seemed pure—but Caleb had been organized, too.

Never trust the performance, she reminded herself.

Justin poured freshly squeezed orange juice from a small thermos, then revealed another thermos and a mug.

"How do you take your coffee?"

Hope, who had switched to tea two years prior, was so touched by his thoughtfulness that she couldn't bring herself to tell him.

"A little milk and no sugar," she replied, a small lie slipping out.

Justin poured the coffee and set it next to the plate.

"Ms. Hope, breakfast is the most important meal of the day. When you said you usually didn't have breakfast, I decided to fix that today. So, here is your breakfast. And don't tell me you don't have time to eat. I will walk Nelson so that you do." That all came out precisely as Justin had rehearsed. "Oh, and one more thing. Here's my driver's license as collateral until I bring Nelson back."

Hope studied his body language, searching for signs of impatience or a performance mask she'd seen in other men, but found only sincere, hopeful earnestness. *Who is this guy?* she wondered, and her heart replied, *I don't know, but I like him.*

"This is remarkably thoughtful. Thank you," Hope said, her voice filled with genuine appreciation, her smile radiating warmth. She consciously fought the urge to quiz him about his day.

Justin took hold of Nelson's leash, and the well-behaved dog readily followed Justin's lead. Hope watched them stroll away, trying to push aside thoughts of her busy day. She wanted to savor the peaceful moment Justin had created. She put in her earbuds, letting Jill Scott's poetry wash over her as she sipped her juice and ate her muffin.

When she finally opened her eyes, Justin was patiently waiting with Nelson.

"I'm running late. Thank you so much for the breakfast. I'll save the apple for later," she said, her voice hurried.

"You're very welcome," Justin replied. "Before you go, could you give me your phone number? I'd like to call you sometime."

His considerate approach took Hope by surprise.

"Well," she said, a playful smile forming, "I know you stalker types are quite persistent. You'd probably find it anyway. So, yes."

Although Hope's stalker comments made Justin somewhat uneasy, he was willing to overlook them to get her phone number. He pulled out his phone, carefully entered the number she recited, then pressed the call button to confirm it was correct. Her phone immediately lit up.

"Thank you," he said, his voice laced with boyish enthusiasm.

"No, thank you for breakfast and walking Nelson. Talk to you later," Hope replied, then turned and quickly headed back to her house with Nelson by her side.

"Mission accomplished," Justin thought, a sense of quiet satisfaction washing over him.

He had successfully gotten her phone number, and the conversation had stayed free of awkward mentions of his late wife. He momentarily wished he could celebrate with a victory lap, but he knew his day, far from being over, was just beginning its complex course.

Chapter 11
Voice of Evil

*H*ope loaded her reusable grocery bags into the back of her SUV and pressed the button to close the automatic liftgate. Her mobile phone rang as she shut her driver's side door and pressed the ignition button. The caller ID on her SUV's control panel displayed an unfamiliar number.

"Hello, this is Hope," she answered casually, expecting a professional call.

A male voice emanated from the SUV's hands-free system. "Hello, Doctor. I trust you are in good health. One of your patients needs your help."

"Really? Who needs me?" Hope responded, eager to help whoever needed her.

"You must do something. She will make a major mistake this week, and you have to stop her."

The words felt more like a command than a request.

"Sir, I don't—"

"Listen, lady," the man said, cutting her off. "Hannah is your client, right? Well, she's supposed to testify later this week. She's going to tell a bunch of lies that will hurt many people."

"Sir, I can't discuss any of my patients. I don't even know who you are or how you got my phone number."

"This is Alexander Domnhall. I tried to talk to you at the courthouse, but you brushed me off. You need to stop Hannah before I get sent to jail for a bunch of false allegations."

"Mr. Domnhall, we should not be talking. Please do not ever contact me again."

"Careful, lady. You better do as you're told. I'm not someone to be messed with."

"Sir, I'm hanging up now."

Alex's already agitated voice rose, growing increasingly threatening.

"You better not hang up on me! Do you hear me? You better not, you—"

Hope abruptly ended the call, cutting him off mid-insult.

Her heart slammed against her ribs in a frantic, sickening rhythm. Her breath hitched as she instinctively hunched her shoulders, shrinking into the leather seat. A cold dread, sharp as a needle, pierced her mind. She thought of her years-ago hospitalization—the betrayal of vulnerability—and a quick, angry flash of her own powerlessness washed over her.

She wrestled with a sudden rush of adrenaline. Should she call the police and report the harassment? Or should she handle this predator herself? The urge to shield Hannah, to take responsibility for the threat, won out.

She frantically locked her car doors and scanned the parking lot, searching for any sign of Alexander Domnhall before slowly maneuvering out of her parking space. Hope knew, with a chilling certainty, that this was not the last she would hear from him.

Chapter 12
Soccer Game Reconciliation

The late morning in Houston was beautiful, the kind of day that made you forget the city's concrete heart. On a sprawling soccer field bustling with activity, Hope searched for her father's team. Hope had invited Rachel, hoping this would be a small way to reconnect, show support for their half-brothers, and spend some time with their father, Craig.

Hope and Rachel found a spot a few yards from the sideline and set up their lawn chairs. They deliberately placed the chairs several feet apart, creating a moat of turf between them, as if years of silence required a physical safety buffer. The silence between them was thick and uncomfortable, stretched thin by years of unspoken anger. Hope gripped the arms of her chair, rigid and staring straight ahead, while Rachel meticulously adjusted the angle of her seat every thirty seconds, unable to look at her sister.

Hope started the conversation, mentioning how their stepmother, Alejandra, was always so good about emailing her the boys' soccer schedules.

"She's very organized," Hope offered, the tone meant to be complimentary, but it landed flat, sounding instead like a stiff, professional assessment.

Hope made it to a few games a year, but it was never enough.

"I missed those invites," Rachel said softly, her eyes fixed on the field. "I suppose I'm not known for my organizational skills," she added, an edge of defensiveness in her voice.

The admission was barely audible, yet it carried the weight of old hurt from feeling excluded. Rachel assumed she had never actually been invited, but she hid her disappointment.

"I will check my e-mail more closely," she added.

The silence returned, heavier than before. The referee's shouts and the parents' cheers were deafening in the vacuum between them. It took a long, strained minute before either of them dared to mention the past aloud. The tension eased slightly, giving way to a shared nostalgia. The fluid movements and competitive spirit of the twins on the field reminded them of their own days on the church volleyball team.

Rachel, the younger sister, had always been the better athlete. They laughed about a particularly memorable game against a rival church, a fierce but fond memory that seemed to dissolve the years of silence. They both cherished these moments together, especially the times when their emotionally abusive mother, Gina, was not around.

Their different skin tones had been a normal topic of conversation since they were children.

"Hey, don't you need to put some sun tan lotion on

that light skin of yours?" Rachel quipped, a familiar jab.

Hope just smiled. "Don't worry about me. We can't all be blessed with an abundance of beautiful melanin like you."

Rachel ran a hand down one of her sculpted arms. "It is beautiful, isn't it?"

The two laughed together, sharing a moment full of years of history.

Hope turned to face Rachel, her voice dropping a little. "Confession time, I was always a bit jealous of your mocha skin and high cheekbones. You look like some masterpiece an artist dreamed of and put on canvas."

Rachel's expression showed her surprise. Hope had never said anything like that before.

"Thank you, sister dear," Rachel said, her voice trembling with warmth. "But I'm not going to let you downgrade yourself. You're a knockout and always have been. All my life, I've heard guys rave about how pretty you are, your dimples, and that butt of yours. No younger sister wants to constantly overhear guys talking about her sister's impressive backside."

A fresh wave of laughter overtook them, loud and unrestrained, until they shushed each other, remembering where they were. Rachel paused and reflected on the past few weeks. She bit her lip, looking away for a long beat before speaking.

"Hope, I'm sorry," Rachel said, her voice barely above a whisper. "The way you found out about the baby… it wasn't right."

Hope's heart ached. She accepted the apology and wished her sister nothing but the best for her and the baby. But inside, a persistent, dark voice whispered that the best thing for Rachel and her baby would be to get Caleb out of their lives forever.

As the game wore on, Rachel began to open up, her guard noticeably lowering. Her voice softened as she shared her feelings about being a new mom, a mix of excitement and fear. Then, leaning in, she dropped her voice to a conspiratorial tone.

"I have no doubt Caleb will be a great pastor and a great father," she said, her eyes fixed on the twins on the field. "He's amazing with people."

Hope waited, sensing there was more.

Rachel paused, biting her lip. "But...I'm scared, Hope. A great father is one thing, but a good family man? That's what worries me."

The vulnerability in her voice shocked Hope—a crack in the polished façade she'd always seen. In that moment, seeing her sister so uncertain, so close to the same pain that had defined her own life, Hope's confession died on her lips. She had come here to tell her everything, but the secret about Twila and Caleb would have to wait.

The twins won their game, celebrating with high-fives and shouts of triumph. Craig approached, beaming with pride, and hugged Hope.

"You should come over to the house sometime, Hope. We can fire up the grill."

"I'd love that," Hope said, her eyes meeting his.

She saw Rachel's face fall, a brief shadow of hurt crossing her features. Craig had always seemed to favor Hope, and Rachel had always carried the burden of believing she was to blame for her parents' divorce. Her interactions with Craig were strained, cold, and distant.

As they packed up their chairs, Hope and Rachel

watched Craig and Alejandra, who were now laughing and celebrating with their boys. It was an effortless, natural scene of family joy. They marveled at, and even felt a bit envious of, how wonderful parents Craig and Alejandra were. They served as an example of everything their own family had never been.

Chapter 13
A Shared Pain

*I*t was 12:30 p.m., and Hope was on her way to the office. She was still battling a mix of anger and deep concern for Rachel, and she found herself looking forward to the distraction of her patients' problems. Just as she entered her office parking lot, her phone rang. Using her car's hands-free system, she answered.

"Hello, this is Hope."

"Hi, Hope. Hannah just canceled her one o'clock appointment, so you're free until two," April informed her.

"Thanks, but that would have been helpful sooner. I'm already here," Hope replied, slightly annoyed.

"Oh, sorry. She literally just called."

"It's fine. I'll be right in. Bye." Hope ended the call and parked.

While gathering her belongings, Hope noticed a car parked several spaces over. Despite a vehicle partially blocking her view, she immediately recognized Hannah's distinctive long, curly brown hair. Hannah's head was bowed, resting on her hands, as she gripped the top of the steering wheel. Her hair created a curtain that hid her face. Hope, purse in hand, stepped out of her car and approached Hannah's. She tapped lightly on the driver's side window.

Hannah slowly lifted her head, revealing puffy, tear-filled eyes with red veins in the whites. Her expression was vacant.

"Can we talk?" Hope asked, her voice gentle.

Hannah remained completely still for a few tense moments. Then, Hope heard the distinct click of the car doors unlocking. Interpreting this as an invitation, Hope walked around to the passenger side and got in. The air inside the vehicle was heavy and stale, thick with an unpleasant odor. Hope fought back a wave of nausea and tried to stay focused on the situation.

"Hey, how are you doing?" Hope asked, keeping her tone casual.

"Abigail and I aren't friends anymore," Hannah stated, her voice flat and her attention remaining fixated on the windshield.

"What happened between you two?" Hope asked gently.

"She told me I ruined her life and that she hates me." Hannah paused, her gaze unwavering. "And you know what? She's right. I did ruin her life. Alex, I mean Mr. Domnhall, is on trial because of me. He could go to jail for twenty years."

"Hannah, it wasn't your fault he sexually assaulted you," Hope reassured her.

Hannah exhaled slowly, pursed her lips, and lowered her head slightly. "Assault? That's what everyone keeps saying. But, you know, I liked it when he said nice things.

He was funny, kind, and gentle. I liked it when he touched me," she trailed off into silence.

"Hannah, you were fourteen years old! He's a grown man!" Hope's voice rose, her professional composure momentarily cracking. She took a deep breath, regaining control. "Let's go inside. We'll be more comfortable there," she suggested.

"Would the world be better off without me?" Hannah asked, ignoring her.

A million alarms sounded in her chest. She didn't need a degree to know that hollow stare; she'd seen it before, staring back from her own mirror. The various step-by-step approaches to talking to a suicidal person were well ingrained in her mind. However, this moment was different somehow. It was very personal to Hope. She shared an unspoken bond with Hannah, and Hope would not let Dr. Castillo interfere. Her following words could not be found in any psychology journal.

Her breath caught in her throat as she fought an intense internal battle. She had sworn to bury that memory, but Hannah's despair was too close to her own. She knew a professional response wouldn't save this girl—only a raw, painful truth would work.

"You are not alone in your feelings. Several years ago, I asked myself that same question. The night my fiancé broke off our engagement to be with my sister, my answer was to swallow several bottles of pills. It was the wrong answer. My best friend found me on the floor the next morning, unconscious." Hope's words cracked as they left her mouth.

Hannah's head snapped up. Her tear-filled eyes widened in pure, unadulterated shock. She stared at Dr.

Hope Castillo as if she had just seen a UFO in the night sky. The connection the two shared was not out of mutual respect or love, but rather out of a kindred spirit of pain deep inside their very being. The shock slowly gave way to a dawning recognition, a terrifying but binding intimacy.

"Can you help me?" Hannah requested, which sounded more like a prayer than a question.

"Yes, I can," Hope comforted, then verbally pivoted. "But first, can we go inside or at least crack a window? It's musty in this car!" Hope said with a chuckle, waving her hand in front of her face.

Hannah's face lit up with a slight grin.

"Okay, let's go inside," she said with a small laugh that lifted both of their spirits.

Hope cleared her schedule for the rest of the day, and they spent the afternoon in her office. Their conversation proved a healing balm for their wounded souls. Hannah had gone through eight months of therapy and countless sessions, but it wasn't until today that she finally felt seen and truly understood.

Chapter 14
Mr. Eyes

"Chica! Let me get this straight. He gave Nelson a treat yesterday and brought you breakfast at the park this morning?" Anna exclaimed, her Puerto Rican accent thick with excitement.

Hope nodded, a hint of pride in her smile. "Yes, he did."

They sat together on the expansive couch in Hope's living room. Her two-bedroom condo was ideally suited to her needs, with one room serving as a guest room and a secondary office. Hope always felt her house reflected her personality: easy to enjoy, sophisticated yet not pretentious, well-organized, adorned with inspiring African American art, and undeniably charming.

"Well, a man that thoughtful must be gay or ugly," Anna said with a crooked smile. "But that's okay. We can work with ugly."

Hope shook her head. "No, not at all. He looks good! He's tall and well-put-together. His shoulders and arms have muscles in all the right places. His hands are large, working man's hands, but he keeps his nails immaculate. His head has a tight fade and a neat beard."

"Oh, that sounds nice." Anna exhaled.

"Wait, I haven't even told you the best part. Justin has these eyes," Hope said, almost in a trance. "I can't describe them. They seem to change depending on how the light hits them. They're brown and hazel and sparkle all at the same time."

"Wow, he sounds like my kind of man if I liked men. If he has a brother, maybe I'll switch back," Anna said sarcastically.

"Girl, you crazy. I'll tell you. He left me speechless. I didn't know what to say. After I gave him my number, I just got out of there."

"You should have said, 'Here's my number and address. Come over tonight.' Justin should be here right now, and you should give him the gift that keeps giving." Anna demonstrated exaggerated hip rotations, playfully instructing Hope. "Oh, wait a minute. Are you going through that 'reclaiming your virginity' phase again? You do remember how well that worked out for you last time, don't you?"

"I know, I know. Don't remind me. I was celibate for almost two years. Then I fell off the wagon," Hope confessed.

"It was actually only fourteen months. Then, you fell off the wagon onto about four or five bozaks, right?" Anna questioned.

Best friends develop their own language over the years. Hope found it interesting how many times her gay girlfriend would bring up men's "bozaks." But Hope's many sexual misdeeds with men when she was in pain were not a source of pride for her.

"You better stop it. It was not that many bozaks. But,

yes, I did date more than a couple of guys back then. I was in a bad place. An awful place," Hope responded flatly.

Anna realized her snappy comeback had almost gone too far. They both tended to speak before thinking, which sometimes led to trouble. Considering their sharp tongues, it was amazing they were still friends after ten years. But they'd been through so much together—incredible highs and dark lows they didn't discuss. They were each other's lifeline, really.

Anna attempted to lighten the mood. "What happens now with Mr. Eyes?"

"I don't know. Maybe I'll see him in the park, or he'll call me in a week or so," Hope said.

Hope's cell phone rang then, and she looked at the caller ID.

"Or maybe he's calling me right now!"

"Oh, put him on speaker. I want to at least hear what Mr. Eyes sounds like," Anna said eagerly, like a puppy waiting for a treat.

"No, you go on and get out of here." Hope pointed to the door.

Anna popped up and gave a parting shot. "Chica, you better jump on him. I mean, jump on him!"

Hope held back her laughter and answered the phone in her professional voice. "Hello, this is Hope."

Anna gave Hope a thumbs-up of encouragement before slowly closing the front door behind her. Hope felt a burst of genuine, unburdened joy just from Anna's presence and their laughter. This friendship, steady and fierce, was proof that she had people who cared for her.

"Hi, Hope. It's Justin. Sorry to bother you. Is now a good time to talk?" he inquired.

"It's a great time. I was relaxing with a good friend, but she just left. So, now is perfect."

"Great. I thought I would check in and see how you're doing. Did you eat your apple?"

Between Alexander Domnhall's call and ensuing Hannah's session, Hope had forgotten about the apple, which was still sitting in her purse.

"Why? Are you trying to take it back?"

"No," Justin replied with a chuckle. "I want to ensure you get your daily nutrients."

She contemplated telling a little white lie, but the truth emerged in its place.

"I got caught up in meetings today and forgot about the apple. I promise I will eat it before I go to bed tonight. Is that okay with you, sir?"

"Yes, it is, young lady."

"Wait a minute. Aren't you breaking some rule?" Hope asked. "You are supposed to wait a standard minimum of seventy-two hours after getting someone's phone number before calling."

"Well, a couple of things. First, my son went to bed early, so I had some time to talk and could think of no one better to talk to than you. Second, nothing about you makes me want to do the minimum or the standard. I want to exceed all your expectations."

Hope paused. That was good. She liked everything he said and the way he said it.

"Well, then, Mr. Thompson, I am happy you called," she responded.

"That reminds me, Ms. Hope. I was looking at your number in my contacts and realized we haven't exchanged last names. How did you know mine?" Justin inquired.

Hope grinned, "I read your driver's license. You didn't think you could leave your license with a sistah and she not squeeze it for all the details, did you?"

"You know, that never crossed my mind. So, you know it all. My height, weight, age, address, eye color. You know everything about me, and I still don't know your last name."

"Actually, I might have done a little more digging," Hope said, slightly embarrassed. "I googled you earlier today."

Justin's brain immediately started working overtime, picturing news articles that might be out there about his role in his wife's death. He'd been so caught up in everything back then that he'd had no idea what was being written.

Trying to sound casual, he asked, "So, did you stumble across anything…interesting?"

"Yes, I did. I saw many articles on you, mister," Hope replied, then stopped for dramatic effect.

"Hmm, really?" Despite feeling the knot in his throat, Justin maintained his steady tone.

"You were quite the athlete in high school. First-team all-conference in basketball. You led the team to a league championship, and if I recall, you won two sectional games in the state tournament."

"That's correct; we lost in the regionals," Justin said, relieved that the conversation was in safe territory.

"You also were a pretty good cross-country runner."

"I wish I had liked it more. I'm a natural long-distance runner but hate running long distances."

"I did see something a bit strange." Hope's words gave Justin pause.

"You won some music contest. Do you sing or rap? All I could see was a picture and a caption with you on a stage."

Justin laughed. "It was a contest I won for best DJ. I had a pretty unique style. Back in the day, I could mix old-school jams with Ja'Rule, Missy Elliott, and Common songs. You haven't jammed until you've danced to Nelly with a Parliament Funkadelic beat." He reminisced with satisfaction.

"That does sound cool. Do you still deejay? I would love to hear you jam."

"I still do wedding receptions here and there. While I don't like most of the new hip-hop, the line dancing is getting more fun. At a wedding, I run a line dance set, starting with the Bus Stop and ending with whatever is hot. Collect my fee and go home. Pretty easy. My mixologist skills are of no use."

"So what else do you do? How do you pay for such elaborate breakfasts for strangers?"

"I own a small warranty repair business. Companies and private homeowners can get a warranty from me. When something breaks in their building or home, my team and I fix it. Nothing special. I am just a repairman trying to make a dollar out of fifteen cents."

"Nothing wrong with being an entrepreneur. Small businesses are the backbone of this great nation. I'm proud of you. Where did you go to school?"

"Wait a minute. You've been interrogating me, googling me. Time to balance this out a little bit. Can I at least get your last name before we continue?" Justin stated, pleading his case.

"It's Castillo," Hope replied.

Usually, when she told someone her last name, they would scrutinize her face more closely and give her that "What race are you?" look. Before, they just saw a brown-skinned, 5-foot-6-inch-tall African American woman; afterward, they tried to determine whether she was Latina. Per her norm, she didn't offer any additional commentary. She always liked to keep people wondering.

"Ms. Hope Castillo. I like that," Justin replied.

"It's Dr. Hope Castillo," Hope said with a hint of pride, which was her tendency when she said her name and title.

So often, people assumed she could not be a doctor because of her brown skin. Therefore, she used her title in introductions as a first punch in the fight for respect. This time, however, Hope immediately regretted jabbing her name and title at Justin. Her mouth was always faster than her brain.

"Wow, a doctor. Nice," he responded.

Hope tried to listen for any trepidation or intimidation in his voice. More than once, a new relationship had been killed at inception as soon as the man found out she had a PhD. He would run toward someone he thought he was "better than." She reassured herself that only a weak man would be intimidated by her credentials.

"What type of doctor? Are you a brain surgeon?" Justin asked, going deeper.

"In a sense, I suppose. I'm a psychologist. I focus primarily on family and adolescent behavioral issues because I believe the nuclear family is crucial to society. My job makes me feel like I'm doing my small part to make the world a better place," Hope said with an optimistic tone.

"That's cool. I know you can't tell me names, but can you tell me about a family you helped?" Justin asked.

Without using any names, Hope described a family she was counseling, highlighting the challenges faced by their daughter, Hannah, who was battling drug addiction and engaging in risky behavior. Through therapy, Hannah revealed a history of molestation by her best friend's father, Alexander Domnhall. This traumatic experience was identified as the catalyst for the family's ongoing struggles. Alexander's trial for statutory rape had just begun. Hope continued to provide individual and group therapy for the family, supporting them as they worked to heal and move forward.

Justin was quietly encouraged. He was deeply reassured by the knowledge that individuals like Hope were dedicating their lives to making a tangible difference in the world, one person, one family at a time.

The night unfolded in this fashion: Hope would try to learn more about Justin, and he would deftly redirect the conversation back to her. Hope had never talked to a man who was such a good listener. Sharing stories about of her cases with him made her feel good, and she started to believe she was making a positive difference.

Justin felt privileged to talk to Dr. Castillo. He thought the work she did was amazing, especially compared to his job of fixing air conditioners and toilets. He decided this time he was not going to let any self-doubt get in the way of learning more about this beautiful woman. He was tethered to the phone and had to hear more.

Their conversation flowed smoothly, filled with laughter. The call lasted until 1:00 a.m., when the responsibilities of the next day began to weigh on both of their minds.

"I will be walking Nelson at the same time tomorrow. Will I see you?" Hope asked with anticipation.

"God willing and the creek doesn't rise, ma'am, I will be there," Justin replied.

"Okay, good night. And don't let those bed bugs bite," Hope said.

"I won't because I don't have any," he responded, and they both laughed.

After ending the call, each lay in bed, a few miles apart, thinking about what the next day might bring.

Chapter 15
The Missed Appointment

As Hope entered the park, she noticed Nelson's accelerated pace. His legs moved with unusual urgency, nearly breaking into a trot. She realized he was mirroring her heightened anticipation. She had arrived fifteen minutes earlier than usual, eager to see Justin. Only a few hours had passed since their lengthy phone conversation. Yet, Hope felt a youthful excitement, reminiscent of her high school days when she would secretly chat with a boy in her room.

"We're early, Nelson. Should we take a quick lap around the park?" Hope asked.

Nelson wagged his tail and gave an attentive gaze, as if to say, *I'm game.* Hope decided a lap would be a good idea. Her pedometer showed it was roughly nine hundred steps. From the path, she could see the bench where she was supposed to meet Justin. Walking would help her appear casual and burn off some nervous energy.

After completing two laps, Hope decided to stop before breaking a sweat. She didn't want to ruin her carefully applied makeup, a step up from her usual workday look.

Hope sat at the picnic table, inserted her earbuds, and let Prince's "Let's Go Crazy" fill her ears. She instinctively smiled and started bobbing her head to the music, even serenading Nelson with her favorite song. Nelson simply watched her with his usual non-judgmental gaze.

Hope glanced at her watch as the last notes of another favorite Prince B-side faded. Justin was now fifteen minutes late. She had been waiting for nearly thirty. An internal debate raged within her: should she be angry or understanding? She knew not everyone shared her punctuality, but she had made a considerable effort, dressing up and arriving early.

He better get here soon before I give someone else a chance, she thought, a touch of humor masking her growing agitation. However, as the minutes ticked by, concern started to take root in her mind. *He wouldn't forget, would he? We spoke just hours ago. Could he be ill? Or his son?*

She considered sending a text, but doubts held her back. *Maybe he changed his mind? Is my Ph.D. always going to be a barrier? I was the one who suggested this. Did I come on too strong?*

Her thoughts spiraled. After almost an hour, she accepted he wasn't coming. A wave of sadness washed over her.

"Let's go, Nelson," she said, her voice heavy. Nelson, sensing her mood, followed with a subdued gait.

The perfect weather, the birdsong, the children's laughter—all starkly contrasted with the emptiness she felt.

"I wish it would rain," she murmured

Chapter 16
Women's Shelter Confrontation

"I don't know if I can do this," a frail, uncertain voice said, doubting her ability to go on.

"Of course, you can do this. You are already doing it and have been doing it for the last month," Hope reassured the young mother of two preschoolers.

The small meeting room was heavy with silence. Hope and Kerry tried to make sense of the chaos that had become Kerry's life, but words failed them.

With no family, job, or money, Kerry Blackman found refuge at the Sisters Helping Sisters women's shelter. She had fled her abusive boyfriend, the father of her youngest child, weeks ago after he assaulted her older child one too many times. The shelter provided a temporary haven for her family.

"I'll be back here a week from Tuesday. We can talk more then. I'm here two to three times a month and on the first Sunday of every month. You have my number; you can call me anytime."

Hope wished she had more time to volunteer at the shelter.

Kerry stood up and opened the door. "I need to get back to my boys," she said as she shuffled into the hallway.

After completing her notes on Kerry, Hope closed her notebook. She knew these situations were never simple, but the wrong choices too often made haunted her: returning to the abuser, the desperate decision to sell one's body, the oblivion offered by drugs, and the final, irreversible mistake of suicide.

Hope made her way down the short hall toward the back of the building. She saw her sister, Rachel, through the doorway of the back-storage room, skillfully folding a pile of donated clothes. The sight of her brought a small, genuine smile to Hope's face.

"Thanks for helping out, Rach," Hope said, stepping into the room. "People call me anal retentive, but I have nothing on your meticulous clothes folding."

Rachel looked up, her hands busy. "Reduces the ironing later. You know I hate ironing. As for helping out, I'm happy to help. It feels so good to do something that actually makes a difference, you know?"

Hope nodded, a shared memory flickering between them. "It reminds me of when we were teenagers, volunteering on the weekends at the food bank. Sorting through all those cans and boxes. Honestly, I even miss riding next to you on that old church van. You remember, the one that made us feel every bump in the road."

A rare moment of familiar camaraderie hung in the air, a whisper of a time before everything changed.

Rachel's expression softened. "It really does. We would laugh and giggle all the way down and back."

They both paused, lost in the memory of when their

sisterhood was easy and their laughter was loud.

Rachel looked past Hope into the hallway. "By the way, Amira's waiting for you out in the lobby. I like her a lot. She reminds me of you."

With that compliment and a genuine smile, Hope headed to the lobby.

The center's lobby was nondescript, but the scene unfolding there was anything but. Hope saw Amira talking to a man whose predatory aura was unmistakable, his gaze lingering on her with unsettling hunger.

Hope darted across the lobby, her movements precise and purposeful. She took a position between Amira and the man, her back shielding her little sister, her posture radiating a clear warning.

"Dr. Castillo, I'm so glad you joined us. I came by to talk to you," Alex Domnhall said, justifying his unexpected appearance at the shelter.

Hope's nose was close enough to Alex's face to smell the bizarre blend of Listerine and chewing tobacco on his breath. Her rage—usually a cold weapon—now felt hot and immediate, fueled by the instinct to protect Amira.

The demand was a harsh whisper, forced from Hope's tight lips: "You need to leave here now."

Undaunted by Hope's demand, Alex appealed his case. "You have to stop Hannah from testifying. This thing is ruining my life. I'm a family man who fell in love. I am not the first man to—"

"Stop it. Love? It's called statutory rape, you sick bastard," retorted Hope.

The exchange startled Amira as she stood very close to Hope's back.

Alex countered with a pointed finger at Hope's face.

"There you go! There you go again! There was no rape involved."

A question barked from the corner of the room. "Hey, hey, we got a problem here?"

Off-duty policewomen volunteered at the shelter to help the women feel safe and keep unwanted visitors from causing havoc. Although dressed in plain clothes today, Tanisha Ross, known as Tee Tee, was one of those officers. Small in stature, Tee Tee made up for it with a strong, commanding presence.

Alex looked at Tee Tee and quickly sized her up. Towering over her by a full foot and confident in his strength from countless hours at the gym, he figured he could easily handle the loudmouth approaching. He figured wrong.

Alex delivered his complaint with an air of unearned superiority. "I didn't rape anyone. All you liberated women need to stop trying to destroy a hardworking, real American man like me."

A sudden ping—the sound of a telescoping steel baton—startled everyone in the room. Tee Tee held it at her side, her expression unreadable.

"Sir, it's time for you to leave unless you want your skull cracked open."

With her extensive training and experience, Officer Tee Tee knew she could handle men of his size and larger. Non-compliance would be met with immediate and decisive action.

Alex's jaw tightened as he quickly grasped the new reality. He glared at Hope, then spun around and stormed toward the door.

Alex listened to the official trespass warning as Tee

Tee walked him to his car. But it was the unspoken threat—the way she held her baton, the look in her eyes—that truly made his blood run cold. He knew he would have to find another, quieter place to deal with Dr. Castillo, the fierce little guardian who now stood squarely in his way.

Inside the lobby, Hope turned to Amira. "Are you all right? What were you doing talking to that creep?"

"I had finished folding a pile of clothes like I usually do, and then I came out to see what you wanted me to do next." Amira's voice wavered, a crack in her composure. She looked up at Hope, tears filling her eyes. "He approached me and asked me if I knew you. I didn't mean to—"

"No, Amira, I'm so sorry. You did nothing wrong. I am so sorry." Hope hugged Amira close, a gesture of care and protection.

These volunteer sessions were a regular part of their routine, offering Amira a glimpse into a different world. Amira thrived on the work, from washing dishes to sorting donations, leaving the shelter each time with a feeling of purpose.

Hope's final appointment of the day, a one-on-one session with a new resident at the shelter, was about to start. She looked at Amira, then back at the door where Alex had just exited, a cold fury still simmering in her veins. Amira, her usual cheerful demeanor replaced by shock, watched her with wide eyes.

"I didn't know you could be like that, Hope," Amira said, her voice a hushed whisper. "I've only ever seen your professional and fun side. You were a badass."

Rachel, who had stepped out of the back room to

witness the tail end of the commotion, overheard Amira's comment.

"It doesn't surprise me at all," she said, her voice low and steady as she walked toward them. "Growing up, Hope was always my protector. She would step in front of any threat to protect me. She rarely stood up for herself, but she would for me or anyone else she saw as vulnerable."

A quiet moment passed between the two sisters, a silent acknowledgment of a bond that had been strained but never fully broken. Rachel had always admired that about Hope—a quiet strength that only emerged when someone else needed her to be strong.

"Come on, let's go back and finish folding," Rachel said gently, leading a still-shaken Amira back to the storage room.

As Amira fell into the familiar rhythm of the work, Rachel watched her, a deep regret settling in her chest. She thought about all the years she and Hope had lost and the part she had played in their estrangement. The sight of Hope, fiercely protective and selfless, only deepened her regret.

Chapter 17
Justin Needs a Lawyer

*I*t felt as though the instant Justin closed his eyes, the insistent chime of his phone alarm shattered the silence. He tried to ignore the relentless bongs, but each one seemed to pierce his ears with increasing sharpness.

"Damn," he muttered, glancing at the screen. "It's quarter after six."

Justin typically rose at 5:30 a.m. for a quick workout before his morning routine. But the Geeston Corp boiler overhaul hadn't wrapped up until 2:00 a.m. Even as he set the alarm, he'd known that today's workout was a lost cause.

Showered, shaved, and dressed, Justin entered the kitchen. The sight of Deuce brought a smile to his face. Sitting in his booster seat, he clutched a fistful of scrambled eggs in one hand, a strip of bacon in the other, and sported a generous smear of grits across his face.

"Daddy!" Deuce proclaimed with his usual burst of energy every time he saw his father.

"Hey, little boy, can I have some of that?" Justin said

playfully, reaching for the food on Deuce's plate.

"No! Ask Bibi! These are mine, mine!" Deuce declared, covering his plate with his tiny hands and grinning. The familiar game always brought laughter.

Justin turned to his mother, Lorraine, who watched their daily ritual by the counter.

"Bibi, can I have some? Please, please, Bibi?" he asked, mimicking Deuce's playful tone.

"Sit down, boy," Bibi replied, a hint of amusement in her voice.

She walked over with a plate piled high with food and placed it before him. Lorraine always prepared Justin's plate, just as she had for his father before he passed. It was a lifelong tradition, and Justin had never questioned it.

"I heard you come in late last night, or should I say this morning? What happened? You shot out of here yesterday morning like a bat out of hell." Lorraine was trying to figure out what was driving her son's 20+ hour day.

"Well, you know Geeston Corp has an old office building on 43rd Street. Their boiler kinda blew up," Justin explained. "It was a mess in the basement. It took all of us—Me, Hank, and Akil—to fix and clean up the mess. We had to delay two other appointments until today because it was all hands on deck, all day and most of the night."

"Why couldn't you stop at a reasonable time and finish today? You are not a machine." Lorraine's mother bear side was showing.

"Geeston is one of my top accounts, and I cannot afford to lose it. Their tenants need hot water, and it's my job to get it to them," Justin said. "We need the money, so we need Geeston. Besides, a little hard work is good for me."

"You sound more like your daddy every day," Lorraine reminisced.

"I'm going to work hard and get dirty every day so that this little guy won't have to," Justin said, rubbing Deuce's hair, still grinning. "My son's going to be a scientist or a Harvard lawyer, something important. He's going to be a far better man than me."

Lorraine wasn't sure how to respond. She was immensely proud of Justin. He was a good man—raising his son well, caring for her, and trying to build a business. Yet, he still spoke so negatively of himself.

"Are you taking Deuce to school today? I can, but you might want to say hi to your new friend on the way."

Justin's face scrunched up in thought. *New friend? Who's she talking...* Then it hit him.

"Hope!"

His promise to meet her flooded back into his memory. How could he have forgotten?

"Momma, I'll take Deuce to school," he said, suddenly in a rush.

He scooped Deuce up from his chair and hurried out the door.

Lorraine looked up at the ceiling, a silent prayer forming on her lips. "Lord, help that boy. He needs you more than he knows."

* * *

The first clouds in weeks had turned the morning gray, the sun playing a teasing game of hide-and-seek.

Just as Justin and Deuce reached the park, the sun vanished behind a massive cloud, casting a somber light on Hope, who was already heading for the exit with Nelson at her heels. Justin and Deuce hurried to intercept her, blocking her secondary path out of the park.

"Hope, can I have a minute, please?" Justin asked, his voice laced with a soulful sadness.

Hope stopped, Nelson beside her. She stood silent, her gaze cold and unwelcoming. Mirroring her mood, Nelson sat with ears perked, but his tail remained still. They waited in tense silence for Justin's explanation.

Justin, leaving nothing to chance, had decided on the way over to the park to bring out the big guns.

"Miss Hope, Daddy told me to say he's sorry. He forgot," Deuce chirped, his father's small, encouraging nod preceding his words.

Hope's shoulders relaxed, the unconscious tightness easing. She looked down at the pint-sized advocate, his face an image of pure innocence, and couldn't help but smile. Nelson rose and stepped forward, just within reach for Deuce to pet him.

"Wow, that's not playing fair, is it?" Hope said, keeping her gaze on Deuce but directing her words at his father. "Bringing in the world's most adorable negotiator. Though 'you forgot' isn't exactly a stellar defense."

"I know, I know," Justin said, shaking his head. "It's a bit more complicated than that. I know your time is precious. I had a work emergency that took up my entire day and evening. I'm so sorry. But that doesn't excuse me for not calling or texting. I was negligent, practically worthless for standing you up." He lowered his head, genuinely remorseful.

"What's negligent, Daddy?" Deuce asked, his eyes wide with curiosity.

Justin turned his attention to his son, considering how best to explain. He always aimed for complete honesty with Deuce, following his mother's advice. He pondered how to describe being thoughtless.

"Stop. The man I know is built better than that. Don't call yourself thoughtless or worthless. Not even as a joke," Hope interjected, her voice firm.

Hearing Justin call himself thoughtless and worthless triggered a surge of protectiveness in her.

"Your dad is a good man who just made a mistake. I've made a lot of mistakes myself, Little Man."

"Me too," Deuce blurted out, not wanting to be left off the mistake train. "I hid my fish sticks under my seat. I wanted pudding."

Hope crinkled her nose and smiled. She wasn't exactly sure what crime the little assailant had just confessed to, but he would be too cute to convict anyway.

"He is so adorable and cute."

"Yes, he takes after his mother," Justin said, redirecting any possible praise that might come his way.

However, he wanted to kick himself this time after giving his standard response. Just when he was digging himself out of a hole, he went and brought up his deceased wife.

"Doc, I do apologize. I messed up. I—"

Justin's apology was interrupted by Hope raising her hand and shaking her head slightly.

"You don't need to apologize anymore," Hope said, her voice softening. "I believe in showing people a little grace sometimes. Forgive them without needing long apologies. Let's just move forward."

"Thank you kindly for your grace, ma'am," Justin said, a wave of relief washing over him.

"But don't take advantage of my kindness and stand me up again," Hope added, a partial smile playing on her lips, hinting at her seriousness. "Trust me, I can be a real witch."

"No, ma'am," Justin replied, giving a slight bow. "I will do my very best to do my very best."

"I have to go now. I have an early appointment."

"Okay. Can we meet here tomorrow morning at six-thirty? I promise I won't forget this time."

"Better not forget. The witch is not as nice nor as forgiving as I am. By the way, bran is nice, but apple cinnamon is better," Hope said, giving Nelson a slight tug on his leash. Nelson obediently left Deuce to follow Hope.

As Hope and Nelson walked away, the sun emerged from the clouds again, instantly warming everyone's skin.

"Nice job, Deuce. You were a big help." The father and son slapped five. "Let's get you to school. I have a long day ahead of me. I also have to pick up some apple cinnamon muffins sometime tonight."

Chapter 18
The Birthday Kiss

*H*ope's birthdays always evoked a deep-seated dread in her. It was a day she wished she could simply skip, quickly moving on to the rest of the year. Birthdays had long stopped being a cause for celebration, if they ever had been. She hoped today would be uneventful—perhaps a quiet phone call from Craig, a brief visit from Anna with a glass of wine, and the usual mailed drugstore card from Rachel. She just wanted to get through the day without any fuss.

Her hopes were quickly dashed as she and Nelson entered the park. Instead of the usual natural beauty, she was met with a cluster of purple balloons tied together and anchored to a purple-covered picnic table. On the table sat an oversized cinnamon apple muffin with a single small candle, a fruit plate wrapped in clear plastic, a glass of orange juice, and coffee. A handsome server with sparkling eyes stood beside the table.

"Good morning, and happy birthday, Doc," Justin said with a respectful nod.

"Good morning to you, too," Hope responded, shaking

her head in disbelief. "This is quite a surprise. Do I even want to know how you discovered it was my birthday?"

Justin grinned. "Well, I learned from the best. I googled you. You can find the most interesting things online. Interesting things like the Sea of Galilee Church posting monthly birthdays in their announcements. And what do you know? A certain lady doctor's birthday was on that list."

Hope was taken aback, struggling to process her emotions. Justin had clearly put a lot of thought and effort into this. He'd even used her favorite color, purple, for the decorations. She wondered how he'd known. She wanted to tell him it was too much, that she didn't deserve such kindness. This small gesture was, without a doubt, the sweetest thing anyone had done for her on her birthday.

"You..." Hope began, her voice breaking as the words caught in her throat. She tried again, but only silence followed.

"Hope, are you alright?" Justin asked, his voice laced with worry. "I just wanted to..."

He trailed off as Hope closed the distance, her hand softly resting on his cheek. She rose on her toes and kissed him, her lips quivering against his. His lips were warm and comforting.

Nelson nudged Justin's leg, a silent cheer.

Hope still struggled to find the right words. Feeling her legs weaken, she sat down in front of her birthday muffin.

Justin reached into a shopping bag on the bench and pulled out a lighter. As he lit the candle, he said, "I won't torture you with my singing. Trust me, nobody wants to hear that. But I can hum 'Happy Birthday' if you'd like."

Hope smiled, relieved to have something to say finally. "No, that won't be necessary. Just sit down."

"Don't forget to make a wish."

Hope closed her eyes, made a wish, and blew out the candle.

"Now, remember, don't tell me what it is. We want your wish to come true."

"It already has," Hope said, a genuine smile lighting her face. "You're still here."

She was proud of her quick wit, hoping to brighten Justin's day.

"Oh, that was nice. You know how to make a brotha feel good." Justin then gestured to the muffin. "Eat, eat. I know you have important appointments this morning."

"I'm sure you have important meetings, as well," Hope said while picking up her muffin and breaking off a piece.

"I have a full schedule. My first job is at eight o'clock. But what I do does not compare to what you do. You change lives. I change air filters."

There he goes again, Hope thought, a familiar pang of frustration. Of all his outstanding qualities, his low opinion of himself was her least favorite. She wanted to scold and tell him to stop putting himself down. But he'd been so kind, and she decided the pep talk could wait. She hoped there would be many more days like this. So, instead of fussing, she decided to change the subject.

"Where is your little Johnnie Cochran, the defense lawyer extraordinaire?"

"He's at home with his Bibi. He only goes over to Noah's Ark preschool part-time."

John Gary Long

Now, noticing for the first time that she was the only one eating, Hope said, "Oh, I'm sorry. I didn't offer you some of my birthday breakfast. I shouldn't eat all of this huge muffin. Please have some."

"No, I ate before I came. Any day my mother and I are in the same house, she cooks me breakfast. This is true any and every day, without exception. She won't let anyone else do it for me. Not even..."

Justin caught himself this time, with no reference to his deceased spouse. Talking about Chaka would not be suitable for the mood.

"Be happy she does that for you. I have prepared my cornflakes in the morning my whole life. I don't do much in the cooking department. Let's just say I am culinarily challenged."

"Well then, you shouldn't have to cook for yourself today. I know it's short notice, but how about I take you out to eat tonight? Nothing fancy. Real casual. I'm talking jeans type of meal."

Hope had woken up that morning with her usual birthday blues and a strong urge to stay hidden under the covers. Now, she was being offered the chance to spend time with a handsome, thoughtful man. *I might be a little crazy,* she thought, a smile tugging at her lips, *but I'm definitely not a fool.*

"Yes, that sounds good," Hope said to Justin's welcoming face.

"Great. I'm not sure what time my last appointment ends. Can I text you once I get home and take a shower?"

Having just finished her muffin, Hope put a banana from the fruit plate in her purse. "That sounds great. That delicious and massive muffin I just scarfed down may have digested by then."

Hope got up, and Nelson gave her his "What about me, no food?" look.

Sensing the dog's desire, Justin said, "Hey, man, sorry about that. I'll bring you something next time. Okay?"

"Don't worry about him. He is such a beggar," said Hope. "Thank you for making this morning special. I am looking forward to tonight."

"Me too. See you later."

Hope and Nelson disappeared from view, but Justin's eyes followed them until the last moment. He felt a flush of embarrassment at the intensity of his attraction.

Smart, funny, irresistible dimples, and a remarkable badunkadunk. He laughed softly to himself. *I'm going to have to hustle to get through today's jobs!*

* * *

"You smell good," Anna said as Hope walked past her into the kitchen.

"It's French. Eric gave it to me. He brought it back from one of his trips to Europe," Hope explained.

"Eric? Was he the one who couldn't get it up?" Anna asked with a sly smile.

"No, that was Christophe, the county commissioner. Trust fund pretty boy who couldn't close the deal," Hope said, taking a sip of bottled water from the fridge. "Eric was the investment banker. He was the asshole. Turns out he had a wife, kids, and a boyfriend! The boyfriend was the one who told me about the wife and kids. He found me and said, 'Girl, your man's cheating on us. And I don't like being played.' It was wild."

"Oh, right, that's it. Eric was the last one before your man-cation," Anna said.

"Hard to believe it's been almost a year," Hope replied. "I figured I'd put this perfume to good use. It's not the perfume's fault that the guy was a jerk. Besides, I think Justin will like it."

"Oh, he will like it, all right. But I think he'll like that cold shoulder top you have on even more." Anna shimmied her shoulders as she spoke. "And don't get me started on those jeans. Your booty is bangin' in those jeans," she said with her best homeboy imitation.

Hope smiled. "I caught him taking a peek at my butt. You know, but who could blame him for staring at all this goodness?"

Hope patted her derrière. She and Anna shared a burst of girlish laughter.

"Well, you look good. He better take you someplace nice. Maybe that creole fusion place we went to for Jasmine's birthday."

"I don't think so. That place is a bit pricey. He's old school, so going Dutch would be out of the question."

"Are you okay dating a 'Joe lunch pail' dude? You haven't dated anyone broke since college."

"You're right, but I'm not with any of those rich, pretty boys now. All of them wasted my time. They were either stuck up, secretly married, or full of themselves."

"Or limp dicked. Don't forget your boy, Christophe." Anna rubbed it in the only way a true friend can.

"On that note, you need to get out of here. I'm expecting a text from Justin anytime now." Hope gestured toward the door.

"Okay, okay. I would never get in the way of you and

Mr. Eyes. And don't worry about Nelson. I love this dog; he cracks me up. I'll bring him back tomorrow afternoon." Holding Nelson by his leash, Anna opened the door. "I'm looking forward to one day…"

Anna stops when she sees the woman she believes is Satan's first cousin standing in the hallway. It's unclear if she was about to knock or just eavesdropping.

The two glared at each other like two rams about to bump heads, fighting over the same mountaintop. Even Nelson assumed an attack position.

With her eyes fixed on the woman, Anna said over her shoulder, "Be sure to call me if you need me. Happy birthday."

The two women moved enough to their respective rights to allow the other to pass, but neither gave ground.

"Bye, Anna. Talk to you later. Nelson, be good," Hope said, bracing herself for Gina's arrival. She wondered if it would be a mild breeze or a full-blown hurricane.

Gina swept in, the door clicking shut behind her. "Is she still a dyke?" she smirked.

Gina had a knack for asking questions that left no room for a good response, like, *Are you just stupid?* Hope's usual tactic was silence. Gina had a talent for pushing Hope's buttons, making her want to curse. Maybe it was because Gina's presence always made Hope feel like shit.

"I haven't seen a man near you in months," Gina said, continuing her assault. "Have you finally surrendered to her charms? Are you allowing her to explore the same intimate spaces that so many men have occupied?"

"Enough. What do you want? I'm not in the mood for this," Hope said, her voice taut with anger.

"Can't a mother stop by to wish her eldest daughter a happy birthday?" Gina asked, her voice laced with false sweetness.

"A mother with basic human decency can, and that is not you. What do you want?" Hope repeated, her arms folded tightly across her chest, her hands hidden beneath them, clenched into fists.

"We haven't had a chance to discuss Rachel's news," Gina said, her eyes fixed on Hope. "Isn't it wonderful? Rachel has made me so happy. I'm finally going to be a grandmother." She paused, watching for Hope's reaction.

Hope chose her words carefully. "A baby is always a blessing. I wish everyone good health."

"Oh, it's more than just a blessing," Gina countered. "You're going to be the aunt of the heir to a great legacy. A legacy I'll be proud to announce to the world. But don't worry, they can find a place for you in their empire. They'll need nannies and babysitters, you know. You can do that. You don't have anything better to do." Gina snickered, clearly enjoying Hope's discomfort.

"I don't think my babysitting their child is the wisest move," Hope replied, her voice steady.

Gina saw she'd gotten a reaction. "For once, you're right. You don't have any maternal instincts. And Lord knows you can't cook. You can barely take care of yourself."

"And where, exactly, would I have gained any maternal instincts? I've always seen you more as a sow than a mother. You know, female pigs are known to devour their offspring," Hope shot back, a surge of vindication.

"Well, aren't we the intellectual?" Gina spat. "Spelling bee champion. All that intellect squandered on you, with no one to inherit it. Maternal instincts would be a complete waste on you. We all know that wasteland between your legs will never produce a child."

Hope's fists tightened, her nostrils flaring with each breath. She pointed towards the door, her voice trembling with rage. "Get out of my house, you bitch!"

With a swift, predatory motion, Gina's hand clamped down on Hope's arm below the wrist. "Or what?" she hissed, her grip cold and unyielding.

The force of her grasp drained the blood from Hope's skin, leaving a stark white mark. Hope tried to wrench her arm away, but Gina's hold was like a vise. After asserting her control, Gina released Hope's arm. Hope cradled it protectively, rubbing the lingering pain.

"You are, and always have been, weak," Gina said, turning towards the door.

The feeling Hope had harbored for years finally solidified into words. "I hate you!"

Gina opened the door, a cold smile playing on her lips. "I know. Happy birthday."

She closed the door behind her, leaving Hope in silence.

* * *

Justin stood outside Hope's door, breathing into his palm one last time to check his breath. He still needed reassurance despite brushing his teeth twice, flossing, rinsing, and consuming mints. He held a bouquet of six purple roses. Taking a deep breath, he knocked firmly twice.

Hope opened the door with a slight grin. "Hey, come on in," she said, turning to usher him inside.

Hope had mastered the art of switching gears quickly, moving from Gina's brutality to a facade of normalcy. It was a skill often found in those who had experienced childhood abuse, something she had learned in her psychology classes. She had changed into a long-sleeved shirt to conceal the fresh bruise on her arm and had buried her emotional pain deep within.

Justin stepped inside, his words momentarily lost in the sight of Hope. In the park, she was always in her comfortable "morning routine" attire—hair pulled back, casual sportswear, a touch of lip gloss at most. Tonight, she had transformed. Her makeup was flawless, perfectly complementing the French perfume she wore. Her hair, now unbound, flowed freely past her shoulders. Justin had always found her beautiful, but she was simply stunning tonight.

Justin recovered enough to present Hope with the bouquet. "Hey Doc, these are for you."

Hope received the flowers and sniffed them slightly.

"These are beautiful and smell so nice. Thank you! I'll go put them in some water."

Hope headed to her kitchen, which opened to the living room, where Justin now stood. She pulled a vase out of a cabinet and filled it with water.

"You look amazing," he said, his voice filled with childlike wonder.

"You sound surprised. Do I look that bad in the mornings?" Hope teased.

"No, no, just the opposite. You always look great in the mornings. But seeing you now, it's like, wow," Justin stammered, wishing he had a more eloquent way to express himself.

Hope placed the vase on the living room coffee table, her hair cascading over her shoulders as she leaned forward.

Still searching for the right words, Justin added, "Luxurious. Yes, luxurious. You have long, beautiful, luxurious hair."

Amused by his stumbling attempts at flattery, Hope smiled. "You can thank my dad for that. He's half-Colombian. He and his father both had long, curly hair. That's why I don't cut it—it reminds me of him."

Hope's admission surprised her. She had never shared that with anyone before. Her earlier encounter with Gina had stirred up a longing for her father.

"I'll thank him when I get a chance."

Hope settled onto the couch next to Justin, tucking one leg beneath her. "Hey Justin," she said softly, "I'm not up for going out tonight. Could we just stay here?"

"You're not sick, are you? Do you want me to go get you something?"

"No, I'm not sick. I had a slightly more stressful day than expected, and relaxing here would be great. Is that okay?"

"That's no problem. It's your birthday." Justin was yielding to Hope's request. "Have you eaten? I can make you some dinner."

"We can order pizza. They know me very well down at Spagnola's. I'll give them a call."

"If you eat there all the time, it's not special. Let me see what you have here in your kitchen."

Before Hope could protest, Justin jumped up and headed to the kitchen.

"You won't find much to work with in there."

"Don't you go worrying. I got you. If we need something, I'll make groceries at the corner market."

Hope chuckled. "Did you say 'make groceries'? Where you from, Tennessee?"

Utilizing his inner Charlie Pride spirit, Justin spoke fluent Country. "Well, no, ma'am, but my Daddy was from Mississippi. I learnt my good English from him."

They both laughed.

His voice returned to its normal tone, and Justin surveyed the available ingredients. "We've got eggs, a pre-made spinach salad, tomatoes, onions, and green peppers. Wheat bread, turkey bacon, peanut butter, and jelly. Hmm. I think we can whip up a late-night breakfast. How does a vegetable omelet and toast sound?"

Hope, leaning against the counter that separated the kitchen from the living room, replied in a soft, sultry voice, "That sounds perfect."

Her voice made him pause and look at her, struck again by her beauty. She gestured for him to come closer. He did, and they kissed.

"Oh, and by the way, hold the onions in that omelet," Hope said, her voice laced with affection. "I might want to kiss someone later."

"Hold the onions. Check. I hope I know the guy," Justin replied with a grin.

Justin set to work on the late-night breakfast, his movements confident and practiced. Hope watched him slice and dice the vegetables, a twinge of self-consciousness creeping in. She felt ashamed that she wasn't as skilled in the kitchen.

"Would you like some wine? I have a bit of a head

start on you. My friend Anna and I finished off a bottle a little while ago, but I can open another one if you want."

Hope told a partial truth. She and Anna each had one glass of wine before Anna left and Gina came. After Gina slithered out of Hope's apartment, Hope finished the bottle they had opened by herself.

"No, thank you. I'm not much of a wine guy. Sorry. But feel free to have some, birthday girl. If you can't drink on your birthday, when can you drink?"

Hope agreed. "Mr. Man, I like how you think. I will have some."

Hope uncorked a bottle of Pinot Grigio with the skill of a connoisseur. She might not know how to cook, but she could open a bottle of wine.

Hope sipped her wine, her eyes fixed on Justin as he moved around the kitchen. She'd always thought a tuxedo could make even a troll look good, but it took a real man to make a simple polo and jeans look this good. The shirt stretched across his broad shoulders and chest as if custom-made for him. A pleasant tingle ran through her as his triceps flexed and relaxed while he chopped vegetables. She had to suppress a laugh when she caught herself thinking, *I'm not the only one in this house with a nice butt.*

"Here you are, my lady. Vegetable omelet with a side of toast. Ma'am, would you like anything further?" Justin said, standing at attention like a dutiful waiter.

"No, not right now," Hope replied, her voice laced with playful suggestion. "But later, there will be something else I'd like."

Justin smiled, acknowledging the unspoken promise. Then he sat down next to her, and they both started eating.

"These eggs are delicious."

"Yeah, I cooked the eggs in some olive oil in the cabinet. It looked imported, so I gave it a chance. It tastes great."

Hope recalled that her ex-boyfriend, Eric, had brought the olive oil back from Greece. She hoped it wasn't too old or spoiled. *Between the perfume and the olive oil, Eric is actually helping a date go well for once,* she thought, amused by the irony.

The conversation was fast and fun. Each appreciated the other's deep love of music, eventually leading to a Michael Jackson vs. Prince argument. Hope took her title as Prince's #1 fan very seriously. After several minutes, Justin tried to end the argument.

"Wait a minute. Aren't you too young to be such a big Prince fan? *Purple Rain* came out before you and I were born."

"First, loving Prince's music is one of the few things my mother and I have in common. She played it all the time, and it put her in a good mood. Secondly, classics never grow old. Am I too young to listen to Beethoven or Bach? Should I turn off the radio when Elvis or Smokey Robinson comes on? I don't think so."

Justin realized Hope was a much better debater than he would ever be. So, he decided not to press any more points out of fear of her continued dominance.

"Okay, okay, I give. Since it's your birthday, I'll let you and his Purple Badness win."

"On behalf of Prince, The Revolution, and the millions of Prince fans everywhere, I thank you for knowing who is the best of all time."

They both laughed a good laugh.

The air between them crackled with desire as Hope settled on top of him, taking control of the moment. She felt completely safe with him, the kind of safety she hadn't felt in years. The pain of her birthday, her sister's pregnancy, and her mother's insanity were all distant memories, a world away. All that mattered was this moment, this man.

As they kissed, Justin's hands found their way to her butt, and she stopped to look up at him. When he immediately removed his hands, she shook her head and smiled.

"I didn't tell you to stop," she whispered, her voice husky. "I just wanted to look into your magnificent eyes. Now get back to work."

"Yes, Doctor," he replied, a playful grin on his face. His hand returned to its firm yet soft resting place on her.

With her gaze still locked with his, Hope asked, "Do you have any condoms?"

Justin was visibly startled by the question. His eyes went wide as he stammered, "No, I don't. I didn't think to... Well, you know, it's been a long time since I've needed any."

Hope shrugged, her smile not faltering. "I know this is going to sound bad, but I do."

A wave of relief washed over Justin. Part of his mind felt that things were moving too fast, but his body had reached a point of no return.

"That doesn't sound bad at all," he said, his voice raw with need.

Hope slowly lifted herself off him. "Stay right there," she whispered, her eyes promising a swift return.

She came back a moment later with two condoms

from her purse, placing them on the coffee table.

"I'll help you with one of these later," she assured.

She returned to her position on top of him, and as their bodies reconnected, an intense sense of rightness settled over her. This was the first time in forever that she hadn't felt alone. This wrong felt incredibly and beautifully right. The more she took of him, the more she wanted.

She looked into his eyes, and he whispered, "You're so beautiful. This is incredible. You're amazing."

He kissed her with increasing passion, his hands moving over her skin, finding the clasp of her bra. With his eyes closed, he spoke softly, a raw vulnerability in his voice. "Chaka, you're amazing. I want you. Chaka!"

The air turned to ice.

The chasm opened between them.

"What did you just call me?" Hope's voice was flat, hollow.

"It was a mistake," Justin said quickly, his eyes flying open. "I didn't mean it. I swear."

"You said it," Hope replied, her voice heavy with a disappointment that was worse than anger. She fastened her bra, her gaze finding his wedding ring and settling there.

"I'm so sorry. I don't... I don't know why I said her name," Justin pleaded, his face a mask of regret.

Hope reached down, her movements mechanical, and retrieved Justin's polo shirt, holding it aloft. With her gaze fixed on the wall behind him and her voice barely a whisper, she said, "Please go. Please go now."

Justin wanted more than anything to take her in his arms, to beg for her forgiveness, to explain. But he knew he had made a devastating error. He saw the raw hurt in her eyes, a reflection of some deep pain he'd unknowingly touched. There was no easy fix for this. So, he took his shirt from her hand and put it on.

He opened the door and said only, "I am so sorry. Happy birthday."

And then he was gone.

Hope stood alone in the cold silence, trying to reconcile the emotional whiplash of the day—the soaring highs followed by crushing lows. All she could do was cling to one small consolation: all things considered, this birthday hadn't been her absolute worst.

Chapter 19
Hope Confronts "The Devil"

ope didn't sleep a wink. The events of her birthday had only hardened her resolve to intervene in Rachel's marriage, and she decided that today was the day. Today, she would confront the truth. But before she presented Rachel with the proof of Caleb's infidelity, she needed to check one last box. She would confront Caleb directly, leaving no room for doubt. She wanted to see if he would admit the truth or try to hide his actions. Either way, Hope knew that after their conversation, she would be absolutely certain.

Pastor Caleb's study in the Sea of Galilee Church was large and modern, a testament to his success. An adjustable desk stood sentinel against one wall, and a sleek speaker-microphone replaced a traditional phone. He was online when two hard raps on the door interrupted him. Hope stood at the door waiting for her invite into the viper's den.

"Hey, beautiful, come on in," Caleb said, waving her in with a smile that was all teeth and no warmth.

"Don't start! Not today," Hope said, her eyes piercing.

She made her way to the conference table, and Caleb joined her there.

He leaned back in his chair, the picture of effortless calm. "It's been far too long. I've seen you a couple of times around the church. I saw those dimples of yours that always commanded my attention. I'm happy you dropped by so we can catch up."

Hope felt a familiar flash of anger. "Catch-up? That is what we should do? Really?"

"Well then, Cheeks, what should we talk about?" he asked, a hint of a smile on his lips as he leaned forward.

The nickname, Cheeks, hit her with a sudden, jarring rush of memories. She hadn't heard it in years, not since the night he shattered her world. Back in college, Caleb had called her Cheeks because of her remarkable dimpled cheeks and what he referred to as a perfect apple-bottom butt. Back then, the nickname played into her insecurities and made her feel good about herself.

He was a big man on campus, a star football player, and she was just his English tutor. Then he chose her over everybody. She was the "good" girl, the one he claimed to be serious about. She was his first love, and he was her first everything. While she remained loyal to him, he was sleeping with women of all races and demographics across campus and at every opposing team's venue. He was so charming, so beguiling. Hope had always thought no woman could resist his charm—not her and especially not Rachel. Even now, he still managed to make her feel special, and for a fleeting, guilty moment, she felt a pang of nostalgia for that younger, more naive version of herself.

Hope shook her head to dispel the old memories and steel her mind.

"Shall we discuss your nocturnal activities? There are feral alley cats that are more faithful than you," Hope spat, her voice low. "Can't you keep that crooked cock in your pants? Rachel is pregnant, and instead of being there for her and the baby, you're out banging hoes."

Caleb chuckled, a deep, easy sound that made her skin crawl. "Good to know you still think about our crooked friend."

"I know you moved Twila to Houston," she retorted, her voice shaking with rage.

Caleb's smile didn't waver. "Twila? Oh, she's just a big supporter of mine. You know me, Cheeks. I'm a faithful one-woman man." The final words were delivered with a mocking wink.

Of all the things he could have said, that line—a lie so absurd and cruel—was the one that broke her. Hope lunged from her chair, fueled by blinding rage, intent on wiping the smug look off his face. But his reflexes, honed on the football field, were still sharp. He was out of his seat in one smooth motion, catching her wrists and spinning her around until her back pressed against his chest. His embrace was unyielding, and she felt the shocking, repulsive press of his erection against her.

"I remember this," he whispered, his breath hot against her ear. "I know you do, too. Do you still like to get it this way? All you have to do is ask, and I can make that happen."

Hope's rage turned to ice. "Get off me, you nasty motherfucker!" she screeched.

"Hey, what's going on?" the church clerk shouted,

who was now standing in the study.

Caleb released Hope and stepped back. Hope spun around and shot Caleb a glare, noting his smug, still-smiling expression.

"Nothing, nothing at all," Caleb said, a false calm in his voice.

"If you ever touch me again, I will cut off your crooked friend and throw it on the altar!" Hope roared, gesturing toward Caleb's pelvis.

Caleb's eyes held no anger, only a disturbing flicker of desire. He was aroused. He took a perverse pleasure in her anger and her display of strength.

Hope didn't wait for his response. She spun on her heel and stomped out of the study, the sound of her heels echoing down the silent hallway. Behind her, Caleb watched her go. He shrugged at the church clerk, whose surprise was tempered with a familiar look.

"She has issues," he declared, his voice a calm veneer over his twisted satisfaction. "We should pray for her."

Chapter 20
Unforgivable Betrayal

The air in Rachel's sprawling, luxurious home was light and warm, a suffocating contrast to the cold fury seething in Hope's veins. Fresh from Caleb's office, she was a walking storm, and she had come here to unleash it. They sat in Rachel's gleaming kitchen, the marble counters and stainless-steel appliances mocking Hope with their testament to the life Caleb's ministry afforded her.

Hope's heart hammered against her ribs, a frantic drumbeat against the silence. She didn't lead in. She didn't soften the blow. She just launched the grenade.

"Caleb is cheating on you. Her name is Twila Gooden."

Rachel didn't flinch. She took a slow, deliberate sip of her tea, the clink of porcelain the only sound in the room. Then she met Hope's gaze, her expression impossibly calm.

"I know."

Hope's jaw went slack. The breath caught in her throat. "You… you know?"

"Yes," Rachel said, her voice flat and emotionless. "I've known for months."

John Gary Long

"Were you also aware she moved here to Houston?"

"I suspected."

Hope felt the blood rushing to her face, hot with fury. "How can you just take this? What is wrong with you? I knew you've always been soft, but this is a new level of weakness. You are letting this woman ruin your life. Caleb ruined my life when he seduced you, and you were so blind to his charm. Now you're letting him do it all over again."

The words hung in the air, a knife-edge of a sentence that Hope hadn't realized she was capable of saying. The color drained from Rachel's face. She set her cup down with a clatter, the fragile peace between them shattering into a thousand pieces.

"He didn't seduce me, Hope," Rachel said, her voice cracking. Her confession was a whisper, a stark, painful truth that was even harder to hear than Hope's accusation. "I pursued and seduced him, not the other way around."

Hope was so stunned she couldn't speak. Her perfect narrative of Caleb as the slick, predatory villain unraveled. She experienced a deep sense of disorientation, as if the ground beneath her had vanished. All her rage and pain from the past several years had been directed at Caleb, but Rachel's confession turned everything on its head.

"Why?" Hope finally managed to say, the word a raw, guttural sound.

"I was so jealous of you," Rachel said, a tear finally escaping her eye. "Of you and Craig. He always picked you. He always called you. I'd be home, and all I could think about was why he loved you more. When you got engaged to Caleb, it was just…too much. Taking him away from you…it fed some dark, sick part of me."

All the air left Hope's lungs. She no longer saw Rachel as a victim but a manipulator—someone who had willingly participated in a cruel act. Her long-simmering anger finally boiled over, and the words ripped out of Hope, laced with years of festering bitterness.

"You destroyed me!" she spat, her voice rising to a piercing shriek. "You destroyed us! All because of some sick, pathetic jealousy? You're just as fake as he is. All of this," she gestured wildly at the gleaming kitchen, "this perfect house, this perfect life—you built it on my broken heart! You're a liar, and now you're going to teach your baby to be one, too."

The verbal assault was too much. Rachel's composed facade didn't just crack; it shattered. Her face crumpled into a mask of grief and shame.

Hope didn't wait to see if she would respond. The rage and betrayal burned like fire in her veins. She stood, grabbed her purse, and stormed out the front door, the slam echoing through the silent, perfect house. She got into her car, her hands shaking on the wheel. The tears came then, hot and furious. Her heart wasn't just broken; it was annihilated, and her bond with her sister was now more fractured than she ever believed possible.

Chapter 21
Seizure

Hope was up before dawn, another restless night behind her. Her fury at Justin and Caleb was a dull ache compared to the raw wound of Rachel's deception. The chaotic stew of her mother's cruelty, Caleb's smug malice, and Justin's betrayal now all paled next to the staggering lie her sister had confessed. Nelson, however, was a constant, and his need for a morning walk was a command she obeyed on pure instinct. Her mind felt fried, and she moved as if in a daze, her body an empty vessel on the well-worn path to the park.

Hope sat at what she had come to think of as the Justin table. She needed a moment to gather her bearings.

"May I join you?" a familiar voice asked from behind her.

Hope flinched. She wasn't in the mood for apologies or conversation; she wanted to be left alone with her rage and grief. She looked up and saw Justin, but said nothing. She didn't have the energy for a single word— not a yes or a no.

Justin decided to sit across from her. He had thought of a couple of things to say, but he somehow knew not to say anything he had practiced. He stared at Hope's blank face, which was focused on something in the distance over his shoulder. Justin scanned the area where Hope was looking and saw nothing of particular note.

"Hey, so what are you—"

Justin abruptly stopped. He now realized Hope had not moved since he sat down. She wasn't even blinking.

"Hope... Hope, are you okay?" His voice splintered with notes of concern.

Justin reached out to touch the one hand she had resting on the table, adding a gentle tug to his voiced concerns. "Hope, what's wrong?"

Justin stood up and moved to Hope's side of the table. He put his arm around her. "Let's get you home."

As he lifted her, her legs involuntarily supported her weight, but they didn't extend fully. Justin moved her away from the park bench when he realized he was now entirely supporting her. Hope was unresponsive, but her eyes remained wide open.

Justin laid her on the park grass as gently as he could. "Hope, are you okay? Please be okay."

Her lips began to move—a frantic, silent struggle. Then, a single, raspy word escaped.

"Hi."

"Do you need some help?" a male voice came from above Justin, who was hovering over Hope.

"Yes. I don't know what's wrong with her," Justin said.

"Looks like she's having a seizure. I'll call 911. While I call, look at her medical necklace and see what it says."

Hope's necklace was almost entirely concealed by her

T-shirt during her morning walks. In the prone position, a set of medical dog tags had slipped out from under her shirt and was lying beside her head. Justin's concern for Hope had made the necklace invisible to him until the good Samaritan pointed it out. He picked up the dog tags and read the engraved words:

Hope Castillo
Lupus
ALGY: Amoxicillin
ICE: 781-555-3348

Lupus? Hope has lupus? Justin questioned in his mind, a look of confusion on his face.

"The dispatcher said an ambulance is on its way," the stranger told Justin while still holding the phone to his ear. "He wants to know if she's responsive at all. Call her name again."

"Hope, it's me, Justin. Can you please say something?"

Hope's face gave the slightest attempt at a smile as she whispered, "Hi."

Her lips continued to move slowly, but nothing could be understood.

"She can only say hi. She doesn't appear to be in any other distress," the stranger explained to the dispatcher, then said, "Okay, thanks," before disconnecting the call. "An ambulance should be here in less than ten minutes. St. Agatha's is just eight blocks away."

Justin knelt beside her, holding her hand. A bone-deep fear settled in his chest as her eyes slowly closed and did not reopen. He squeezed her hand, a silent plea.

Please, no. Not this.

His terror transformed into determination. Justin decided he couldn't wait one more second. He scooped Hope's limp body into his arms, the weight surprisingly light. He turned toward the direction of St. Agatha's and began to walk briskly. After only a few strides, he knew it wasn't fast enough. The silent fear inside him felt alive in his chest. He broke into a jog, then a full run, holding his precious cargo close to him. Nelson, loyal and frantic, kept pace just behind his heels.

Due to Justin's run, Hope's head bobbled up and down, hitting Justin's arm. Justin slowed momentarily to adjust her head so it rested between his arm and his chest. Now, with Hope safely cradled in his arms, Justin ran at a sprinter's pace. Dog walkers and other street inhabitants marveled at his strength and speed.

Six blocks into their journey, Hope briefly opened her eyes and looked up at Justin who—focused on avoiding traffic at the street corners—did not notice. Hope was too weak to have any coherent thoughts, but she felt the safety of his arms.

Justin didn't stop running until he reached St. Agatha's parking lot. The sight of an ambulance pulling out of the bay sent a fresh jolt of fear through him. He waved frantically, yelling until a paramedic noticed him. He gently laid Hope on the ground, and a swarm of paramedics immediately began their work. Justin and Nelson could only stand there and watch, their hearts aching with a shared, desperate prayer for the one they both loved.

* * *

Justin sat in the emergency room waiting area chair, a hard plastic shell that offered no comfort. He rocked back and forth, the cold, unyielding back pinching his spine with each movement. Every three minutes, he got up to take a sip from the water fountain, a futile attempt to wash away the bone-dry feeling in his throat. The wailing of babies and the commotion of the busy waiting room were just background noise, a distant buzz beneath the deafening roar of his own anxiety. Hospitals, he knew, were where God was at His cruelest. And experience had taught him to dread them.

On his return from his fortieth trip to the water fountain, Justin was stopped by a smiling yet concerned Latin face. "Excuse me, are you Justin?" the face asked.

"Yes," Justin replied, unsure why he was being questioned.

"Hi, my name is Anna. I'm Hope's friend," she said, extending her hand.

Her presence was like a lifeline, pulling him out of the spiraling vortex of his anxiety.

"Nice to meet you," Justin managed, his voice still tight with tension. "Hope has told me a lot about you."

"I hope she didn't tell you everything," Anna responded.

"No, I don't think she told me everything." Justin briefly smiled, but the expression was fleeting, his face immediately returning to a serious mask. "She's been back there for over two hours, and they won't tell me anything. I don't know what's happening or how she's doing."

Anna heard the desperation in Justin's voice and saw it on his face. She quickly noted two things. First, his eyes were magnificent, just as Hope had described. Second, and more importantly, *He cares for my girl Hope. Yes!*

"The hospital called me because I'm Hope's ICE, or In Case of Emergency contact," Anna disclosed. "I'm on file here at St. Agatha's as a person they're allowed to give personal information regarding her health situation. Unfortunately, we've been here more than a few times. I'll go see what I can find out."

Anna left Justin standing in the middle of the waiting room and headed over to the receptionist's desk. Justin could not hear much of the conversation, but he soon realized they were conversing in Spanish. While he did not understand what was being said, he felt a little relief that Anna was making considerably more headway than he had in the previous two hours.

Anna returned to Justin. "They're still evaluating her. She said I could go back and see her. Once I get an update, I'll let you know. Okay?"

"Okay," Justin answered with the only reply he could give.

Anna walked away and entered the back area after being buzzed in.

Justin slowly paced around the waiting room. He could no longer sit in the confining plastic scoop of a chair. The dryness in his throat that had eased while talking to Anna had now returned. He could hear his short, quick breaths as he inhaled and exhaled through his nostrils. As he paced, Justin kept glancing at his phone, hoping for a text with news about Hope.

After about thirty minutes, the backroom door opened, and Anna appeared.

"So Hope had a seizure," she explained after walking

over to Justin. "The doctors aren't sure what caused it. These episodes in the past have been triggered by things like her levels getting out of whack, lack of sleep, or stress."

"Her levels getting out of whack? What does that mean?" Justin questioned.

Anna realized she was working with information Justin did not have. He didn't know about Hope's medical condition. Anna gestured to the loveseat, and they both sat, perched on the front edge of the cushions as if ready to flee.

"Hope has lupus," Anna explained, her voice soft but steady. She watched his face for a reaction. "She was diagnosed back in college. From time to time, she has episodes that can take the form of seizures, severe pain, or extreme fatigue. She's on medication that usually keeps everything in check, but stress and lack of sleep can throw her body out of balance."

Justin tried to process what he was being told. He had heard of lupus but had no idea what it was. He just knew it was severe. He wondered why Hope hadn't told him she was sick. Whatever reason she had, he was sure it was his fault.

"Is she going to be all right?" he asked.

"She should be. She's getting her bearings but is still far from one hundred percent. The doctors are going to keep her overnight for observation. Once she's admitted, you can see her in her room. That will take several hours."

"Well, I want to see her as soon as possible," Justin said.

"I planned on staying with her tonight," Anna added.

"By the way, can you take Nelson home with you? I have his food, a portable water bowl, and poop bags in my car."

Justin's eyes widened, then lit up with a mix of relief and horror. He had completely forgotten about Nelson, still tied to the bicycle rack outside. The guilt was immediate and crushing.

"Yes," he said, his voice a rush of new purpose. "Absolutely. Can we go and give him food and water right now?"

"Sure, let's go."

Anna and Justin headed out to the car. For a brief moment, his worry for Hope was superseded by his concern for Nelson.

This is all Hope needs. While she's in the hospital, I kill her dog, he thought.

Chapter 22
Justin's Realization

*I*f God were cruel in emergency rooms, hospital rooms were where He executed His most diabolical plans. They were sterile torture chambers, places where both Chaka and Justin's father took their last breaths.

Justin sat at the foot of Hope's bed, the room's silence a cold shroud. Concern enveloped him, its tentacles squeezing tighter and tighter. His eyes darted between the heart monitor and the subtle rise and fall of Hope's chest, watching for any sign of a faltering beat or an unsteady breath.

It was now mid-morning. The family of the woman with whom Hope shared a hospital room had just left. Justin was happy they were gone. They were kind enough, but their laughter and talking might disturb Hope's rest. Fortunately, the commotion did not affect Hope, as she had slept the entire time since Justin had relieved Anna at about 7:30 a.m.

Hope's eyelids fluttered open, then closed again. Justin sprang from his seat and stood over her, debating whether to rouse her from her fragile rest. Just as he decided against it, her eyes opened again, this time wide and fully present.

"Hey Doc, how are you feeling?" Justin kindly asked.

Hope looked at him, smiled, and whispered, "Good."

Being mildly drugged and having recently experienced a seizure, "Good" was just a reflex answer because Hope wasn't currently capable of high cognitive thinking.

Justin reached down and held her right hand between his two massive ones.

"Great. I'm sure they'll take great care of you," Justin said in an attempt to convince himself that today's visit would not be like his last two visits to the hospital.

Hope looked around the room, then back at Justin. Her voice remained small. "I'm sorry."

"You don't have to apologize. You just get better," Justin responded.

Hope spoke even more softly as she closed her eyes again. "Thank you."

Hope then drifted off to sleep. Justin wanted her back. He wanted to talk to her.

He continued to hold her hand, finding a sense of grounding in her warmth. It was soft and impossibly small in his large hands. He leaned over, gently lifted it, and pressed the back of her hand against his cheek. Then, with a tenderness that surprised him, he kissed her skin before returning her hand to its comforting place against his face. The touch of her hand, warm and delicate, was a sudden balm to his turmoil.

He couldn't take his eyes off her face, a beautiful canvas stripped bare of make-up. Though a little color had returned, her skin lacked its usual radiant glow.

Every time he tried to look away, a sharp pain pierced his soul. His heart pounded in his ears, a frantic drumbeat he couldn't understand. Then, as he stood there watching her, a profound silence fell.

It was in that moment—in the middle of a sterile hospital room, looking at a pale, unconscious, and helpless Hope—that the truth hit him. He wasn't just concerned. He was in love—completely, irrevocably, falling-off-a-cliff in love.

He faintly whispered, "I love you," to the sleeping Hope. To his surprise, she returned a small smile but never opened her eyes.

The realization that he loved her terrified Justin. He wondered if he could hide his feelings from God because God had taken away everything and everyone Justin loved.

Chapter 23
Hospital Battlefield

amiliar voices, engaged in an all-too-familiar argument, clawed their way through the haze and woke Hope.

"Why are you here? Aren't there some packages that need to be delivered?" Gina's voice, sharp and laced with disdain, sliced through the quiet of the room.

"I'm here to see about Hope and make sure you don't pull the plug on my daughter," Craig shot back, his tone a low, growling defense.

He and Gina stood on opposite sides of Hope's bed, the sterile hospital room now the latest battlefield in their seemingly ancient war.

"Your daughter, your daughter…" Gina repeated, a sneer twisting her perfectly done-up face. "Oh yeah, you must protect your daughter from her mean old mother. That's right. I'm such a horrible person that your daughter needs protection from me." Her voice dripped with sarcasm.

Gina was uniquely gifted at pushing every one of Craig's wrong buttons. He and his ex-wife were stuck in a destructive cycle that started in their dating years, continued through marriage, and carried into their bitter divorce. Gina's words were a poison he couldn't resist, carving hurtful wounds deep inside Craig. He couldn't even remember why he once loved her. All he could recall were the heated arguments and her words that degraded his very existence. She had set a verbal trap and, as always, he had taken the bait.

"Horrible does not begin to describe you. There's a long list of words I don't like to use anymore that better describe who and what you are. In fact, here are a few—"

"She's awake," Rachel interrupted, her voice cutting through the malevolent verbal barrage.

She had been standing in silence near the window, a silent spectator to a war she'd witnessed her entire life. Their arguments had confused and hurt her as a little girl, and they still did now. She would remain silent and pray for the storm to pass. When the barrage and wind would move on, Rachel would feel like she was the one hit by lightning bolts.

Craig stepped forward toward the top of Hope's bed. His kind eyes, framed by worry lines, searched her face.

"Hey, girl, how are you doing?"

Before Hope could respond, Gina stepped in front of Craig. "How's she doing? She's in the hospital after having a seizure. How do you think she's doing? I see being married to that accountant hasn't made your naive ass any smarter!"

A vein pulsed in Craig's forehead as he glared at Gina, but he swallowed the bait this time. He turned back to Hope, taking her hand in his and placing his other hand on her forehead.

"Hi, Craig," Hope said, the words a dry whisper between two minor coughs. She had not spoken much in the last twenty-four hours, and her throat was dry.

"Hi, Craig? Is he the only person you see in here?" Gina asked, continuing her role as the chief instigator, her eyes a mix of fire and calculation.

Hope gave a quick scan of the room. "Hi, Rach," she said to her sister, who was standing in the corner, trying to remain invisible.

Hope knew it was a petty jab at her mother, but from a hospital bed, there were so few joys. Her seizure-induced disorientation made her momentarily forget her sister's betrayal, and she seized the small victory.

Gina's nostrils flared. When Hope had been under her roof, a smart-aleck comment like that would have earned a smack across the mouth. The impulse was still there, but the hospital setting gave her pause.

"They came by earlier and gave us the results of your blood tests. Your levels are close to being back to normal, and you should be going home either late today or first thing tomorrow," Craig explained to Hope. "They're not sure what brought on this episode. Anything out of the ordinary happen over the last couple of days?"

Again, before Hope could answer, Gina interjected, her voice sharp as a tack. "Yes, something happened. She has been getting into shit that is none of her damn business." Gina now stared directly at Hope, her gaze a heavy weight. "You need to stay out of married folks' business and try to get some business of your own."

Rachel shot a glare at Gina, a flicker of outrage on her face. She confided in Gina that she and Hope had discussed Caleb's infidelity. Now, Gina was weaponizing it.

Craig extended his arm across the bed, shielding Hope from his ex-wife. "Hey, hey, you better cool it!"

Gina scoffed and smacked Craig's hand away. "You never have and never will tell me what to do. I will do what I want when I want."

Unnoticed by the combatants, the machines monitoring Hope's vital signs started to beep with renewed distress. However, a man now standing in the doorway detected the change.

"Excuse me," Justin said, his voice firm and his posture resolute.

The argument ceased instantly. All three turned to look at the man with strikingly familiar, kind eyes.

"I'm not sure what's going on, but I know Hope needs to get some rest," Justin said, his voice now gentle but unwavering.

All three wondered, *Who in the hell is this?* Before anyone could ask, another figure entered the room.

"I must agree," the white lab-coated Dr. Bamenda said in his distinct African accent.

His confident walk and air of authority commanded immediate respect. Everyone in the room stood a bit more upright. Gina adjusted her designer pantsuit jacket, and her face softened.

In an angelic voice, she said, "Hello, Doctor. I am so glad you're here. I know my daughter is in excellent hands with you."

"Hello, Ms. Georgina. It's always a pleasure to see you," Dr. Bamenda said, his voice warm as if he were greeting an old friend.

Neither Hope, Rachel, nor Craig was surprised by Gina's sudden change of demeanor. They had witnessed the two-faced monster in action many times.

"So, how is my dear daughter doing?" Gina inquired, continuing her performance.

"Well, that is why I'm here. Can you all step outside, please, while I examine Hope?"

Gina spoke quickly, not allowing anyone else to comment. "Of course, we can. Please let us know if you need us to do anything."

She then ushered the group out of the room, giving the doctor a warm pat on the chest as she passed. Once everyone was standing in the hallway and the door was shut, all eyes turned toward Justin. Without a word, he felt the need to introduce himself.

"Well, I'm Justin, a friend of Hope's. She was with me in the park when her seizure started."

Craig, a man with a weathered but kind Latino face, extended his hand. "Hi, I'm Hope's father, Craig. Thanks for getting my baby help so quickly."

Rachel, an image of beauty but with a guarded expression, extended her hand next. "I'm her sister, Rachel. Nice to meet you."

"Nice to meet you, too, and congratulations. I heard you and the Reverend are expecting."

Rachel smiled, a genuine flicker of light in her eyes. "Thank you."

She was still growing accustomed to being the first lady and everyone knowing the details of her personal life.

Gina stood silently with her arms folded across her chest. She was a stylish woman in her early fifties, but her face, though beautiful, carried a hardness that spoke of a life spent in sharp judgment. She was still deciding whether this man was worth her time. The only thing Gina liked about Hope was that she usually paired herself with well-educated, prosperous men—the same kind of men Gina exclusively dated after divorcing Craig. When Justin turned to her with an extended hand, Gina reluctantly reciprocated.

"I'm her mother," Gina said curtly, her voice a glacier that refused to melt.

"Nice to meet you, ma'am," Justin said with a charming voice that usually warmed women up.

"Don't call me ma'am. I am not that old." Gina's cold response was a final barrier.

"Okay," Justin said, a bit taken aback by her abruptness.

The four of them stood in an awkward silence, connected only by the patient in the room behind them.

Dr. Bamenda emerged from the room. "She's doing much better. Lupus manifests itself in different ways in people. I would like to keep her overnight for observation. She needs rest and not visitors. I recommend that only one of you stay with her."

To Justin's dismay, Craig said, "I will."

Justin felt that somehow Craig was taking a job that should be his and his alone.

"Yes, Doctor. Unfortunately, I cannot stay. But Craig is sure to call if she needs anything," Gina said to the group in her practiced, cherub voice, batting her long eyelashes.

"Okay, Mr. Castillo. The nurse is going into the room for some additional tests and housekeeping. Please wait until she's out before you go back in. As for the rest of you, have a good day," Dr. Bamenda said, then hurried off to his next patient.

Justin reached into his pocket, pulled out several of his business cards, and handed them to the group. "Please call me if anything changes."

"Sure, man," Craig said.

Gina read the card and mentally turned up her nose. *He's a grease monkey. Hope is lowering her standards.*

She departed from the group without so much as a grunt. Rachel gave a small wave and quickly followed after her mother. Craig and Rachel's eyes never met as she exited.

"Nice to meet you, young man," Craig said, giving Justin a firm farewell handshake.

"Same here, sir. Again, don't hesitate to call me if needed. Oh, and if she asks, tell her I have Nelson. Okay?"

"Got it," Craig said, giving Justin a man-to-man head nod.

Justin walked away feeling like he had abandoned his guard post. While he left Hope in her father's care, he now only trusted himself with Hope's well-being.

Chapter 24
Twila's Moral Conflict

The hospital at 3 a.m. was a ghost town. The only sounds were the quiet hum of machines and the hushed whisper of rubber soles on tile. The halls were deserted, and in Room 417, Hope was totally alone. Her roommate had been discharged, and Craig was asleep on a couch in the visitors' lounge. Hope was alone, the nurse's resentment standing over her.

Twila Gooden, the emerald-eyed nurse from St. Agatha's and Caleb's not-so-secret lover, looked down at the sleeping Hope Castillo. Getting rehired by St. Agatha's was easy; with a nursing shortage, they were happy to welcome her back. It was a pure, dangerous coincidence that her return had afforded her this unique opportunity—an opportunity to fix a problem that had just emerged.

Twila's thoughts, a bitter stream of consciousness, turned to the woman in the bed.

"You and Rachel have it so easy," she muttered, her voice barely a breath. "You both act like you're better than me, treating me like trash." She saw their little group today, all arguing in the hallway. "Must be nice to have so many people who care. And, Hope, I see you have a boyfriend. A new one?"

She took a step closer, her focus shifting from Hope's face to the IV drip beside the bed—the clear pouch and the thin tube connecting it to Hope's arm. Her plan, once a fleeting thought, now felt solid and sinister.

"So many things I could put in this IV," she mused. "Something to give you a worse seizure, something permanent. How would Rachel feel if you died here tonight? Would she blame herself and leave Caleb? Then I could take her place. I'd be a better first lady than she could ever be."

"And your new boyfriend," she whispered, the malice in her voice unmistakable. "Would he mourn you? Who would he seek comfort with? An old flame, perhaps? A fascinating experiment."

The thought of inflicting harm, of wielding such power, fueled the bitterness festering within her. It gave her a sense of twisted control. Yet, as she held the prepared syringe in her hand, the memory of his face surfaced. Not Caleb's, but the man from the hallway. The man with the captivating eyes who she had noticed from afar. His gaze was a phantom of a much happier time in her life. A part of her, buried deep under years of bitterness, ached for that old, uncomplicated feeling.

Twila took a few steps back from the bed, her hand lowering. The syringe felt cold and heavy in her palm.

"Hope, you truly don't know how fortunate you are," she whispered, her voice laced with a raw, unexpected regret.

She carefully put the prepared syringe back in her

medicine bag, tucked it away, and quietly exited the room, leaving Hope to sleep, unaware of just how close she had come to not waking up.

Chapter 25
Justin Keeps It Moving

The aroma of bacon in his mother's kitchen had always been the most enticing smell Justin could imagine. The scent alone was enough to make Pavlov proud; it was an automatic trigger for him to find his seat in the kitchen and eagerly anticipate breakfast.

In front of Justin, Lorraine set the plate of bacon, two eggs over easy, and buttered toast beside the bowl of steaming hot grits already there. Justin promptly picked up the plate and slid the eggs into the bowl of grits. Lorraine smiled. She loved it when her son had a full belly to take on the challenges of this world.

A panting Nelson sat by the kitchen table beside Justin, staring up at him. Whenever Hope made turkey bacon in her microwave, she would give him a slice or two. Nelson sat, hoping Justin knew the drill. Unfortunately for Nelson, Justin had other things on his mind than his salivating friend.

Justin started eating but kept staring at the messages on his phone. "I'm not sure how to get all of these jobs done today and pick Hope up from the hospital," he said in a burdened voice.

"So your friend is getting out today? That's good. How is she doing?" Lorraine asked, her eyes twinkling as she saw her opening for more questions. Justin hadn't shared much information about his newfound friend, but her instincts told her this was no ordinary friendship.

"Her dad has sent me a couple of texts updating me on her status. She is much better, except she woke up around three-thirty this morning and couldn't get back to sleep. He said she should get released about four o'clock if she has no setbacks," Justin explained.

"Oh, that's good to hear," Lorraine said. "It's amazing she trusts you with Nelson. I would have thought she would've had her family take him for the night."

Choosing not to elaborate on the family dynamics he had witnessed the day before, Justin simply stated, "Well, he was with me already. So, it was easiest for me to keep him for a few days."

"That makes sense," Lorraine said, refraining from asking additional Hope questions. She moved her cross-examination to another part of the investigation. "You mentioned work. Is today going to be another one of those 'leave the porch light on' for you days?" Lorraine asked with equal parts humor and concern.

"I don't know yet. Based on these messages, it doesn't look good. I need to go into the shop and coordinate with Hank before he heads to the first job," Justin said as he inhaled an entire slice of bacon. He barely had the whole piece in his mouth before he had already started spooning the grits and eggs in.

"Okay. Well, let me know if you need help or want

me to pick up your friend for you," Lorraine said, expressing support. "Deuce and I will be here all day."

Justin was in the last few steps of his breakfast-eating sprint when another message popped up on his phone. He stopped dead. A smile, sudden and bright, spread across his face as he read the message. "Hope says good morning. She also wants to know how Nelson is doing."

He typed his reply, muttering the words aloud as he wrote. "Mom says good morning to you, too. Nelson is fine. He is sitting next to me, watching me eat."

Justin waited a moment for Hope's response: *He is a greedy little thing. ☺ Feel free to give him any of your breakfast leftovers...but don't worry about him. He'll be fine.*

OK, Justin texted back, and Hope's reply came quickly. *I can have Anna pick me up if you're too busy.*

Justin sent his response just as quickly: *No, it's no problem. Is four o'clock still okay?*

Yes. See you then. Bye.

Bye.

Justin set down the phone and glanced up at Lorraine, who was smiling. She had been watching him the entire time. Seeing the excitement on her son's face as he texted with Hope warmed her heart.

"Boy, look at you. You are grinning from ear to ear. This Hope must be something mighty good."

Justin dropped his shoulders and confessed, the words pouring out like a man unburdening a heavy secret. "I think she is."

Justin stood up, grabbed his last piece of bacon, and held the strip a few inches in front of Nelson. After a few quick sniffs, Nelson caught the bacon and plopped down into a comfortable position to enjoy his breakfast treat.

"I gotta go. Tell Deuce I said bye. I'll see you both later when I come by to pick up the dog."

With one last grin, he jogged out the door, his steps lighter than they had been in years.

Lorraine looked at her canine house guest, who was staring at her. "So, I guess you want some more breakfast. Well, let's see what I can do."

Lorraine started toward the refrigerator. She had another boy to take care of today.

* * *

Justin stared at the long list of backlogged jobs, a knot of dread tightening in his stomach. He wasn't prioritizing by client urgency; he was prioritizing by who could pay him in cash. His bank accounts were empty, and his credit line was maxed out. Friday was coming, and he didn't have enough money to pay Hank and Akil for all the overtime they had worked.

The shop door swung open, and Hank walked in with his usual steady pace, setting his large metal thermos down on his bench with a familiar thud. The thermos was a throwback to the days when men built skyscrapers with their bare hands, just as Hank was a reminder of simpler times—a time before debt, before this suffocating pressure.

Both men prepped for the long day ahead. Hank readied his tools for his first call while Justin, hunched over his phone, rearranged the afternoon schedule so he could pick up Hope. Every change had a domino effect, causing more overtime for either Akil or Hank— overtime Justin couldn't afford to pay. The mental jigsaw puzzle was interrupted by Hank's voice.

"I had to replace the feed to the Geeston boiler again. I used a Yates boiler feed this time," Hank said matter-of-factly, his voice a low rumble.

A Yates. Justin's head snapped up. Yates boiler feeds were the best in their class and the most expensive. He stared at Hank, who did not look back, continuing to pack his bag. Justin knew the argument was coming. He'd tell Hank they couldn't afford the $2,000 upgrade. Hank would say the generic feed was crap, and buying another was throwing good money after bad. He'd remind Justin that a client like Jake wouldn't tolerate a boiler that broke down every other week.

Justin closed his eyes. Hank was right. But what Hank didn't know was that the purchase had officially pushed the business over its credit limit. The decision had been made for him. He'd have to take on all the overtime work for the next week or two. He just wouldn't pay himself.

"I'm going to text you a new schedule for today. I need you and Akil to clock out no later than six o'clock. So, please plan to have everything done by then." Justin's voice was strained as he typed the new schedule into his phone.

Hank's movements slowed. He looked at Justin, a flicker of concern in his eyes. "I guess I'll be starting my Uber shift earlier. But I know Akil could use the cash. Are you sure you can pick up all the slack?"

"He needs to learn how to save his money. He can't keep relying on me giving him overtime to get him extra cash," Justin retorted, the words a bitter defense.

"It's not like he's asking for a handout. He puts in a full day's work for a full day's pay." Having spent a few years as a union representative, Hank was always ready to defend someone else's rights.

Justin felt his hands ball into fists. He knew Hank was right. The fact that Hank always seemed to be right was getting under Justin's skin, a constant reminder of his own failings. Frustration with the conversation and the crushing weight of his financial burden had him wringing his hands.

Hank put down his tool bag and walked over to Justin's seat, his expression softening. "Hang in there. I know it's tough, but now is not the time to give up. Keep pushing forward, my friend."

Forward was the last direction Justin wanted to go. Forward meant more issues, more bills, a business on the verge of collapse, and a new love who would surely leave him once she found out he was just an uneducated, broke grease monkey. He returned Hank's overture with silence.

Both Hank's and Justin's phones pinged almost simultaneously. The text was from Akil, saying he was on his way to his first job.

"I'm gone," Hank said, a finality in his voice as he headed out the door.

Justin sat, trying to catch his breath, but he knew he couldn't sit long. An extended list of jobs would take him well into the night. He also had to pick up Hope from the hospital. The thought of his work truck—battered and covered in grime—next to her luxury SUV filled him with a fresh wave of humiliation. They were in different classes, and he feared she would eventually see that he wasn't worthy of being in hers.

Chapter 26
Big Preach Pays a Visit

The sterile white walls of Hope's hospital room felt like a cage, a stark contrast to the life she knew outside. Though she was due to be discharged later that day, her mind was a whirlwind of worry. She sat propped up in bed, a small, fragile figure against the crisp sheets.

A gentle knock on the door broke the silence. "Come in," she said, her voice still a little weak.

The door opened, and a small salt and pepper-haired, spry man with a kind, weathered coffee-toned face entered. He carried the familiar, fresh scent of old-school cologne. Reverend Dr. M. John Rice, known to everyone as Big Preach, smiled warmly. He was a man who, at barely 5'6", had earned his name not from his stature but from the profound weight of his words.

"My dear child," he said, his voice a gentle baritone, "I heard you were in a bit of trouble."

"Pastor John," Hope said, her eyes welling up with tears of relief. "I'm so glad you're here."

The sight of him—a man she had admired and trusted

her entire life—was a big comfort. He was a second father to her, the man who had always been a source of wisdom and strength. He had been a significant reason she remained at Sea of Galilee Church when Rachel returned with Caleb.

Big Preach pulled a chair to her bedside. "Hope, my dear, I heard about your episode. I'm concerned about you. How are you feeling?"

"Better," she said, managing a small smile. "I'm just...tired. And confused. Everything feels like a mess."

He nodded, his expression one of deep empathy. "Life's trials, they can leave us feeling like that, can't they? Troubled on every side, yet not distressed. Perplexed, but not in despair."

He spoke the scriptures from 2 Corinthians 4, a message he delivered every year on the Sunday after her birthday, a sermon he once told her he had crafted just for her.

"I have been worried about you," he continued. "I know things have been difficult. Your heart, my dear, is parched. Your tears have become your food because the people closest to you are causing you to question the very love and mercy of God."

He saw the pain in her eyes, the same pain that King David wrote about in the Psalms. He knew this feeling well, and Hope was experiencing it.

"Do you know what it says in Psalm 42:1-3?" he asked gently, then began to recite the verse. "As the deer pants for streams of water, so my soul pants for you, my God. My soul thirsts for God, for the living God. My tears have been my food day and night, while people say to me all day long, 'Where is your God?'"

He paused, letting the words sink in. Hope's own tears had been her food these last two days. It was a feast that only intensified her pain.

"Hope, we, as God's children, shouldn't dwell on 'why' these trials befall us," Big Preach said, his voice now a low, comforting rumble. "Instead, we should ask, 'What will God do through me now?'"

Hope thought about her work with patients, Hannah's family, the women's shelter, her little sister Amira, and the many lives she'd touched. Her empathy, born from her struggles, fueled her ability to help others. Her greatest pain was the wellspring for her deepest purpose.

"And now, you have a new struggle," Big Preach said, a twinkle in his eye. "A new love, is that right?"

Hope's face flushed. She had no idea how he knew.

"I am not asking for details. I'm just here to give you advice that you can hold on to. Do not be confused, my dear. If you want to be strong, you have to lift something heavy. You are in training to be a modern-day Samson. Trust in the Lord with all your heart and lean not on your own understanding; in all your ways acknowledge Him, and He will make your paths straight."

"I'm sure this new relationship with this young man is a scary and exciting new chapter," Big Preach continued. "I have no doubt that you will approach this new season with all the faith and perseverance I have known you to have all of your life. Do not let your past pain with your mother and sister keep you from moving forward. Do not let fear rule your heart. Open your heart to the love God has sent you. He has a plan to prosper you and not to harm you."

Hope, comforted by his words, felt a sense of clarity settle over her. "Thank you, Pastor John."

"You are a precious child of God, my dear. You are loved, and you are not alone."

He gave her a warm hug and then walked out of the room, leaving her with a renewed sense of purpose and a spirit ready to face the challenges ahead.

Chapter 27
Chaka's Story

Hope unlocked the door to her condo, the sound a quiet click against the humid air. Justin stepped inside, his arms full with a duffel bag and a small backpack. He gently placed the bags on the floor.

"Thanks for doing all this, Justin," Hope said, her voice soft.

The scent of her own space—a warm, inviting aroma of vanilla—was a welcome comfort after the sterile smell of the hospital.

"No problem," he said, setting the crate down and giving Nelson a scratch behind the ears. "He's all set up. I took him for a long walk this morning and gave him a good breakfast. I don't want you to have to do too much for a while. Doctors said no heavy lifting, and an hour-long walk is a lot. I will swing by in the morning to take him out again. You stay put."

Hope's heart swelled. He was so considerate. "Thank you, Justin. Really."

He simply nodded, his eyes scanning the room. The

last time they had been here, the air had crackled with a different kind of tension, one that had ended with him saying another woman's name and Hope telling him to get out. The memory hung in the air like a ghost.

A heavy, torrential rain beat against the large window, a drumming that filled the silence. It was a rhythmic, relentless downpour, as if the heavens themselves were weeping.

"It feels like we're back at the scene of the crime," Hope said quietly. "All that's missing is the police tape."

Justin's shoulders slumped. "I know. I will be taking off in a minute. Just need to sit for a moment."

He walked over to a comfortable chair in the living room and sat down, his posture slumped.

"Don't go," Hope said, a note of urgency in her voice. She walked over to the chair across from him. "Before we talk about anything else...I want to talk about her."

Justin's breathing turned shallow. He looked at the rain, then back at Hope.

"I… okay," he whispered.

He had thought about this moment, but he still wasn't prepared.

"Her name was Chaka," he began, his voice a low rumble. "We met at a wedding reception I was deejaying. She was a bridesmaid, and the groom and I go way back. Chaka dragged the bride and groom out to the dance floor and led the wedding party in what seemed like a thousand line dances. She was like some kind of step master."

He smiled—a genuine, sad smile that creased the corners of his eyes.

"Later that night, I asked my boy about her. He said

she was cool and that we should meet. He introduced us. Fifteen months later, we were married at St. Mathews, a small church down on Emancipation. The church was packed with her friends. They filled both the bride's and groom's sides, and people stood along the wall. That was Chaka. She had a million friends and no enemies. She was raised in foster care, so she didn't have anyone to walk her down the aisle. But she walked down that aisle with such elegance. Man, she looked so good."

Justin had lost himself in the memory—the condo, the rain, and Hope all fading away. He paused, a flicker of something in his eyes as he returned to the present. He took a deep breath and continued.

"Once married, she moved into my one-bedroom apartment. She immediately transformed it from a bachelor pad into a home. Chaka was a preschool teacher and ran an arts-and-crafts business on the side called MommyTime. She could make anything from flower baskets to macramé. I used to tease her by saying she was part Amish." He laughed, a short, hollow sound. "She used her skills to make my old place something special we could share. Then, after just a few months, Chaka gave me the greatest news I had ever had. She was pregnant. When we found out it was a boy, she insisted we name him after me. She said she wanted him to be just like his father. She was always pumping me up like that. I needed that boost, too. Work-wise, I bounced around a bit. Well, actually a lot back then. But she always had my back. She never once gave me a hard time. But with her being pregnant, I had to stop messing around. I started working for Mr. Kim. He died soon after Deuce was born, and I bought his business on a kind of lease-to-own arrangement with his widow.

"I was at work when she called and told me she needed to go to the hospital," he continued. "She was probably in labor before I left for work, but she wasn't the type to complain about some back pain. By the time I got home, Deuce was well on his way into this world. He was born about ten minutes after I walked in the door. There was baby, blood, and goo everywhere. It was the scariest, craziest, messiest, most amazing moment of my life. She had made me so happy."

He looked at his hands, twisting them together in his lap. Hope noticed the faint indentation on his ring finger where his wedding band had been. He took several deep breaths, as if preparing to dive into a deep pool.

"Chaka was a great mother. She breastfed the little man for the next seven months. Looking at her holding him was an amazing sight. I never felt worthy enough to watch."

He fell silent, his eyes closed. Hope could see his mind trying to pull a painful memory back into focus. He turned his head to the side, then to the other, as if wrestling with an unseen force.

Hope had seen these moments before with her clients. She knew better than to push. The only thing she could do was offer comfort. She reached out and gently laid her hand on his right hand, her touch soft.

"It's okay," she whispered.

The rain outside seemed to intensify, matching the storm brewing within him. Justin withdrew his hands and put them in his lap, pressing them together.

"Then she died."

The words were pushed out in one breath, and his

breathing turned into heaving gasps. His eyes were open, but he was looking through Hope, a vacant stare that broke her heart. Hope had never seen such a strong man look so vulnerable.

Hope's mind was a whirlwind of emotion. The psychologist in her wanted to dig deeper, to help him find a pathway to healing. But the woman in her felt an overwhelming sense of inadequacy.

Could I ever measure up to a memory this amazing? she thought. *Chaka gave Justin more love in a couple of years than I could do in a lifetime. I can never take Chaka's place.*

Her conflicted emotions told her this was not the time to ask clarifying questions. He needed compassion, not an inquisition.

Hope stood up and moved to the floor, leaning against his chair. She put her arms around his waist and placed her head on his shoulder. He was trembling. She hugged him tightly, trying to hold him together like a broken toy. He rested his face on top of her head, and she started to feel a warm liquid on her face, like the rain showers outside. The tears streaming down his face now overflowed onto her.

She lifted her head and began wiping the tears away with her thumbs.

"Oh, baby. It's okay. It's okay," she said. "Thank you for sharing your story with me."

"I'm sorry. I don't know why I said her name," Justin pleaded, his face a mask of regret.

Hope gently touched his face.

"That name was a reflex, a ghost limb of a wonderful life that's regrettably gone," Hope comforted. "You know, when I told you not to apologize...I said that because I should apologize," she continued. "The other night, I was angry and hurt, and I moved too fast. I'm sorry. How about we start over? Give me a chance to go slower?" she asked.

"Sure," Justin said, a shaky breath of relief escaping him. "I'm working late tonight, so I don't think I can call. I will see you tomorrow morning when I get Nelson."

"Perfect," Hope replied.

"I better let you go," Justin said, his tone a little stronger now. "I don't want to keep you from anything important."

"This is important. If you have a few minutes, can we sit here and listen to the rain?" Hope requested.

Justin blinked and gave a slight nod.

They sat together on the loveseat as they listened to the rain continue its relentless assault, a steady waterfall from the sky. It seemed as if the heavens held nothing back. Amidst this oppressive storm, Justin carried a heavy secret—one he was unable to share with Hope: he was responsible for Chaka's death.

Chapter 28
A New Beginning

*H*ope opened the door to her condo and was greeted by a sight that made her heart flutter. Justin stood in the hallway, his face flushed from the brisk morning air, while Nelson happily panted.

"Hey, Doc," Justin said, a genuine smile lighting up his face. "We just finished our morning walk."

"You guys were gone for over an hour and a half. I started to get concerned."

Hope's eyes softened. He was so thoughtful. The past few days, Justin's actions had done more to heal her heart and mind than any therapy session or medication. The old anger at the "scene of the crime" had dissipated, replaced by a quiet sense of hope. Her talk with Big Preach had given her the courage to move forward.

Justin handed her Nelson's leash. "How are you feeling today?" he asked, his voice full of concern.

"Much better," Hope said. "I'm just a little tired. This whole thing has been a lot."

"I can only imagine," Justin said, his eyes filled with

empathy. He took a deep breath and squeezed her hand. "I...I don't know much about lupus, Hope."

Hope smiled, a sad, weary expression. "To be honest, I don't think doctors understand it either. It affects everyone differently. Every new doctor means a new prognosis, medications, and therapy plan." She sighed, the frustration evident in her voice. "Lupus is like having an alien living inside me. I never know what it will do or when it's going to erupt and ruin everything." She looked at Justin, a hint of vulnerability in her eyes. "The alien has a knack for destroying relationships."

Justin looked at her, and his grip on her hand tightened. "In the movies," he said, "the good guys always team up to defeat the alien. So, how about we team up?"

A genuine smile bloomed on Hope's face, and her dimples appeared.

"You'd do that?" she asked, a sense of amazement in her voice.

"Absolutely," Justin said, his own spirits lifting. He knew she had been struggling with this illness on her own for a long time. "And we can get help. Pastor Caleb is your brother-in-law. Somebody that close to God should be able to get you a hookup."

Hope's mind, honed by years of listening to others' emotional turmoil, nearly short-circuited. However, she had learned the skill of listening without revealing her true feelings.

She gave a little laugh. "You'd be surprised by what Caleb can do," she replied, keeping her disdain for him completely hidden.

"Can't you go tomorrow to the church and get special prayer? Isn't that what you church folk do?"

The casual talk, which started as a friendly conversation, became a nightmare for Hope. She had to move this conversation away from that wolf in pastoral clothing.

"Maybe another time. I love my church, but I'm not up for all those people."

"You're right. You need something a little more lowkey. How about I take you to a low-key, low-stress church service tonight? That way, you can get your 'worship on' and sleep in tomorrow."

"Service on a Saturday night? Are you taking me to a Mass?"

"No, it's not a Mass. It's very informal. Please wear jeans and comfortable shoes. I'll come by about five-thirty to pick you up."

Hope was caught up in the moment. She wasn't sure what she was signing up for, but she signed up anyway.

"Sure. I'll be ready."

"Great. I have to head out. Even though it's Saturday, I have a couple of service calls to make this morning. See you tonight."

"See you then."

Justin jogged back down the hallway, leaving Hope with a renewed sense of purpose. He no longer felt the need to run away from his problems. A smile spread across his face as he thought about the night ahead. He was ready to team up with Hope and face the aliens in their lives, together.

Chapter 29
Gina's Diagnosis

*I*n her home office, Hope stared at her mother's psychological diagnosis—a document, penned shortly after Hope completed her Ph.D., that attempted to explain Gina's often inexplicable behavior toward her daughters and others. For Hope, the diagnosis was a strange salve, offering a measure of understanding for the emotional bruises Gina inflicted.

Psychiatric Evaluation
Subject Name: Georgina (Gina) Castillo
Evaluator Name: Hope Castillo, Ph.D.
Reason for Evaluation:
To assess the subject's personality functioning and determine the presence of any psychological or personality disorders.

History:
- Developmental History: Gina was born to Mabel Carter. Mabel was considered a good mother. Gina's

father was never in the picture. Mabel and Gina lived in the housing projects. Mabel was diagnosed with ALS when Gina was 8 years old. Mabel died 2 years later. Gina watched her mother go from very active to no physical movement; her mind was alive and present, yet she could not communicate with Gina. The ordeal was painful and confusing to watch for the young Gina. Gina was placed in foster care. Gina moved often from one foster home to another and had to fight to keep possession of the small bag of personal items she had. Gina was molested/statutory raped by the 24-year-old son of one of her foster mothers. Gina loved him. Gina competed with another foster child in the house for affection from her foster brother, who was approximately 2 years older than Gina. The foster brother ultimately moved the older girl in with him when she turned 18.

- Educational/Occupational History: High School Diploma. Dropped out of nursing school after becoming pregnant with her first child.

- Relationship History: As a teenager, she had a sexual relationship with her foster brother. She married her first high school boyfriend at age 17 after a relationship with her foster brother. Marriage ended in divorce after 10 years. Marriage produced two daughters.

- Hobbies: Physical fitness. Participates in "Tough Mudder" hardcore obstacle course events. Foster mother to special needs animal shelter dogs.

- Medical History: Physically fit. No major surgeries. No major illnesses.

- Psychiatric History: No information.

- Substance Abuse: None. The subject finds people who rely on drugs or alcohol as weak.
- Legal History: No record.

Assessment Procedures:
- No formal clinical interviews or standardized assessments utilized.
- The evaluator is the subject's daughter. The evaluator used personal observation of the subject to gather data.

Diagnosis:
<u>Narcissistic Personality Disorder with Malignant Features</u>
o Sadistic and Antisocial Traits: Enjoyment in the suffering of others, a lack of remorse, and a history of aggressive behavior.
o Ego-syntonic Aggression: Views their aggressive and exploitive behaviors as justified and even necessary.
o Pronounced Grandiosity and Entitlement: An inflated sense of self-importance and the belief that she deserves special treatment.
o Lack of Empathy: An inability or unwillingness to recognize or understand the feelings and needs of others.

Prognosis:
- Subject is unredeemable. (Evaluator acknowledges her own bias, but has not seen any improvement in the subject in twenty years of observation.)

John Gary Long

A name on a page can't capture the years of damage, Hope lamented. *This isn't a diagnosis; it's a birth certificate for the demon that haunts my life.*

She wondered why her little treasure chest of knowledge hadn't saved her from her mother.

Chapter 30
Akil's Paternal Crisis

Justin could see an animated conversation between Akil and his girlfriend, Andrielle, through the garage window. After several minutes, a frustrated Andrielle left, clearly aggravated. Moments later, Akil entered the shop and sat on his bench, leaning his back and head against the wall. On entry, Justin could feel a heaviness in the air around Akil, whose face matched the room's atmosphere; no smile, only a somber expression.

Something had gone down between Akil and his lady love. Usually, he would try to find out what was ailing a sad soul like Akil's. But Justin felt the weight of bankruptcy, a burden that could crush his dreams of being a business owner and providing a better life for his son. He had no time or desire to discuss the puppy love games of these barely twenty-somethings.

Sticking to business, Justin said, "Thanks for getting both the Perez and Boyce jobs done this morning. I wasn't sure that was possible."

"No problem," Akil responded with minimal life in his voice. "Hank stopped by between his jobs to help. He gave me ten minutes, saving me about two hours of work."

Justin was not surprised at all by Hank's fairy godfather's repair magic. Before they died, Justin had learned quite a bit from his dad and Mr. Kim about repair. But working with Hank was like learning the piano from Beethoven.

The room fell silent for several minutes. Justin was trying to come up with new search terms to find a source of cash infusion. Akil had finished his work for the day, and Justin knew Akil was aware that he was free to go home. Justin feared Akil would pull him into some trivial conversation.

Akil finally broke the silence. "Hey, shouldn't you be home with your son? I thought on Saturdays you took him to the park."

Justin had just stumbled upon a URL for small-business grants. He wanted to explore the website, and the last thing he needed was the distraction of chatting with Akil right now.

"No, not today" was all the response Justin could muster.

His eyes never left the computer screen. He thought any further explanation about why his mother cared for Deuce today would only lead to more questions. To Justin's chagrin, Akil kept pushing to have a conversation.

"Being a father must be hard. It seems like a lot of responsibility and pressure."

"Yes, it is," Justin blurted. "A lot of responsibility. Very stressful every step of the way. I would not recommend it to anyone who is not ready. It will change a man's life."

Because Justin's eyes remained fixed on the computer screen, he didn't notice the change in Akil's posture when he heard Justin's words. Akil shifted from lying against the wall to sitting forward, elbows resting on his knees and his head in his hands. Justin's eyes and ears weren't tuned in for cries of help today.

After a few minutes, Akil picked up his tool bag and slung it over his drooping shoulder. His steps were slow and deliberate towards the door. A baby cries when it needs the attention of someone close by. A man shows his need for care through subtle hints and body language. Since Justin was not in a caregiving state of mind, Akil left without a word, thinking he should cry out loudly for help next time.

Chapter 31
Gina's Manipulation

"Please come in, Sister Gina," Big Preach said, gesturing for Gina to enter his home, his smile a practiced mask he was already growing tired of.

Gina entered the foyer, her eyes immediately scanning every detail of the gracious old home. She moved toward the large family room, which opened into a well-appointed kitchen. The combined space, furnished with plush couches, bar stools at the center island, and a long dining table, was clearly designed for hosting a crowd. Gina was unimpressed.

"I haven't been here since Dora's tea party five years ago," she said, her voice dripping with judgment. "Your wife had a quaint decorating sensibility. I see you haven't changed much."

The mask of Big Preach's smile fell away. "Gina, how can I help you today?" he asked, his tone clipped.

Gina chose a plush couch, sank into it, and crossed her legs, resting her hands on her knees. The movement was deliberate, a show of control.

"John," she began, her voice leaving no room for argument, "you can no longer stand in the way of the church's north side expansion."

Big Preach's hands began to rub together, his teeth grinding audibly. "Gina, I have known you for thirty years, and you rarely surprise me. But this is the exception. You don't care about saving anyone's soul up north. Why do you care now?"

"Careful, pastor," Gina warned, her eyes narrowing. "First, it has been thirty-three years, not thirty. But back to the matter at hand. Caleb and Rachel are starting a family. The souls that need to be saved on the north side of town would also provide good tithes and offerings. Rich people need the Lord just as much as poor folks do. You should not stand in the way of expanding God's kingdom. We all need to think of the future."

"Now that sounds exactly like the Gina I know," Big Preach said with a half-smile and a knowing nod while pacing back and forth, his hands still rubbing together. "As a matter of preference, I have always felt the church is best served in one building. In the community, creating community. That was the vision we built this church on. A vision I was still committed to before a certain faction of the search committee controlled by you used strong-arm tactics to push Caleb through."

Gina stood, her expression calm and unbothered. She moved closer to him, her voice dropping to a conspiratorial whisper.

"As the new pastor, Caleb has ambitious expansion plans. As pastor emeritus, I'm here to ask you for a personal favor. Please, don't obstruct him. Caleb and Rachel's child is my grandchild," Gina said, emphasizing each word and pointing to herself. "That child deserves every luxury. I expect your continued support of my family whenever and for whatever I ask. Now is not the time to disrupt our arrangement—an arrangement that has benefited us both over the years."

Big Preach flinched as Gina's words landed with the precision of a surgeon's scalpel. Her mastery of wielding secrets to her advantage had always been a thorn in his side, a constant source of impotent rage. The quiet of the house felt suffocating. Gina's victory was palpable.

"No need for an answer now. I'll be at the next church meeting. Your support, or at least your silence, is expected. I'll see myself out. Goodbye."

Big Preach remained motionless, a fierce battle raging within him between his convictions and his guilt.

Chapter 32
Open Sky Church

The sun still had about an hour before its work was done for the day when Justin pulled his truck up to the curb. His vehicle joined several other cars lining the street next to the parking lot of an abandoned convenience store. The store was a relic of when The Ward neighborhood was a thriving community. The closure of the engine plant was the last of several factory closures that had disproportionately impacted The Ward. When jobs moved out, unemployment, drugs, and homelessness moved in.

"Hey, are you okay?" Justin asked his passenger, his voice laced with concern as he tried to gauge her tolerance for the surroundings.

"Don't give me that look. I've been down in The Ward before. In fact, many times," Hope said with a touch of defiance.

She wanted him to know that just because she had a Ph.D. didn't make her an out-of-touch "Buppie" or Black American Princess. Her roots ran deep into the streets of The Ward.

"I also do pro bono work over at the women's shelter on MLK," she continued.

With his hands up in a gesture of surrender, Justin smiled. "Okay, okay, I got it. You're good in the hood."

Hope shook her head and thought, *That was the corny Justin, but he's still cute.*

"A guy I met a few years ago started a church service here. His name is LaTavious Liddel. Most of his friends and I call him T'bone. People here at the church call him Reverend T."

Hope looked around at the empty lot, where about eight to ten people stood as if waiting for something.

"So where's the church?" she asked.

Justin's smile widened. "It's called Open Sky Church, and you're looking at it. Let's get out."

Justin and Hope got out and stood on the curb. A truck pulled a trailer into the lot. The driver jumped out, and the people waiting in the parking lot approached it. Once the container was open, Hope could see several stacks of folding chairs and tables.

"I'm going to help them set up. You can wait here for a few minutes."

"No, I want to help. Don't worry. I won't break."

Hope and Justin walked toward the trailer. The truck driver saw Justin and hurried over to him.

"My man! What's up, man!" the driver said.

He and Justin gripped hands and shared a firm man-hug. Justin, grinning, lifted his smaller friend slightly off the ground because of the tight embrace.

"I'm good. I'm good. I see you doing very good," Justin said, stepping back and giving his friend a light punch in his round gut. "Janice is feeding you some of that good bread pudding?"

"You know she is. Where have you been? I haven't seen you in a few weeks. I texted you several times, but got no response. We always miss you when you're not there."

Paying attention to word choice was critical for Hope's occupation. She noted that Justin's friend said "there" and not "here." *Where is "there"?*

Hope quickly pushed aside her investigative instincts as two friends just chewed the fat.

"I've been busy," replied Justin.

"I see you've been busy. Are you going to introduce me to your lady friend or just stand there?"

Before Justin could speak, Hope extended her hand. "Hi. I'm Hope."

Justin's friend grabbed Hope's hand, placed his left hand under her elbow, and pulled her closer.

"Hello, Hope. I'm LaTavious, but please call me T'Bone or whatever a lovely lady like you would like to call me."

Hope's new admirer had a playful charm that she couldn't resist. She was about two inches taller than T'Bone with his original Jackson 5 afro. His glasses, which kept slipping down his nose, his toothy grin, and his round belly somehow all came together to make him adorable.

"I'll call you LaTavious. I like that name," Hope said, her smile broadening.

LaTavious' toothy grin widened even more as he continued to hold onto Hope's hand and arm.

"Reverend! Reverend Liddel," Justin called out, his voice a playful mix of warning and affection, breaking up the moment. "We have a service to get set up for. The crowd is starting to gather."

John Gary Long

Reverend Liddel released Hope's arm. "You're right, you're right. Let's get going."

All three walked to the trailer. The people waiting in the parking lot were volunteers to help with the service. When T'Bone came upon each volunteer, he greeted them with handshakes, hugs, and laughter. Hope realized his warm welcome was not exclusive to her. T'Bone would make everyone he met feel special.

The volunteers took the folding chairs and set them up in rows facing toward the old store. About fifty chairs were set out in all. Hope carried one chair at a time, marveling at Justin's ability to carry three chairs in each hand on each trip. After all the chairs were in place, a row of four folding tables was set up behind the chairs. A single podium was placed on the sidewalk by the store's former front door.

Feeling a little weak, Hope decided she'd better sit in the back row of chairs. She watched Justin as he continued working. He went to the back of his truck and pulled out his two deejay speakers. He placed them about twenty feet on either side of the podium, facing them outward toward the chairs.

Then Hope witnessed a sight that deeply moved her, affecting her mind, body, and soul. Justin emerged from the trailer, carrying an old, six-foot-tall oak cross over his shoulders. The rough, weathered wood looked heavy, but Justin's broad shoulders made the weight seem light. He carried it alone and leaned it against the store door behind the podium. Hope, having observed countless men in her life, never understood their tendency to bear their burdens alone. She felt a strong urge to help Justin carry his.

Goosebumps pricked Hope's arms, and her stomach fluttered. She became acutely aware of her own breathing, and her eyes welled with tears. The inexplicable power of the moment—the way this man stirred her very being—remained a mystery to her.

Before making his way to Hope, Justin stopped to talk to T'Bone.

"Are you preaching today?" Justin asked.

"No, I was at the dollar store the other day and ran into Deacon Ross from down at St. Mathews. He said he had a Word to share. I always appreciate the help."

Justin nodded. "I remember him from Chaka's funeral. He may be a hundred and fifty years old, but he has wisdom."

"Yep, that ole' time religion."

Justin took a seat next to Hope in the back row. The crowd of about twenty-five people began to take their seats. Before sitting down, each person received a numbered slip of paper. Hope later learned that the paper could be redeemed after the sermon for dinner. The parishioners were all either homeless or down on their luck. Hope recognized their situation by their walk. She took heed to what Big Preach would always say: *If you want to be a good Christian, you better learn to love people who walk, talk, and even smell different than you. Jesus loves and wants you and me to help everyone. If you're always around people who are just like you and smell of expensive perfume or cologne, you probably aren't doing enough work in God's mission field.*

Reverend T. took to the podium. He spoke into the microphone and was clearly heard through the speakers Justin had set up. Reverend T. gave the customary opening and prayer. He also played a music track from his phone via the speakers, leading the group to an upbeat version of "Amazing Grace."

"Most of you will be happy to hear I'm not the one preaching today," Reverend T. said with a smile. "You've heard me enough over the years. Deacon Ross will bring you the Word. But before I take my seat, I would ask for a special prayer for my wife, Janice. She's home under the weather today. You know she hates to miss service. In fact, today is the first time I've had service here without her. Y'all know our story. I've been an alcoholic for over fifteen years. My disease caused me to lose family, friends, and jobs. Janice found me at my lowest point. She helped me clean myself up, and I've been clean and sober now for seven years. I owe it all to that woman. I am here to tell you God will send you what and who you need when you need it." Reverend T. gave a shout and a wave of his hand, then another shout. "I better sit down before I start preaching. I can talk all day about how good my God is."

As Reverend T. took his seat and Deacon Ross approached the podium, Hope and Justin exchanged glances and a smile. During Reverend T.'s talk, they started holding hands. Neither had given it a thought; reaching out to one another and holding hands felt right.

Deacon Ross spoke with authority and deliberate wisdom gleaned from years of living. His sermon was from the Book of Luke, a message so clear that the text almost preaches itself:

Luke 12:2-3 (NIV) — ²There is nothing concealed that will not be disclosed or hidden that will not be made known. ³What you have said in the dark will be heard in the daylight, and what you have whispered in the ear in the inner rooms will be proclaimed from the roofs.

* * *

On the ride home, Justin and Hope stopped at a light.

"That was amazing," Hope said, patting Justin on the leg. "Thank you for taking me. Getting back to the basics of worship is just what I needed. You have no idea how much good tonight did for me."

It was dark out, but a streetlight shone through the truck's window. It illuminated Hope's face, and in Justin's eyes, she was a bright light in his darkness.

"De nada, Señorita Castillo. El gusto mio," Justin replied in Spanish with a very clumsy English accent.

"You never cease to surprise me. Our first actual date was to church, and now you're showing off your Español skills. Me estoy enamorando!" Hope responded.

Justin wished he knew what she had said. All that remained of his two years of Spanish in high school were just a few phrases. Because he didn't want to spoil the mood, he didn't ask her what she meant in English.

The rest of the ride home was mostly quiet. Both Justin and Hope reflected on the sermon and how its message rang true in their lives. They both considered the secrets they were hiding from each other—secrets that, as the Word says, will eventually be brought into the light.

Chapter 33
The Lost Son

A morning call from McReynolds Company postponed their HVAC overhaul by two weeks, leaving a sudden gap in Justin's schedule that was too late to fill with other appointments. The long hours and busy weekends meant Justin had spent far less time with Deuce than he wanted. With this unexpected free time, he knew exactly who he wanted to spend the day with.

The day was perfect for a visit to an amusement park. The sun shone brightly, adorned with a few playful clouds. A Texas "cold front" had swept through, banishing the humidity while maintaining a comfortable seventy-eight degrees. The park's attendance was light, a typical midweek crowd.

Throughout the drive to the park, Deuce maintained a non-stop monologue filled with questions and facts about the world outside the window, his preschool classmates, and his favorite snacks. As they entered the park, his eyes widened, trying to take in all the fantastic sights.

"Maybe we should start my little man on the Big Dip

Rocket Ship roller coaster? It's the biggest in the state and will make a man out of him," Justin deadpanned to Hope, a mischievous glint in his eye.

Hope could not help but smile and shake her head. "You are so silly. If we were going to do that, we should have had Deuce drive us here."

"He can always do that on the way home. I need a break," Justin responded with an ever-growing smile.

"Before you win parent of the year, let's take Deuce to the kiddie section. I think you and he will feel right at home with all the kids," Hope said, then took each of her companions by the hand and escorted them to the expansive Kids' Zone.

The Kids' Zone is a four-year-old's dream. Bounce houses, carousels, famous characters in costume, and miniature rides highlighted the area. Deuce started with the bounce house and quickly moved from attraction to attraction.

"Wow, this is nice. We didn't have anything this good when we were kids," Justin commented.

"You're right. My dad would have loved to bring me to a place like this. Instead, we had the once-a-year, ride-at-your-own-risk carnival rides. I now know we were taking our lives into our hands just getting on those old rickety deathtraps," Hope said.

Grabbing Hope's hand and giving her a slight turn towards him, Justin said, "I'm glad you survived."

Hope looked up at Justin, his words like a beautiful song. A warmth spread through her chest. In her mind, she could hear Prince's "The Beautiful Ones" playing, the music of his gaze. She was mesmerized, ready to lean in for a kiss, when…

Justin leaned in and kissed her on the cheek, a soft, warm press of his lips. A shiver, not of cold, but of pure feeling, went through her. Hope's legs grew unsteady. She was ready to move in for round two, when…

"Daddy! Daddy! Can I do that again? Please! Please!" Deuce pulled on his dad's hand, doing a little jig as he pleaded.

"Yes, Daddy, can we do that again?" Hope playfully stated.

Justin did not skip a beat. "Yes, son. You can ride the roundabout. And you, young lady, will just have to wait."

Hope crossed her arms and frowned, giving her best spoiled-little-girl imitation. "But I don't want to wait," she said, trying to hide her smile but failing.

Holding his son's hand, Justin walked toward the ride's entrance and said to Hope, "You stay right there, and don't talk to strangers."

Deuce rode the roundabout and about every other ride in the Kid's Zone. After having a lunch of hot dogs, potato chips, and fruit punch, they all agreed the treehouse would be a logical next attraction to visit.

The treehouse was a series of bird nest playhouses connected by catwalks and hanging bridges. Each playhouse had a different theme, along with two or three entrances and exits, allowing kids to travel through the interconnected web of playrooms. Well-placed netting kept the miniature explorers safe as they moved twenty feet above the ground.

Justin inspected it and determined it was more than safe for his son.

"Okay, son, go have fun. We'll meet you over there at the exit."

Deuce quickly ran up the enclosed stairwell to the attraction, waving at his dad through the netting when he emerged from the top.

"Let's stand over here. This way, we can see the entrance and the exit down there. We'll be able to see him come out," Justin said.

Hope was impressed by how Justin cared for his son. He did his best to leave nothing to chance.

"You are a great father. That's good to see," she told him.

Dropping his head slightly, Justin humbly accepted the praise. "I'm just trying to do my best. I've made many mistakes before and want to ensure I get this daddy thing right."

"Well, you've gotten this daddy thing very right. Look at him. He could not be a happier kid," Hope said.

They both looked up as Deuce emerged from one treehouse and ran across a hanging bridge into another.

"My mother has been a huge help. When Chaka died, she stepped in. I, I mean, we would be lost without her." Justin was speaking to Hope but looked into the distance as he talked.

"I'm sure your mom has done a lot, but don't underestimate the benefits of a good dad. My dad means the world to me. When my parents divorced, it felt like a death in the family, though I'm not sure who died. Sometimes it felt like he did, sometimes like my mom did, and other times…" Hope paused to catch her breath. "Other times, it felt like I died. Life was so different once my dad moved out."

Neither was looking at the other but were instinctively holding hands. Then Hope felt like she had just emerged from a pool back into the current reality.

"Do you see Deuce?" she asked.

"No, but I'm sure he's up there. I'll take a closer look. Stay by the entrance."

Justin started moving toward the attraction exit. It had been in his sight the whole time. Justin kept glancing up as he walked to the treehouse exhibit exit to glimpse Deuce. About halfway to the exit, Justin stopped and looked directly to his right. He looked again at the exit and then again over to the right. He looked back at the series of bridges and started calling out for his son.

Hope knew something was wrong. As she quickly approached him, she looked to the right in the same direction Justin was looking. She now understood his concern. There was a second exit from the massive web. It was not completely visible from where they were standing before due to some large bushes that had been unfortunately placed.

"Do you see him?" he asked Hope, his voice trembling.

"No, not yet."

"I'll go up there and look for him. If you go stand by that exit, you'll have a view of all the ways out of that damn contraption."

Justin's voice shook enough for Hope to be concerned for both of her Justins. Running to the exit, she positioned herself to see all the possible escape routes while Justin was heading up the original stairs for a "house-to-house" search.

Hope could feel her heart beating in her ears, a frantic drum against her skull. She knew she was breathing, but somehow, her body felt as if it were getting no oxygen. Her mind raced, conjuring worst-case scenarios: a child wandering off, a kidnapper, a terrible accident.

Looking up, she could see Justin on the first bridge, going to the second treehouse. He moved with the focused determination of a man on a mission. Thinking about what he must've been feeling made the heartbeat noise in her ears grow louder.

Justin exited the second treehouse, and there was still no Deuce. The air filled with fear, and even the birds in the trees seemed silent.

"Please, God, just let—" Her prayer was interrupted.

"That was fun, Miss Hope! Did you see me?" Deuce asked as he ran out of the first planned exit.

Without thinking, she bent over as Deuce ran into her open arms. Relief and joy, so powerful they felt like a physical force, washed over her. She picked him up and hugged him, holding onto him like a shipwreck survivor clinging to a floating piece of wood.

"Where's Daddy?" Deuce asked while also trying to survive the massive bear hug.

"Well..." Hope looked around and saw Justin jogging towards them. "There he is."

"Dad, did you see me? I was up there and there! I was everywhere!" Deuce exclaimed while pointing at the exhibit.

"Yes, son, I saw you. I'm glad you had fun." Justin rubbed his son's head as they talked.

Justin and Hope's eyes met, and they breathed a simultaneous sigh of relief.

"That's probably enough fun for today. Let's go home and have some ice cream. Okay?" Justin said, using the lore of the ice cream to soften the blow of leaving the park.

Justin took his son from Hope's arms and hugged him. Hope thought the sight was a perfect picture. Somehow, the love Justin showed his son enveloped Hope, making her feel safe and secure.

The now exhausted party made their way out of the park and back to the truck.

Deuce quickly fell asleep during the ride home. The adults were quiet and a bit tired from the day, as well.

Hope closed her eyes, her mind drifting as she thought about many things from the day. The kiss, the panic, the relief, and the fatherly love. *Is this what it's like to be part of a family? Daily highs and lows.* If so, she knew she would love such a life.

Chapter 34
A Mother's Blessing

*D*espite it being the start of a new work week, Hope looked forward to immersing herself in her clients' cases. But first, she had to walk Nelson. She'd skipped his walks the past few days, as Anna or Justin had taken him on long excursions. Hope chuckled at Anna's running joke about Nelson: *Unlike men, he doesn't try to hide his stuff.*

She had spoken with Justin the night before and knew he would be heading straight to his shop. While she enjoyed their morning park encounters, she was relieved to walk Nelson in her comfortable park "uniform": leggings, sneakers, an oversized sweatshirt, and no makeup. Since meeting Justin, she'd been putting more effort into her appearance for her walks, and today, she was glad for a break.

Arriving at Webb Park, the unusually cold air hit her, and her breath fogged. The dew still clung to the grass. She hadn't checked the weather, and her sweatshirt was barely enough. She wished she'd worn her warmer college hoodie, but her walk soon warmed her up.

Nelson, unfazed by the chill, pulled her along the

sidewalk. Hope, lost in thought, tried to focus on her caseload. She didn't notice Nelson pulling her toward a specific spot until he stopped, being petted by a little boy.

"Hey there, little guy. How are you doing?" Hope asked, a bit confused.

Her mind was racing. She scanned her surroundings for Justin, wanting to hide her makeup-free face, but he was nowhere to be found.

"Good," Deuce responded.

Nelson and Deuce were now "old" friends. Nelson moved his body into different positions to get the full-body petting he deserved.

Hope's eyes were drawn to a woman seated at a picnic table a few feet away. She had passed her, but her thoughts had been elsewhere. The woman was petite, African American, with short, neatly styled black hair, a warm, inviting smile, and a perfectly positioned mole on her cheek. Her face, etched with the stories of life, spoke of strength and perseverance. The distinct oval shape of her eyes and the prominent structure of her cheekbones left no doubt in Hope's mind: this was Justin's mother.

Lorraine gave a slight "come here" wave, her hand moving with an almost regal grace. Hope released Nelson's leash and walked toward the smiling face. Nelson, meanwhile, was lying on his back, enjoying a full-on belly rub from his junior masseuse.

Lorraine's smile widened into a beam as she reached out her hand. "Well, look at you. You must be Hope. Now I see why my son has been smiling so much lately. You are just a beautiful thing. Yes, you are."

Lorraine's words gave Hope a warm, comforting feeling, like she had been enveloped in a thick blanket.

Lorraine spoke with a slight southern accent and a down-home charm.

Hope shook Lorraine's hand. "Mrs. Thompson, it's nice to meet you."

"Oh, baby, call me Lorraine. Everybody does. Please sit down."

Hope sat down because Lorraine had an unstated authority about her, a way that made you feel compelled to take her direction.

"You brought Deuce to the park for fresh air. There's plenty for a kid to do here," Hope said, starting the conversation on safe, neutral ground.

"Well, ya' know, I did bring him here to play. But the real reason I'm here is to meet you. I am too old to beat around the bush. I wanted to take a measure of the woman my son would drop everything—and I mean everything—to see about her welfare," Lorraine said, her voice direct but non-threatening.

Hope's mind quickly shifted from her previous relaxed state into interview mode. She sat up straighter on the park bench and made sure to look Lorraine directly in the eye. Between college admission boards, summer internships, and her doctoral dissertation, Hope had always successfully navigated an interview. She knew how to be on top of her game when it counted. She didn't expect one of those moments would be today, amongst children playing and elderly power walkers.

Hearing Lorraine say that Justin dropped everything for her made Hope feel valued in a way she hadn't felt in a long time. She returned that value in words.

"Your son did an amazing job taking care of me. He is a good man."

John Gary Long

Hope stopped short of telling Lorraine she should be proud of her son; she didn't want to lecture an elder. It turned out Hope didn't have to.

"I'm very proud of my son. He's quite the young man. Justin works hard, takes good care of me, and is a great father," Lorraine responded with a sparkle in her brown eyes.

Hope took note of Lorraine's light brown eyes. Lorraine's eyes didn't have the spectrum of lights and darks that Justin's eyes had, but they still resembled some exotic, precious stone.

"Now, tell me a little bit about you. I've tried to get the 411 on you from my boy, but Justin has been tight-lipped as Sitting Bull," Lorraine said and leaned in for the details of Hope's life.

Per her interview-skills training, Hope, her hands resting on the table, took a deep breath and began.

"Well, there's not much to say. I was born here in town, and I grew up on the near northside. My parents divorced when I was nine, and I have a sister who is twenty months younger than me. My dad remarried. He and his new wife have twin boys. I have been a member of the Sea of Galilee church my whole life. I participate in the ASL signer ministry there when I have the time. I received my undergraduate degree in English with minors in psychology and Spanish. I worked at a women's shelter for two years before being inspired to pursue my post-graduate degrees here at U of H. Both my master's and doctorate degrees are in psychology. I've been practicing for about three years, and my office is on the corner of Calvin and Haddon. Oh, and you've met my dog, Nelson."

With the face of a poker player, Lorraine smiled but

did not tip her hand. She continued to probe.

"As you know, Deuce goes to preschool at your church. He loves it, and the cost is so reasonable. I hear you're related to the first family there."

"Yes, I am," Hope replied with no additional color commentary.

Lorraine immediately knew there was more to this story, more underneath the surface to delve into. However, she had learned in her sixty-plus years that family matters are sensitive and should be handled carefully. She would get more insight into Hope's family from her son. Instead, Lorraine moved her evaluation to another area that might reveal Hope's inner workings.

"Why did you choose to be a psychologist?"

Hope was ready for this often-asked question. If she had developed an FAQ sheet for herself, this question would have been in the top 5.

"I believe healthy families are the core building block for healthy communities. Psychology lets me help individuals and families learn to cope with the stresses of life," Hope replied in an almost preprogrammed cadence.

Listening to herself, she did not like the sterile response she had provided. While the answer was entirely accurate, it somehow did not convey the depths of why she felt psychology was her calling.

Lorraine listened and sensed a bit of emptiness in Hope's answer. Lorraine didn't want the "graduate school application" answer. Before Lorraine could ask a more delving question, Hope followed up.

"Honestly, mental health is a set of issues that plague Black, minority, and poor communities. We don't know when to seek help or how to get help for our mental issues. In fact, things like depression are a taboo subject. It is never discussed. These issues lead to people self-medicating with drugs and alcohol. Some commit suicide, another taboo subject in the Black community, and we never talk about these important issues. All the while, these issues are tearing apart families and impacting children. I wanted and still want to help people in need. My profession lets me do that."

That's a much, much better answer, Lorraine thought to herself. Her poker face broke into a genuine smile, letting Hope know she approved.

"Baby, that is so true. We do need help from smart, good folks like you," Lorraine agreed. "People are walking around with clinical depression. They think feeling that way is normal, or they are just having a case of 'The Blues.' They don't know it is a very serious disease like cancer," Lorraine said and saw the expression on Hope's face. "Don't look at me surprised. I did a lot of reading on the internet about depression."

Hope nodded her head with respect. As Lorraine lectured Dr. Castillo on the serious nature of depression, Hope thought, *Preach on, my sister! Preach!*

"Not only depression," Lorraine continued. "I think people need to learn how to deal with their anger, too. People stay angry with family and friends for so long that they forget why they were mad in the first place. Their anger blocks them from the blessings God has in store for them. You know something. Right before David fought Goliath, his oldest brother made fun of David's size and occupation and told him to go home, away from the battlefield. Instead of staying on the mountain arguing, fussing, and fighting with his brother, David ignored him. David entered the valley where the real enemy and his destiny were waiting. David's victory was in the valley. There was nothing to be won by staying angry with his brother."

Hope couldn't help but—at least for a moment—think about her and Rachel. "I've heard that story one hundred times, but I never thought of it that way. Is it okay if I use that sometime?"

"Sure, you can, baby. I'll only charge a five percent royalty," Lorraine joked, and they both laughed.

Hope could listen to Lorraine all day. But Nelson's return to her side reminded her that she had to go to work.

"Sorry, I have to go. I can't keep my patients waiting," Hope said and stood with Nelson's leash in her hand.

"Nice to meet you. You are a sweet girl," Lorraine said in an approving voice. "Hope baby, one more thing. Take care of my boys, and you have my blessing."

Hope wrinkled her nose and asked, "Your blessing? To do what exactly?"

Lorraine did not respond. She just smiled and grabbed Deuce's hand. "Tell Miss Hope goodbye."

"Goodbye. See you later," Deuce said, more clearly than expected for a boy his age. Then the cute couple walked off hand-in-hand.

Hope could not get Lorraine's words out of her head: *You have my blessing. What was she talking about?* If someone wanted to bless her, great! She was a woman of faith and would take all the blessings she could get. Maybe this blessing would bring her the family she never had.

Chapter 35
An Unwanted Pregnancy

*A*ndrielle gave herself a final look in the mirror. Her updo was perfect, every braid meticulously coiled and interwoven, sitting pristinely on her head. The hairstyle made her feel like a Nubian queen. But then her eyes fell on her name tag pinned to her shirt, and she was reminded that Nubian queens didn't work registers at mall department stores.

She turned to the side, gently patting her stomach. She could not discern any change in the mirror or when looking down. A hand from behind joined hers on her stomach, and she was gently pulled back until a man's head rested on her shoulder.

"You still look good, baby," the man whispered in her ear as he placed his arms around her in a reverse bear hug.

"Still look good? You say that like you expect that to change," Andrielle retorted.

"No, I didn't mean it that way. I was trying to say you're sexy."

Pushing his arms away, Andrielle turned and said, "Akil, we don't have time for this. We both have to get to work."

"I know, I know. Maybe we can spend some quality time together tonight. In the last few weeks, I've had to take a lot of cold showers. Maybe tonight, I can show you how much I love you," Akil said in a longing voice.

"Quality time is what got us into this mess in the first place. What we should be doing is talking about what we're going to do next. What should we do, Akil? Do you have any answers yet?"

"I don't know. I'm still thinking," Akil said, lowering his head.

"Well, you need to hurry up. We live in a studio apartment with bad plumbing and black mold. We can't bring a baby here. We don't have any money, health insurance, or…"

Andrielle stopped herself. She never wanted to be a nag, but her pregnancy was a serious matter. She wanted direction from the man she loved—a man she was increasingly seeing as a boy rather than a man.

"I know, I know. We're going to talk. I need to work a few things out."

Everything Andrielle thought to say, she had already said many times before since she found out she was pregnant four weeks ago. Instead of repeating herself, she headed to the door without a word.

As Andrielle exited, and right before she closed the door, Akil said, "I love you."

The door locked, and Akil knew he needed more than words to show the woman he lived with how much she meant to him.

Chapter 36
Justin's Fears

Justin took a deep breath as he sat in his truck. The thirty feet from the curb to his front door stretched into a mile. His shoulders felt chained to the concrete, each ache a reminder of a grueling fifteen-hour workday. Even his runner's legs felt weak, protesting the strain of a week with no real rest. The scent of sweat, grease, and grime clung to him like a second skin. All he wanted was a shower and to collapse into bed. But a higher priority trumped Justin's thoughts of rest.

"Daddy!" an excited four-year-old screamed, charging his father with his arms raised, waiting to be picked up.

Deuce had already been bathed and dressed in his favorite superhero pajamas, the Flash. Justin picked up his son, lifted him straight into the air, and held him there.

"Hey, man. How are you doing?" Justin exclaimed.

Now charged with a burst of energy, Justin was holding his little recharging station. Deuce laughed with the uncontrollable, carefree laugh that only small children have—the laughter of not a care in the world and pure joy when they fly in the air in a father's arms.

Justin put his son down without hugging him. There was no need to transfer his work grime onto his little clean heir.

Deuce looked up, smiling. "I played with Nelson today."

"Really? Where?"

"At the park. Miss Hope was there, but I didn't play with her."

"Bibi took you to the park. Did you have fun?" Justin asked, trying to get more facts from his willing witness.

"Yes, he did," Lorraine said, standing in the hallway. Deuce cosigned with a nodding head and a smile. "Now, you go on to your room, little man. Bibi will be in soon to say our prayers. Okay?"

"Okay. Bye, Daddy. See you later," Deuce said, waving like he was going on a long journey.

"As for you, my big boy, go wash your hands. I've kept a plate warm for you in the oven," Lorraine commanded her favorite and only son.

Without a word, Justin obeyed his mother. After washing his hands, he took his customary seat at the kitchen table. Lorraine took a plate from the oven, removed the aluminum foil covering it, and set the meal before her son. She had her own way of keeping food warm—a tradition older than most microwaves. To Justin, his mother's way of keeping food warm was the best in the world.

The intoxicating smell of the pot roast and potatoes filled his senses, and he couldn't wait another minute to dig in. The first bite was immediate comfort, a physical manifestation of his mother's love. But not even Lorraine's pot roast, so tender that a spoon was required to eat it, could make Justin forget that his mother and new lady friend had met for the first time today.

Justin's mouth was full of food. He was torn between his desire to keep shoveling the roast into his mouth and asking about the meeting of the minds in the park earlier. Lorraine broke the tie.

"I like that girl of yours, Justin. She's so pretty and smart. Very smart," Lorraine said, watching him. "I think she's going to be a keeper. Are you going to call her before you go to bed tonight?"

Justin knew to expect directness from his mother. Her nature would not allow her to be any other way.

"Yeah, I like her, too," he replied after swallowing his food. "I will probably send her a text or something before I go to bed."

"I think that's a good idea. You can be the last thing Hope thinks about before she goes to sleep. That will give her dreams about you. You know, I used to dream about your father."

As uncomfortable as it was for Justin to talk about Hope with his mother, listening to his mother talk about her dreams for his dad would be far worse. So, he quickly steered the conversation back to Hope.

"Not only is Hope smart, but she also cares about people," Justin said.

"Yes, I can tell she has a good heart. You don't see many good hearts these days. She reminds me of Chaka in that way. Good hearts—that's what you like in your women," Lorraine said in a soft, reassuring voice.

Mother and son paused in silence to remember Justin's wife, who had gone on to Glory. They shared a small smile. Knowing her son and his penchant for self-doubt, Lorraine was compelled to give Justin some advice.

"Hope has a good job and some degrees. Don't you ever go thinking she or anyone is better than you. We all put our pants on one leg at a time. You have nothing to be ashamed of in your life. Nothing at all."

A flash of painful memory—a dark night, a siren's wail, a terrible mistake—flickered behind Justin's eyes. He heard his mother's words but could not fully embrace her statement. His first thought was, *Actually, I have many things to be ashamed of, and Hope doesn't know about any of them yet.* He then pushed aside thoughts of his past regrets and mistakes.

"I know, Mom. It's funny, but I'm not intimidated by her education at all. It's cool what she has accomplished. She has the type of education that Deuce will have one day. I wish every day that I hadn't dropped out of college, but that's behind me now. Being with Hope has deepened my desire to make my business successful. I want her to be proud of the business I will build. I don't know how to overcome my money issues, but I will. I must make it work. Justin's Warranty and Repair Shop will be successful." Justin had a determined look in his eye as he stared at his mother.

"Now that's what I'm talking about!" Lorraine said and high-fived her son. "Now finish your plate, take a shower, and go give a call to my new friend."

Justin took his cornbread, made one last sweep of his plate, and shoved the now gravy-soaked bread into his mouth. With his mouth full and cheeks bulging, Justin stood and kissed his mother on the cheek.

"Oh, boy. Get out of here," she said, hitting him with a dishrag. Justin absorbed the blow and headed to his room.

Lorraine proceeded to Deuce's room. She reminded herself that as part of Deuce's nightly prayer time tonight, she would thank God for giving her son what he needed, giving him someone in Hope to fill a space in Justin's life that would only grow larger very soon.

Chapter 37
A Dinner Joust

ope's sleek SUV pulled up to the valet stand at Bayou Broil, a newly popular restaurant boasting a fusion of Creole and soul food. As she handed over her keys, Justin couldn't shake the feeling that this was why she'd taken the wheel. His trusty Ford F-250, a workhorse, would have looked decidedly out of place at this upscale establishment. He couldn't help but wonder if he, like his truck, would stand out.

With reservations secured, guests were quickly ushered to a large, comfortable booth. The vibrant pulse of the live jazz band resonated throughout the restaurant. A diverse crowd, encompassing youthful trendsetters and seasoned connoisseurs of New Orleans flavors, filled the dining room. The waitstaff, impeccably dressed in crisp white shirts and blouses paired with black bottoms, moved with practiced efficiency, delivering fine wines, premium bourbons priced at fifty dollars a shot, and elaborately crafted tropical cocktails.

"I'm assuming you've been here before?" Justin asked.

"Yes, a couple of times. The food was delicious. As I said before, I just wanted to thank you for taking such good care of me over the last few weeks. And you've fed me multiple times, so I thought it was time to return the favor," Hope said with an appreciative smile.

"Neither my homemade chicken soup nor the turkey omelet I made for you can compare to this nice place," Justin said as he looked around with impressed eyes.

Hope reached across the table and pulled his hands toward her. "You're right. It can't compare. The food you made for me with your hands is much better than this place could ever make."

Justin exhaled, visibly releasing tension from his shoulders. He smiled. Her words struck a chord deep inside him.

"Aw shucks, ma'am. You make a brotha feel good," Justin replied with a playful Southern tone.

The time at dinner flew by like a summer breeze. They discussed Justin's old deejay career, which inevitably led to a discussion of Hope's favorite artist, Prince. Justin was also a fan, but he loved teasing her about "His Purple Badness." Also, Hope took the opportunity to tell Justin about her Little Sister, Amira, and how great an actor she was. She invited him to Amira's upcoming performance of *The Lion King Jr.*, and he accepted.

The dining room was filled with jazz music, and people were having a great time. Justin and Hope's continuous, spontaneous laughter went unnoticed; everyone seemed to be in a party mood. All was great until…

"Hello, Cheeks," Caleb said as he loomed over the table.

Hope and Justin were having a good time and did not notice him approach.

"Hi," Hope responded morbidly, in sharp contrast to the energetic conversation she had just engaged in with Justin.

A wave of cold dread washed over her, and her body tensed. She felt her carefully constructed composure shatter. The man who had destroyed her world stood before her, and she suddenly felt exposed, like a raw nerve. Hope's mind raced back to the night Caleb destroyed her world. He had not only ended their relationship, but he also took her sister away from her. That night was almost her last night on Earth. Hope viewed Caleb like a serial killer in a horror movie. He was here to kill another one of her relationships.

"I'm here with a few community leaders discussing business. I had to leave Rachel at home, as her morning sickness is starting to be more like an all-day sickness. I hate being around someone puking all the time. The smell is horrible. I'll be glad when she gets past this phase," Caleb said with an astonishing lack of self-awareness. Caleb then turned toward Justin but was still talking to Hope. "And who is this?"

Justin sensed the change in the atmosphere. A flash of anger mixed with a deep, protective instinct surged through him, his muscles tensing. Before Hope could say a word, Justin stood, grabbed Caleb's hand, and shook it.

"Hi. I'm Justin."

Caleb was surprised by the strength of Hope's companion's grip.

Looking over his shoulder, Caleb questioned Hope, "Your friend?"

Justin squeezed Caleb's hand a little harder and gave it a slight tug back toward him, drawing Caleb's eyes toward the excruciating grip owner and away from Hope.

"Yes, I am Hope's friend."

Hope could not help but enjoy the jousting match, mainly because her knight was winning.

Caleb released the handshake and took a small step back. He used his left hand to rub his now sore knuckles on his right hand. Caleb sneered as he decided to charge Justin, using words as a lance.

"Well, Jackson, I think my wife mentioned you once. You're a custodian or something, right?" Caleb said, his voice dripping with condescension. "I'm sure you know who I am, so no introduction is needed."

Justin knew Caleb had deliberately called him by the wrong name. Justin had been sizing up Caleb since his arrival at their table. When Caleb first arrived, he was a larger-than-life sports and community icon to Justin. Now, Caleb's poor taunts and his air of privilege made him look very small in Justin's eyes.

Justin instinctively felt the need to mark his territory and stand his ground. Having played competitive sports his entire life, Justin knew trash talk from a punk when he heard it. He also learned how to win a round by saying almost nothing.

"You're right. No introduction is needed."

Caleb was surprised by his new adversary's willingness to assert himself. He was accustomed to people being deferential to the former football star turned megachurch pastor. He decided to finish this match with Justin another day—a day Caleb could move the game to his home turf.

"Hey, I'd better get back to my meeting. You should order the peach cobbler. It's great here," Caleb said, providing one last piece of unwanted advice.

"No, we'll share the chocolate bread pudding," Justin replied, his voice calm and deliberate, a direct counter-attack to Caleb's suggestion. "She loves chocolate, and I love bread pudding. It's like the dessert was made just for us."

Hope's grin turned into a full-on smile. *Yeah, you tell him, baby! You sexy beast, you!*

Both knights gave each other one last stare, evaluating and searching for weaknesses in the other for potential jousting matches in the future. Caleb ended the standoff and strutted back to his social group. As Hope watched him leave, she saw in the distance that Twila Gooden was amongst the diners in Caleb's group. Hope and Twila's eyes met momentarily before Twila quickly moved her eyes away. A hot wave of burning anger flared through Hope, and she contained her impulse to go and smack down the hussy who was screwing her sister's husband. She was not going to let a tramp or Caleb ruin her evening.

Hope, now refocused on her knight in shining armor, loved how Justin shielded her from Caleb. Not until Justin protected her did she realize how vulnerable Caleb made her feel—a vulnerability she always hid but that Caleb's predatory nature could still sense.

Now, she wanted to be close to Justin. "Since we're going to share the chocolate bread pudding, why don't you come on this side of the table and sit next to me in the booth?" Hope requested.

A good knight never refuses a fair maiden. Justin

took his place at her side, and she lay her head on his shoulder after giving him a small kiss on the cheek. Justin breathed deeper than usual. His adrenaline flowed freely, and his protective instincts were on high alert. Justin was conflicted. Part of him wanted to respect his girlfriend's pastor/brother-in-law, and the other part of him wanted to punch that jerk in his face. Little did Justin know, Hope would have loved to see Caleb knocked flat on his ass.

Chapter 38
Doing the Right Thing

*H*ope parked her SUV in her reserved carport outside her condo. Justin exited the vehicle and made his way to the back, where Hope met him. Before words could be said, Hope grabbed Justin's hand and led him into the building and up the one flight of stairs. Justin was preparing to thank Hope for dinner, receive a good night kiss, and then drive home. But once they arrived at Hope's door, she already had her key in hand. She quickly unlocked the door and pulled Justin in.

As soon as the door closed, Hope spun around, placed her hand behind Justin's head, and pulled him into her waiting lips. The kiss was warm and soft, the release of a desire that had been building like a ticking time bomb since he had run Caleb off. Hope could not wait another moment.

Hope stopped her kiss and placed her head on his chest. Her arms wrapped around Justin in a tight embrace, and he reciprocated the hug.

"Thank you," she whispered, her voice trembling slightly as she held him.

"No, thank you. That was some kiss," Justin responded.

"No, not for the kiss. Just for being, you know, you," Hope said, her arms still around Justin.

He didn't know exactly what Hope was talking about. What he did know was that he loved her being in his arms. Her curves pressed against his body meshed ideally like a lock and key.

Hope released her embrace and led Justin to the couch. Justin became nervous, feeling as if he were returning to the scene of a crime he had committed. Hope sat down, one leg folded under her. Then she reached over and held both of Justin's hands.

She looked Justin in the eye and said, "I'll do my best to exercise self-control tonight. They say self-control is doing the right thing instead of the easy, pleasing thing. And right now, it would be effortless and very, very pleasing to take you into the bedroom and make love to you until the sun comes up."

Justin's eyes widened, and his pace of breath increased. He was not sure if he was blushing or not. Hell, he was unsure if he could blush, but he would be right now if it were possible. No words came to his mind to say, so he sat waiting for Hope to continue.

"But I want to do the right thing. I want you and me to do the right thing. I want our foundation to be built on more than just physical pleasure. I want our relationship to be special," Hope stated in a tone filled with possibilities.

"That's what I want, too," he finally whispered, and like the ending of some romantic comedy, both stared into each other's eyes.

Hope thought about the number of men she wished

she had not had sex with so early in their relationship. She recalled a fleeting image of a man's face she barely remembered—a stark contrast to the man sitting before her now, a man she cared for deeply. The thought of giving him what she had given so freely in the past made her feel cheap. She knew denying herself and Justin pleasure tonight was somehow right, that this was the way to build something real.

Suddenly, Hope jumped up and bolted into her bedroom. Justin sat, imagining what was next. His mind started generating possibilities: *Is she going to get condoms? Will she be wearing a nightie or just her birthday suit? Should I start getting undressed?* All the options had a happy ending.

When Hope emerged from her room, she had selected "none of the above" as the answer. She was dressed in a warm, comfy, long-sleeved cotton pajama set. She carried a comforter and a large bed pillow. She handed the entire ensemble to Justin.

"Please stay. I want you to spend the night. I want you close to me. Just not too close, if you know what I mean."

Justin smiled, unsuccessfully hiding his disappointment. "Sure. Let me text my mom and tell her I'm not coming home tonight."

"Oh no, what will your mother think of me?" Hope joked, with a tinge of truth, as Justin typed on his phone.

Justin's phone pinged back immediately.

"I don't think you need to worry. Mom just texted me back with her smiling bitmoji saying, 'Go for it.'"

Justin shook his head with happy thoughts of his straight-shooting mother.

"I know you need to get some sleep because you have work in the morning. I'm not going to kiss you good night. If I kiss you again, I…" Hope shuttered and gave herself a restraining hug. "Good night," she said with a slight wave, then headed into her room, leaving the door open.

Justin stared at the open door, a potent symbol of trust, an invitation to a different kind of intimacy. His body was a storm of conflicting emotions—the primal urge to follow her and the deep, abiding respect for her wishes. Unlike the conflict portrayed in movies, the devil on one shoulder and the angel on the other were in complete agreement. They both wanted to see if Hope really could make love until sunrise. Justin subdued every primal urge in his body. He, too, wanted this relationship to work, even if that meant a night on the couch.

Conversely, Hope lay in her bed and fell into a deep, restful Princess Aurora sleep. She felt a sense of peace she hadn't known since the night with Caleb. She had a Prince Charming nearby and could slumber knowing she was safe and secure for that night.

* * *

Justin's sleep was interrupted by the loud clanging of pots. He stood up from Hope's couch and looked over the counter into her kitchen. What he saw initially brought a smile to his face and a laugh to his heart. But on closer inspection, he realized he needed to show compassion, not amusement.

Flour covered Hope's face, hair, and pajamas. In front

of her sat three pancakes on a plate. Each had its unique deformity. One was blackened, one folded on top of itself, and the last looked like a black-and-white sugar cookie. Next to the pancakes were three thoroughly burnt strips of turkey bacon that Hope had cooked on the stove rather than her usual microwave method. Lastly, there was a bowl of raw eggs, filled with more eggshells than yolk.

"Hi. I was trying to make you breakfast, but I…"

Hope's words started with a smile and an attempt at humor, but her voice quivered, migrating to an emotion-filled squeak. A single tear ran down her face. Hope slumped her shoulders as she looked at the catastrophe that was her attempt at breakfast.

Justin sprang into the kitchen and ran to Hope. He hugged her, but she did not reciprocate. Her arms remained at her side as she continued to look at the mess in front of her.

"It's okay. No big deal," Justin said, his voice soft but dismissive of her pain.

Hope's internal monologue flared with quiet shame. *It is a big deal,* she thought. Her inability to cook was always a point of pain for her. It was the fruit of a horrible relationship with her terrible mother. Despite the fact that Gina was an excellent cook, Hope was never allowed to serve as an apprentice in Gina's kitchen. When Hope was very young, Gina would chase her out of the kitchen whenever Hope came near. As Hope grew older, avoiding Gina was one of her top priorities. The kitchen was no exception. The two of them never so much as made Rice Krispies treats together.

To Justin, the kitchen was just a few burned items and

some raw eggs. To Hope, it was a monument to her deepest insecurities, a physical manifestation of Gina's interference. This ruined breakfast was yet another proof of a virus that infected everything good in her life.

"You should go ahead and go home. I'm sure your mom will feed you," Hope said, her voice flat as she walked toward the door.

Justin had been married and had a mother. He knew there were times to say nothing, to leave a woman alone with her thoughts, and not try to be Mr. Fixit. He was torn between his protective impulse to fix the disaster and his knowledge that he needed to give her space. He took a small step back, his shoulders slumping in defeat.

Justin slowly kissed Hope on the forehead. "Thank you again for dinner last night. It was great." He turned toward the door. "I don't know when I'll have free time during the day, so I may not call you. I'll work late tonight so that I can attend Amira's play tomorrow night."

Hope had forgotten about her Little Sister's upcoming performance.

"Okay. Be safe today, and I'll talk to you later," Hope responded while instinctively brushing some flour off Justin's chest, which she had transferred to him during their earlier hug.

Justin headed out the door, and Hope closed it behind him. Hope then turned and looked at the debacle in the kitchen.

She shook her head, lamenting, "Dr. Hope Castillo. Summa Cum Laude. Distinguished scholar. Able to diagnose and treat serious, complex psychological disorders. Yet, I can't successfully make scrambled eggs. How odd can one person be?"

Chapter 39
The David and Bathsheba Defense

"Hope, come on in," Big Preach said, gladly receiving Hope into his office. Hope sat in one of the two large leather armchairs before Reverend Rice's stately mahogany desk.

Big Preach's office was a sharp contrast to Caleb's pastor study. As Pastor Emeritus, Reverend John Rice kept his office in the church after passing the pastoral responsibilities to Reverend Caleb Moore. The room contained no computers, flat screens, or modern trappings. Next to one wall sat a small three-person couch and two matching armchairs arranged around a coffee table. Two other walls, and half of a third, were lined with bookcases from floor to ceiling. Each bookcase was a testament to homiletics. Numerous versions of the Bible—several in Greek and Hebrew—and multiple commentary series analyzing every word, verse, and book in the Bible, as well as lexicons and Biblical concordances packed every inch of shelf space. Near the bookshelves stood a small two-step ladder that helped Big Preach reach the top shelf of his study materials.

His desk had several open Biblical reference books and a notebook where the Reverend Doctor wrote his sermons longhand.

"How are you, my little treasure?" Big Preach asked. "I hope you are feeling better."

He had called Hope his "little treasure" since before she could remember. The term always made her feel special because he referred to no one else in that manner.

"I'm fine. I hope I'm not bothering you too much. I know it's late, but the Sign Language Ministry met briefly this evening. When the meeting concluded, I saw your light was on, so I decided to say hi," Hope explained.

"First, young lady, you are never a bother to me. I always have time for you. Always. Second, I have known you your whole life. After the doctor and your father, I think I was the third man to hold you as a baby. I know when something is on your mind. It's on your face as clear as that mud was the day you fell into a creek at the church picnic when you were seven. So, go ahead and spill it. Don't go acting shy around me now. Look me in the eye and ask your question."

Big Preach's words pried open a question that had smoldered in Hope's head intensely after her most recent run-in with Caleb. Hope took a deep breath, her hands clasped tightly in her lap.

"It's Caleb. You know the disturbing history he and I share. I'm sure you also know many of the other heinous acts he has been rumored to have done. With that said, why did you and the church pick him of all people to succeed you as pastor?"

Big Preach, who had been leaning forward on his desk, sat back and paused. He could not speak off the top of his head without giving a subject proper thought.

"Do you remember when you were about eleven or twelve years old, and the Sunday school class studied the story of David and Bathsheba?" Big Preach asked.

Hope shifted in her chair, a hint of frustration on her face.

"Yes, but I'm not sure how that matters now," Hope replied with a hint of a side-eye toward her former pastor.

"Well, you came running to me after class. You were confused, like now. You asked me, 'How could David, who had sex with a friend's wife and then had that friend killed, be considered a man after God's own heart?'"

"I remember that," Hope said with a small smile. "I also remember not fully understanding your answer."

"The three years Caleb was a youth pastor in Dallas for Reverend Scroggin's church, the children's ministry flourished. Reverend Scoggin and I go way back, and he gave me his highest recommendation for Caleb to succeed me down here in Houston," Big Preach explained.

Hope retorted, "I remember all the other marvelous tributes to Caleb that the search committee put forward when they nominated him. You still aren't answering my question. I'm not asking about his accomplishments; I'm asking about his character."

"In those two years, nine hundred people joined. Five hundred and fifty were candidates for baptism," Big Preach continued, ignoring her last statement. "Caleb relates to teenagers better than anyone I have seen in years. The few weeks he has been here, how would you assess the youth department?"

"Thriving," Hope admitted. "Even teenage boys are active."

"What about how he cares for his brother Eli and sees his every need? He has taken on the mantle of being his brother's keeper in every way possible."

Big Preach paused, then continued before Hope could speak.

"Caleb's fundraisers for muscular dystrophy collected over two hundred and fifty thousand dollars in the last year alone. He's getting an award from the National MD Foundation in just a few nights."

Hope listened to the list, but so far, Big Preach's words were just a list of accomplishments that had no bearing on her question.

"I know you listen intently to every sermon preached from that pulpit. You know the Bible and scrutinize every syllable of a speaker. I know you do when I preach, so I can only imagine your inspection of Caleb's sermons is even more intense. From the sermons you have heard, have you ever heard Caleb say one thing contrary to God's Word from the pulpit?"

Hope thought hard but could not think of anything significant beyond Caleb's attacks of egotism and self-promotion.

"No, not really. Nothing that matters anyway."

"So, he is preaching God's Word, not his own, drawing people to be saved and positively impacting the community." Big Preach paused before emphasizing, "God uses imperfect people to complete His perfect plan. Just as he used David, a man of great faith but also great sin, He can use Caleb's gifts for His purpose."

Hope sat quietly. She pondered his words in her heart. She recalled the same answer from Big Preach almost twenty years prior.

"Little Treasure, we all sin. Believe it or not, Caleb and I are more alike than different. He sins. I sin. And I am sure even you, my little treasure, sin. God calls men not because they are perfect, but because they are willing. Caleb is a national sports hero who received the call to preach the good news of Jesus Christ. He can relate to youth and leverage all these social media outlets. His charisma can command an audience of thousands, both in person and online. He was made for a time such as this. I did not pick Caleb to be the pastor; God did."

The room fell silent for several counts. Hope considered her next question but decided now was not the time.

Still deep in thought, Hope stood slowly, her mind still trying to reconcile her moral objections with his faith-based logic.

"I am going to go now," she said deliberately.

"Feel free to stay and talk some more if you want."

"No, I need to get home and let out my dog. As always, you gave me something to think about. See you Sunday."

"Be blessed, my treasure," Big Preach said as Hope exited.

Hope walked to her SUV, thinking that the answer she received from Big Preach today left her more unsettled than when she was twelve.

Chapter 40
The Unspoken Abortion

"Just as I thought, the evaporator coil needs to be replaced," Justin said as he knelt on one knee, looking into the oversized HVAC unit.

Akil, looking over his shoulder, had come to the same conclusion.

"Yeah, that thing is shot. It looks like this whole unit could use a complete overhaul."

"I'll make that recommendation to the building manager. I'm happy this pet store isn't one of our warranty clients. The parts and labor for this job will run about thirty-five hundred dollars. I would've had to eat that money if they had purchased a warranty plan. Give me a minute to call Bruce and tell him what we found. He may not want to overhaul the whole unit," Justin added, then dialed his building contact on his mobile.

Akil sat deep in thought on the floor off to the side in the building's maintenance room. The pet store had called in an emergency order earlier that day. The store's air conditioning was not working correctly. While most of the animals were doing fine in the heat of the Texas afternoon, employees and customers were wilting like lettuce.

Akil and Justin initially had under-warranty preventive maintenance jobs scheduled for completion elsewhere today. When the emergency call came into the shop, a request to generate immediate cash, Justin quickly changed the team's schedule. The cash proceeds from repairing the broken evaporator coil would allow Justin to make payroll and put gas into his truck for one more week.

"Bruce needs to talk to his boss before he can authorize us to do a complete overhaul. He'll call me back in a couple of minutes," Justin explained as he put his phone in his pocket.

"Hey, since we have a few minutes, I need to talk to you," Akil announced.

Justin felt trapped. He and Akil were stuck in the maintenance room until Bruce called him back. He had no good excuse to say no, so he had to listen.

"Okay, what's going on?"

"It's Andrielle. She's pregnant." Akil admitted. "About six weeks. I don't think I'm ready to be anybody's daddy. I don't even know how to be a daddy. My father took off before I was born. I used to be mad at him. Now, for the first time, I understand him. I want to take off and fly away. What do you think I should do?"

Justin initially thought he had neither the time nor the energy to deal with Akil's situation. He had enough problems without adding Akil's burdens.

"Man, that is serious stuff. I don't know what to tell you."

"Do you think we should have it? Should we get an

abortion? I mean, I love Andrielle and all, but we shouldn't have kids until we're both ready, right?"

The mention of abortion unearthed a deeply buried high school memory for Justin, a memory he'd fought to keep hidden. Like a submerged threat, it rose to the forefront of his mind, destroying any semblance of peace. The resurfaced pain manifested as a sharp outburst.

"I can't tell you what to do," Justin said, his voice laced with anger. "You're a grown man. Make your own choices!"

Akil lowered his head and closed his eyes.

"I'm sorry I bothered you," he said, then left the maintenance room and headed to the restroom.

Justin immediately regretted his harsh words to Akil. He turned to follow him, intending to apologize, but his phone interrupted him. It was Bruce authorizing the evaporator coil repair, but with a catch: payment wouldn't be possible until the end of the month. Justin grimaced. He'd already sunk much of his morning into tearing down the unit. Accepting the terms was the only practical option, but it compounded his financial woes. Now, not only did he have to scramble to make payroll by the end of the week, but he also had to find a way to cover the cost of the new evaporator coil until Bruce could pay. The weight of his financial predicament settled heavily on his shoulders.

Justin and Akil finished the repair. Justin focused on fixing the unit and thinking of ways to generate short-term cash—cash that would allow him to pay his employees and keep Ms. Kim from turning the lights out on him. There was no room in Justin's head for another set of problems. Akil's problems were just that—Akil's problems.

Chapter 41
Broadway Jr.

*A*mira felt lightheaded, caught in her mother's crushing embrace. Esther was overflowing with pride, her joy practically radiating outward. Though she couldn't hear Amira's voice, her eyes were glued to her daughter's performance, and she felt the music's rhythm vibrating through her skin and resonating in her heart. Finally, Esther released her daughter from the hug, stepping back to allow Hector to join the celebration. Hector presented Amira with a bouquet of flowers, his voice filling the silence that Esther couldn't bridge.

"That was amazing," he said, his eyes shining. "You were great!"

Hope and Justin watched the joyous scene unfold before them. Ten minutes earlier, the final curtain had fallen on the opening night of *The Lion King Jr.* The theater lobby was now a whirlwind of activity. Parents, friends, and family members congratulated the young performers, who were beaming with pride. The air buzzed with excitement, punctuated by squeals of delight from children and adults.

Amira turned to the person whose opinion mattered the most to her. "Hope, what did you think?"

"What did I think? Are you kidding me? That was wonderful. You are the best Nala ever. I cried when you sang 'Shadowland'. Not to brag, but I think you were the best thing in the play. Watch out, Broadway."

Hope's praise was music to Amira's ears.

"Really? You thought I was good?" Amira asked again, needing to confirm the words were truly meant for her.

She had performed in school plays and junior theater productions for three years, but her singing voice had dramatically transformed in the last six months. Gone was the soft, childlike sound, replaced by a powerful, almost operatic tone. A voice that could resonate with such force, it could make fine china tremble and warm the hearts of her listeners.

"Yes. We all thought it was excellent," Hope said and motioned her hand to include Justin in the conversation. "Amira, I want to introduce you to my friend Justin."

Justin extended his hand, and Amira grabbed it.

"You were really, really good. I had seen *The Lion King* animated movie, but what you and the cast did was much better. I'll be singing those songs all next week," Justin said with a smile.

"Thank you." Amira accepted the praise. "We were all nervous before the show, but then…"

Amira stopped mid-sentence, looking over Justin's shoulder.

"Pastor Caleb!" she screamed and ran a few feet, jumping and hugging Caleb around the neck.

He instinctively caught her and held her in the air. Hector and Esther rushed over excitedly at the sight of the icon holding their girl.

Hope's gaze was fixed on the embrace, her eyes blazing with an intensity that could have seared a steak. The hug struck her as far too intimate. The entire scene left Justin disconcerted, a swirl of conflicting thoughts leaving him unsure what to make of it.

Now, returned to the floor, Amira smiled from ear to ear. "Wow, I can't believe you're here."

"I saw your IG post about opening night, and I thought I would surprise you," Caleb said as he hugged Esther and shook Hector's hand.

With Justin in tow, Hope made her way over to the group.

"Hope, Pastor Caleb is here. Can you believe it?" Amira repeated as if the moment was too intense to be real.

Hope donned her familiar mask of emotion and smiled. However, her smile did not betray what was in her heart or on her mind.

"I have to go and change out of costume. Thank you all for coming. Thank you. Thank you," Amira repeated and ran off, following her fellow castmates backstage to change.

In the distance, Justin saw a familiar face.

"I'll be right back," he told Hope and headed towards his former friend. The person was changing the trash bag in the back of the lobby.

"Hey, CJ," Justin said.

It wasn't until Justin was right upon CJ that he realized how awkward this moment would be. The last time they had talked, Justin had just laid off CJ. Justin headed toward CJ to say hi to an old friend, but now he stood before him as CJ's former employer.

Justin could now see CJ's grey jumpsuit. His name tag rested above his left pectoral muscle, and "Joe's Janitorial Services" was printed above his right pectoral. Justin concluded that the theatre had contracted with Joe's Janitorial Services, and CJ worked as a contract custodian.

"Justin," CJ responded flatly.

Despite the noise in the lobby, there was momentary silence between them.

"I thought I would say hi. Sorry if I'm bothering you," Justin stated, trying to make the best of an uncomfortable situation.

"You're not bothering me. Did you enjoy the show?" CJ asked.

The question released some of the tension in the air.

"I did. Those young people are talented. I was surprised."

"Yeah, one of the few benefits of this job is seeing the shows. Last week, they closed out the play *The Music Man*. These kids are something else," CJ explained.

CJ asked about Akil and Hank, and the conversation remained light chit-chat for a few more minutes.

While Justin was across the room with CJ, Hope turned to Hector and Esther and signed, "Please excuse me while I talk to my brother-in-law. See you later. Amira did great."

Hector and Esther smiled and waved goodbye as Hope grabbed Caleb by the elbow and pulled him off to the closest corner.

"Hey, Cheeks, careful. Handling me a bit rough, aren't you? Oh yeah, I almost forgot. That's how you like it," Caleb said with a crooked smile and fake charm.

With a pointed gesture, Hope confronted Caleb, her voice tight with a fury that felt like a hot wire running through her veins.

"That hug was not appropriate. It was wrong. Very wrong."

Her anger was fueled by the knowledge gained in her sessions with Hannah, a deep understanding of how older men groomed young girls. The charm offensive towards parents, the supposed gatekeepers, was a well-worn path for abusers. And too often, those gates were left wide open.

Caleb's demeanor completely changed. He dropped his fake charm, and a look of intensity covered his face.

"Have you lost your mind? I can't believe you would even suggest that. First, I happen to agree with you. That hug was not appropriate. She jumped into my arms before I knew what was happening. I interact with people and the youth a million times a day, and I fist-bump everyone. Especially the girls. I don't even want the appearance of anything being wrong. Please teach your little sister how to give a 'holy hug.' I mean it; please do that. You are the one who is making this weird. Second, you have accused me of many bad things, Hope. Hell, I've done a lot of bad things. But to accuse me of harming a child? Well, that hurts me more than you can imagine."

Caleb's face held an unfamiliar expression, a confusing blend of pain and frustration that Hope couldn't decode. He had deceived her before, and with Amira now involved, she was adamant: Caleb's manipulations would not touch her little sister.

"I wouldn't put anything past you," Hope said, her

words tight and low. "Just know I'm watching you. If you touch Amira or any young girl, I will personally see to it that your black ass ends up in jail."

She spoke through clenched teeth, her gaze locked on Caleb's. Neither of them yielded; the tension between them was a palpable force.

"Is everything okay?" Justin arrived on the scene, inquiring about the fierce exchange he could see but couldn't hear from a distance.

Caleb turned to Justin, gave him a quick glance, and said, "Yes, it's all good."

Then Caleb promptly walked away and headed out the door.

Justin turned to Hope. His inquisitive eyes let Hope know he wanted to know what was going on. He could discern a serious issue between Hope and Caleb.

Hope turned to Justin. "I have much to tell you about my brother-in-law, just not now. Can we talk another time? I want to go home."

"Sure," Justin conceded.

While driving Hope home, Justin could not stop thinking about the lively exchange he witnessed from a distance. He wondered what could make Hope so upset. Justin decided Caleb must be mistreating Hope's sister, Rachel, or something along those lines. Only a family mess can make someone that angry, he concluded.

Hope wondered how to tell Justin about her family's trials and tribulations. The closer she grew to Justin, the more afraid she became of losing him. She wondered if her dark secrets would come to light and drive away this remarkable man.

Chapter 42
Love Defined

*L*ove *illuminates life and cannot be hidden.*

This conclusion poured into Hope's mind as if she had a livestream connection with divinity. It was so clear and simple that she was shocked she had not thought of it before.

Hope had spent her entire life pondering the elusive concept of love. She remained adrift in her understanding with no positive examples to draw from. The relationship between Gina and Craig presented a chilling contrast. Their animosity was a toxic brew of hatred and disgust, so intense that words like "hate" seemed insufficient. If a sudden chasm opened and one of them were to vanish, the other would revel in the world's newfound reprieve from a loathsome blight.

Her college experiences only served to complicate her opinion of what love could be. In her English classes, poets and writers pondered the multifaceted and layered aspects of love. Shakespeare said, *Love is blind, and lovers cannot see.* Plato thought love was *"divine madness."* Maya Angelou wrote, *Love recognizes no barriers. It jumps hurdles, leaps fences, and penetrates walls to arrive at its destination full of hope.* Three different perspectives, yet none of them helped Hope understand love.

Hope's studies in science and biology had prompted her to ponder whether love was any more than a complex interplay of chemical reactions within the brain, a set of evolutionary directives embedded in our DNA to drive procreation and ensure the continuation of the human race. While this explanation provided a logical framework, it felt too devoid of warmth and too clinical, even for Dr. Castillo's pragmatism.

Today, the meaning of love had become clear to Hope. She rested her head on Justin's leg and watched the sunset paint the sky above the pond. She felt the warmth of the fading sun, the comforting weight of his hand on her shoulder, and the gentle, caring strokes of his other hand in her hair.

Hope had arrived at the park that evening earlier than she and Justin had discussed. She wanted time to set up the beach blanket and beach chairs near the water. The chairs were the kind with the short legs that had allowed Hope and Anna to set their drinks next to them on those days when they sunned along the gulf's shore. Today, Hope set a tray of assorted salty meats, cheeses, and crackers between the chairs. A bottle of Merlot was also opened to allow it to breathe.

She sat in one of the chairs and people-watched until Justin arrived. In the evening, Webb Park was very different from Hope's daily morning visits. People of all ages filled the park with laughter and playfulness. Somehow, parks bring out one's carefree nature, which is buried deep inside everyone during work and school.

Her people-watching led her to her often-asked question: *What is love?* Look at the teenage couple leaning against the tree, kissing and pushing the boundaries of heavy petting. Was that love? Or were they acting on primal instincts?

How about the elderly couple walking on the path out for their evening exercise? They were not holding hands or locked in an embrace like the teenagers. But apparently, they had been together for decades. The couple had probably been caring for each other through good times and very difficult times. Was that love?

A group of soccer moms sat at a picnic table, watching their toddlers and grade-schoolers play on the jungle gyms and swings. The children would take turns running to their mothers, each seeking to have a need addressed. Hunger, a bandage for a boo-boo, or just a hug. All came in search of Mom to fix their problem. Was that love?

Hope had spent time in her beach chair, overthinking definitions of love and countless potential examples. Her thoughts lingered on the subject until Justin arrived. She shifted gears, focusing on welcoming him and making him feel at ease. She worried she had failed at the comfort part when she offered him a seat, and he had to plop his six-foot-three frame onto the low chair. Fortunately, he stretched out his long legs, leaned back, and smiled.

He apologized briefly for being a few minutes late, explaining he had stopped by home for a quick shower and a change of clothes. Hope hadn't even registered the slight delay; her attention was immediately drawn to his shorts, which revealed the impressive musculature of his legs. A playful thought flitted through her mind, a momentary envy of the teenagers' unrestrained passion against the nearby tree. She inwardly chided herself, reminding herself to maintain a semblance of ladylike behavior, at least for the time being.

Hope sat down, as well. She fixed a small paper plate of snacks and handed it to Justin. She then produced two ice-cold bottles of Mexican Coke from her small cooler and turned on a Prince playlist on her phone.

Justin shared his mother's warm reception of Hope, eliciting a grateful smile and a quiet "thank you." The conversation lingered, then faded, both sensing an unspoken understanding that this was not the moment for a deeper discussion about mothers. They attempted half-heartedly at small talk, mentioning movies and television shows, but the words felt hollow. They drifted into a comfortable silence, a shared serenity that enveloped them, a respite from the turmoil of their lives.

Justin directed Hope's attention to a young boy valiantly attempting to launch a kite. They watched him run, his small figure a testament to persistence, each attempt ending in frustrating failure. Hope saw herself in the boy, trying so hard to grasp something so elusive, only to fail over and over again. On what seemed like his twentieth attempt, the kite finally caught a benevolent gust of wind and ascended gracefully into the sky. Hope and Justin were caught up in the moment and shared a spontaneous cheer, feeling an unexpected sense of shared triumph as if they had personally guided the kite's ascent.

Hope felt this was a perfect moment. Merely watching a kite flying with Justin was terrific. Justin reached over and held her hand. When their hands touched, a wave of warmth—not just a jolt of electricity—emanated from Hope's hand and ran up her arm, giving her whole body a warm charge. She wanted to kiss him, and he knew it. Justin leaned over, and their lips met. The kiss was long and slow. The kiss pushed all other thoughts out of their consciousness. They were oblivious to the world and its harsh realities. Somehow, the kiss neither of them wanted to end ended. Hope moved from her seat and sat on the picnic blanket.

She rested her head on Justin's leg and watched the sunset paint the sky above the pond. She felt the warmth of the fading sun, the comforting weight of his hand on her shoulder, and the gentle, caring strokes of his other hand in her hair. She thought of all that Justin had done for her in the short time they had known each other. He had brought much-needed light into her all-too-dark world. His actions were not just for her to see but for everyone to witness.

Hope then realized, *Justin loves me! And I now know what love means.* She finally understood what Maya Angelou was talking about.

Love illuminates life and cannot be hidden.

Chapter 43
Gala Invite

The morning air at Webb Park was crisp, carrying the scent of dew and freshly cut grass. Hope and Justin walked alongside Nelson, a comfortable rhythm to their steps. The usual small talk about work and Deuce gave way to a brief, comfortable silence.

"So, my friend Anna—you know, my best friend—had two tickets to the Muscular Dystrophy charity gala this Friday," Hope began, breaking the quiet. "She's a big supporter of MD research, and I was her plus-one. But she came down with a nasty virus and is quarantined for the week."

Justin listened, nodding as she spoke. He already knew about the gala from Caleb and Eli's podcast.

"Anyway, she insisted I still go and told me to take a friend," Hope continued, looking over at him with a soft smile. "I was hoping you would come with me."

Justin's easygoing posture stiffened slightly. "A gala? You know I don't own a tux, right? I don't think I'd fit in at a place like that."

A flicker of a memory, of him feeling out of place in her SUV, passed through his mind. Hope, sensing his hesitation, reached for his hand.

"Justin, look at me," she said, her voice firm but gentle. "This isn't about what you're wearing or how much money you have. It's about being with me. And besides," she added with a playful wink, "I already have a solution for the tux situation. Anna's mom is a tailor, and she makes magic with a needle and thread. She'll have you looking like a movie star."

Justin chuckled, but his brow remained furrowed. "I don't know, Hope. Are you sure you want me there? It sounds like a pretty high-profile event."

"Look at me. This isn't about the room—it's about the war. I need you to be my shield in that room. I need you standing next to me when I face them."

The sincerity in her voice disarmed him. It wasn't about the gala or the tux; it was about her choosing him, her wanting to stand with him, unafraid.

"Okay," he said softly, a small smile finally breaking through. "A tux, huh? Just as long as you promise not to turn me into a prince."

Hope's laugh filled the air, a bright, clear sound that carried on the breeze.

"No promises, my knight in shining armor. Now come on, we have a date with a tailor."

Chapter 44
Questions for Caleb

Late Sunday afternoon, Eli sat in his apartment, facing the green light on the top of his laptop. With microphone-enabled earbuds in his ears, he introduced his show.

"Hello and welcome to the historic two hundredth episode of my podcast 'Eli on Everything.' Those of you watching me on our streaming broadcast or my YouTube channel, don't be alarmed. Yes, I shaved my beard and mustache. I am going clean-cut for now."

"Today's special guest is no stranger to all of you and definitely not me. He's been a guest on this podcast, counting today, fifteen times. My favorite pastor, sports hero, and most importantly, my favorite brother, Reverend Caleb Moore."

The streamed screen split into two sections. On the screen's left, Caleb appeared opposite Eli, dressed in a casual black linen-collared shirt. He wore high-end Beats headphones trimmed in gold. Caleb was broadcasting from his home office.

"I'm your only brother, man," he chuckled. "I think

you've told that joke every time I've been on the podcast."

Eli smiled. "You always do a great job, and I'm superstitious. It's worked every other time. Therefore, I'm going to keep telling the joke. Can you believe we started this podcast over two years ago? You were my first guest. Helping out your wheelchair-bound, trying-to-figure-out-life brother."

"The time has flown by, that's for sure. You started once a month and now post new episodes twice a week. You have over one hundred thousand subscribers. Congrats, baby bro. I'm proud of you."

"Thanks, man. By the way, the Muscular Dystrophy charity gala taking place on Friday is completely sold out. I'm sure it's due to my more famous but less handsome brother being the guest of honor." Eli laughed.

Caleb closed his eyes, dropped his head, and chuckled.

"Now that's enough about us. These segments are called 'Questions for Caleb.' We should get to the questions."

"Sure, fire away," Caleb responded as if he were about to hear a question for the first time.

In actuality, once Eli chose a question from tweets and emails, he would send them to Caleb. Caleb then had at least a day to prepare a response to the questions that would be posed to him on the show.

"Caleb, we have here an email from Alex D. He states, 'I'm having a consensual sexual relationship that is a little inappropriate. We care for each other and don't want anyone to get hurt. But now, the relationship is very public, and my family, particularly my wife and daughter, are devastated. I still believe what I am doing is only a little wrong, but to see the impact on my family is killing me. I cannot look them in the eye or myself in the mirror. Please help,'" Eli finished reading and then looked into the camera. "Reverend Caleb, do you have any thoughts on this matter?"

Caleb paused and began to speak. He spoke, his posture shifting, and a more authoritative tone entered his voice, appearing to spontaneously form words of wisdom: "Alex, your situation is all too familiar. The moment we start justifying our actions, we've already lost the battle. We convince ourselves that a little wrong is just a temporary detour, but that detour takes us miles from God's grace."

"I think we all get caught by that one, Caleb. We think what we are doing is somehow less wrong than what others do. We're not the most impartial jury in judging our actions."

"Exactly. We are our own best lawyers, but everyone else's judges."

Eli continued his inquiry. "Okay, if Alex can acknowledge he's wrong, what's next?"

"Well, admitting you're wrong is not an easy first step. One has to be humble enough to admit wrongdoing. It is often some outside catalyst that makes us realize the wrongs we have done. Getting arrested or caught having an affair are two obvious ones. Others can be like a death or illness in the family. These events cause you to reevaluate your relationships with others and God."

"Okay, Pastor. We knew you were going to bring God into this conversation. How can the Big Guy help mere mortals like us?"

"Well, God was always in the conversation. My absolute favorite scripture is 2 Chronicles 7:14 — [14]If My people who are called by My name will humble themselves, and pray and seek My face, and turn from their wicked ways, then I will hear from heaven, and will forgive their sin and heal their land.

"Eli, people ask me all the time, *'How do I seek His face? I don't know where He is.'* I tell them, look for God like He's a lost set of car keys."

Eli had heard Caleb's key analogy dozens of times but feigned ignorance for the audience's sake.

"Look for God like my car keys, man. Are you kidding me?"

"No, I'm serious. Think about it. What do you do when you lose your keys? By definition, you don't know where they are. So, you start looking everywhere they might be. You even go back to places you've already looked at two or three times. You look high and low. It weighs on your mind until you find your keys. You are relentless until you find your keys. Now, car keys can only open a car door and start a car. God is the key to opening doors to joy and the road to salvation, and we should look for God until we find him. The good news is that He is not hiding and is unlike Zeus or Apollo, living up on Mt. Olympus, far from everyday folks. If you look for Him, He will find you."

"Okay, I understand what you're saying, but how does that help my man Alex D.?"

"Once Alex reconciles with God, he can fix his relationships with his wife and daughter and look at himself in the mirror. Not before, but only after."

"You make it sound easy."

"There are just a few steps, but first, Alex must start looking for his God keys. Without his keys, he will not be able to open any doors or get anywhere he wants to go. Know what I'm saying? Do ya hear me, man?"

"I hear you, my brotha. Thanks for your insight. Alex, I hope those words helped you. We're going to let Caleb go on with his day. I'll now transition to a segment on how long to smoke a beef brisket. Please plan on joining us again soon, Reverend."

"Only if you promise to come to the house and bring some brisket."

"It's a deal. Peace."

Chapter 45
The Gala Catastrophe

The ballroom of the Grand Hyatt was a shimmering sea of black tuxedos and elegant evening gowns. The air, thick with the scent of expensive perfume and gourmet food, buzzed with the hum of polite conversation. At a glance, it was a picture of refined charity, but for Hope Castillo, it was a battlefield. She stood by Justin's side, a vision in a midnight-blue silk gown that draped her form like liquid moonlight. The dress was a triumph of Anna's mom's tailoring, a perfect match for the man beside her. Justin, too, was a revelation. He wore a perfectly tailored black tux, the fabric a perfect complement to his dark skin, highlighting the strong lines of his shoulders and chest. He carried himself with a quiet confidence that radiated from him—a man completely at ease in his own skin, despite his initial misgivings. Hope looked at him, and the word magnificent floated through her mind. He was every bit the knight she had imagined.

"I can't believe you pulled this off," Justin said, his voice a low rumble just for her ear. "I feel like a whole new person."

"You are not a new person; you're my man." Hope smiled, her hand finding his.

They were a stunning couple, a beacon of authenticity in a room of carefully curated personas. A waiter approached them with a silver tray of champagne flutes.

"Champagne for the distinguished couple?" he asked.

Hope took a glass, her smile sparkling. "Yes, thank you."

Justin, however, gave a slight shake of his head. "No, thank you," he said politely, his hand resting on Hope's back as if to guide her away.

Hope didn't notice the refusal; she was already caught up in the moment.

Across the room, Rachel, a vision of elegance in her own right, felt a familiar wave of nausea. The eight-week-old life inside her was a constant reminder of her fractured reality. As she sipped ginger ale and endured tedious conversation, her gaze, however, was fixed on a more immediate source of her distress: Caleb. He was holding court among the city's elite, his charm a familiar, potent force. But standing at his left, like an unofficial co-host, was Twila Gooden. Rachel seethed. The sight of Twila's unsettling familiarity with her husband turned her stomach more than any pregnancy symptom.

Suddenly, a new presence caught her eye. Gina, her mother, was approaching with a practiced smile. But Gina's gaze wasn't on her. It was fixed on a couple standing near the entrance—a tall, handsome man in a tuxedo and a striking woman in a blue gown. For a moment, Gina's eyes widened. She didn't recognize the man from the hospital waiting room. All she saw was a confident, elegant couple—the epitome of wealth and success.

As Hope watched the scene unfold—Rachel's isolated sadness, Caleb's performance, and the way Twila laughed and touched him—a jolt of her old protective instinct for Rachel surged to the surface. It was a reflex, a ghost limb of a bond severed years ago. Her logical mind, the part of her that remembered all of Caleb's manipulations and Rachel's own complicity, told her to let it go. But her heart, that illogical muscle that still ached for her sister, rebelled. She quickly suppressed the feeling, the memory of her own pain and Rachel's betrayal, a cold blanket over the embers of her compassion.

Her attention was then drawn to Twila, who, for a moment, had broken from her orbit around Caleb. Twila's eyes, not on Caleb, scanned the room. When they landed on Justin, her gaze lingered, a flicker of interest in her eyes. It was a fleeting moment, but Hope saw it. When Hope met her stare, Twila's eyes darted away, a look of fleeting guilt on her face as she refocused on the crowd.

"Rachel, you look absolutely stunning tonight," a smooth voice said.

It was Eli. As Caleb's brother, he shared many traits: charm, quick wit, and striking good looks, though his eyes held a softer, more inviting warmth. Despite his confinement to a wheelchair, Eli possessed a magnetic presence, a charisma that rivaled even his older brother's.

"Thank you, Eli. Mr. Councilman, please allow me to introduce you to my favorite brother-in-law, Eli," Rachel said, gesturing with her hands for both to shake hands, which they did.

"No need for you to introduce me. I met Eli a couple of years ago at the celebrity softball tournament his brother organized. We raised a lot of money for MD that day. Eli was our honorary team captain."

"Yes, we did. Over twelve thousand dollars, if my memory serves," Eli chimed in.

"I also watch Eli's weekly podcast. I tell you, Eli, you have a unique perspective on just about everything. I look forward to seeing what you'll talk about next. I hope it's something regarding getting out and voting for me in November." The councilman smiled, looking for an endorsement from the brother of the room's star.

"You know, I usually stay out of local politics. But maybe I can make an exception," Eli slyly stated. As always, Eli left the person he talked to feeling encouraged.

The councilman grinned and pointed toward the dais. "I think it is time we all take our seats," the councilman said, then headed to the bar in the corner to get one more drink before taking his seat.

"Please rescue me after the program and take me home. Don't leave me with these people," Rachel whispered to Eli.

Eli winked at her, and they both made their way to the front of the ballroom.

Rachel walked toward her husband so he could escort her to the head table. Caleb's scrum was breaking up.

As he turned and began making his way to the front, Twila lightly patted him on the butt and said, "Go get'em, tiger," making sure to say it loud enough for Rachel to hear.

Caleb turned to Twila, smiled, and gave her a slight, knowing nod.

Rachel's eyes snapped open, her breath coming in rapid, ragged gasps through her flaring nostrils. Her heart pounded against her ribs, a frantic rhythm like the beat of distant African drums. Her fists were clenched so tightly that her knuckles lost their color, mirroring the rigid tension in her jaw. A wave of icy numbness washed over her, the sheer force of her rage leaving her devoid of sensation.

"Hey, are you okay?" Eli asked as he saw the color drain from his sister-in-law's face.

Rachel ignored Eli's words and continued her march behind her husband. As Caleb reached the three stairs leading up to the platform, where the main table was set up, he suddenly remembered he had a pregnant wife and turned to her abruptly. He reached back to hold her hand up the stairs. The scene made him look like a doting husband for the world to see.

The room was filled with forty enormous round tables, each accommodating ten people. The tables were all draped in long white tablecloths, with china and fresh-flower centerpieces. Each table was numbered to facilitate the assigned seating.

Table #1 sat directly in front of the podium. Seated there, in addition to several of the charity's most significant patrons, was Rachel's mother, Gina. Gina was flanked to her right by Caleb's brother Eli and to her left by her date, Samuel Vincent Roberson III, Esq. Samuel was a partner in the city's most significant litigation law firm.

Samuel was one of Gina's key benefactors, and their relationship was a mutually beneficial arrangement. A fifteen-year marriage and two children had ended abruptly when Samuel's wife discovered his long-term affair with a male law clerk from his firm. In their conservative state, a gay partner could devastate the firm's reputation. To avoid scandal, Samuel agreed to a generous divorce settlement, and his ex-wife, prioritizing her financial security, remained silent. She understood the value of maintaining the source of her alimony.

Samuel required a female companion for social events to uphold a respectable public image. Gina readily filled this role as his public consort. When Samuel needed a date, he would call, and Gina would visit Le Mademoiselle's dress shop to have a custom-made evening gown made. She would then purchase the necessary jewelry, favoring diamonds and emeralds, along with matching Christian Louboutin shoes. She would forward the total bill to Samuel, adding a $2,500 fee for "time and incidentals," which was an insignificant expense for the high-earning attorney.

Gina preferred her arrangements with Samuel to those with her other benefactors, as he required no "extra effort" after the event. At the end of the night, Samuel would escort her to her door, offer a platonic hug, and return to his home and hidden relationship.

Hope and Justin were escorted to a table on the opposite side of the ballroom from the head table. Justin instinctively pulled out a chair for Hope. He waited for her to sit before he gently pushed the chair under her. As she settled into the chair, he briefly rested his hand on her shoulder—a small, loving gesture that sent a comforting warmth through her body.

The two of them talked quietly, their conversation a comfortable, easy stream of words that flowed from one topic to the next. The buzz of the other guests and the presence of the dignitaries at their table faded into the background. They were in their own bubble, a shared world of quiet happiness, oblivious to the drama unfolding at the head table.

Everyone sat in assigned positions. The raised head table had a microphone and lectern in the middle, with several people on each side. Immediately to the podium's right was the president of the local Muscular Dystrophy charity's chapter. He would present Caleb with the Community Outreach Person of the Year award. The banquet was an annual charity event, and the recipient was often a local celebrity who drew people to donate $300 per ticket.

Next to the chapter president was Caleb. Then sat Rachel, a board member, and finally, Twila Gooden. Twila, representing the church, was on the program to read Caleb's biography and his community accomplishments.

To the left of the podium sat Mary Weber, tonight's Mistress of Ceremonies, the mayor and his wife, and additional board members. All had minor speaking roles on tonight's agenda.

Mary opened the evening with customary greetings and a pledge of punctuality, eliciting polite smiles and applause from the audience—everyone, that is, except Rachel, the guest of honor's wife. Rachel's gaze was distant, her mind consumed by the earlier scene between Caleb and Twila—a scene that had ignited a furious turmoil within her. She battled the urge to retaliate, envisioning herself plunging a fork into her husband's leg or dousing Twila with a bottle of wine. The more she dwelt on the betrayal, the more her internal rage simmered.

Dinner was served quickly. Caleb conversed constantly with the charity president and the multiple guests between courses, who would stop by the table for an up-close glimpse of him. Rachel's detached behavior went completely unnoticed by him. However, Gina had noticed it and casually approached her daughter.

Gina, her smile a practiced mask, mouthed a silent question: *What is wrong with you, girl?*

Previously fixed on an unseen point in the distance, Rachel's eyes shifted with glacial slowness, meeting Gina's gaze before drifting back to their vacant stare. Gina's practiced smile morphed into a predatory expression, a jungle cat poised to strike its prey. However, her intended attack was abruptly cut short.

"Hi, Mom," Caleb said. "Have you met Peter Schimmelmann? Peter, this is my mother-in-law, Gina."

The jungle cat quickly became the angel of the room. "Hello, Peter. It's so nice to meet you," Gina said, extending her hand.

Peter grabbed her hand. "Mother-in-law? Caleb, you must be kidding me. She looks more like Rachel's sister. I see where your wife gets her beauty from."

"Oh, Peter. I love getting compliments from handsome men like you."

Gina blushed as she placed her other hand on top of the two that were shaking. Peter also added his second hand to the pile. They shared an almost secret smile.

"I'd better get back to my seat. Mary is getting ready to move on with the program," Gina said.

"Till we meet again," the president said, his handshake lingering before he released Gina's hand.

Gina gave Peter one last admiring look before turning and shooting a malevolent glare at Rachel.

Rachel witnessed the entire disgusting exchange between Gina and her new potential benefactor. Adding to Rachel's discomfort, a migraine began to take hold, the familiar ringing in her ears intensifying with each passing moment. The words of Mary and the other speakers faded into an indistinguishable hum, lost in the growing cacophony inside her head. A desperate urge to escape washed over her, but the weight of obligation held her captive until Caleb received his due recognition.

Twila took her place at the podium, passing close behind Rachel, leaving a cloying, cheap perfume trail. She began to read from a prepared speech, extolling Caleb's virtues and emphasizing the "honor" of working "under him" day and night. The phrase "under him" cut through Rachel's nausea, migraine, and the ringing in her ears like a physical blow. A surge of fury washed over her.

Did that hussy just say it was her honor to work under my husband? she thought, her inner voice dripping with venom.

As Twila began to speak, her voice a confident purr into the microphone, Hope felt a chilling sense of duplicity. This woman, who had been watching Justin a few moments ago, was now publicly celebrating the man who had torn Hope's life apart. Twila's words—a prepared speech about Caleb's character and good deeds—felt like a performance. The audience's applause and the smiling faces of people who had no idea what kind of man he truly was made Hope's skin crawl.

Rachel didn't hear Twila's next words, but everyone in the audience started clapping and standing. It was time for Caleb to accept the award. Caleb remained seated as Twila walked behind him back toward her seat. She placed her hand on his shoulder and then across his back as she followed behind him.

That seemingly insignificant gesture was the final straw for Rachel. She abruptly rose to her feet with a sharp, forceful slam of her hands on the table. The sudden movement sent her chair careening backward, striking Twila squarely on the hip. Twila, unsteady on her stiletto heels, lost her balance. She reached behind the dais, expecting to find a wall for support, but encountered only a curtain hanging from the ceiling. Clutching desperately at the fabric, she continued her three-foot descent, dragging the entire forty-foot-long curtain down with her. The resounding thud of her landing echoed through the stunned ballroom.

Rachel's sudden rise triggered a violent expulsion of her stomach's contents. She heaved, releasing every ounce of her appetizers, ginger ale, and chicken cordon bleu directly onto Caleb's head. The vile discharge streamed down his face, now contorted in disgust, and stained his pristine tuxedo.

The audience gasped in unison, but Hope's reaction was a single, defiant laugh. It was a sound of pure, unadulterated joy—a mischievous "ha" that felt like a release of years of pain. In that moment, watching Caleb's perfect world crumble, she felt a deep sense of healing.

Chapter 46
Disrespect

A mischievous smile played on Rachel's lips as she settled into the plush sofa. Her migraine had vanished, and her stomach was now a picture of serene tranquility. She surveyed the luxurious, contemporary space that surrounded her. The ladies' room, located just off the ballroom, was surprisingly spacious, with a large lounge area separated from the toilet stalls by a substantial door. The lounge was tastefully decorated with two deeply cushioned sofas, full-length mirrors on each side, and sleek marble counters with modern vessel sinks.

Rachel knew a sense of guilt should be gnawing at her, yet she felt nothing but a broad, contented smile. Her mind replayed the image of Twila, trapped beneath the fallen curtain, desperately scrambling for an escape. She resembled a mole blindly burrowing beneath the surface of a lawn. The sight of Twila bumping her head twice against the platform legs before being freed from the tangled fabric sent a fresh wave of amusement through her.

Gina stormed into the room, bringing an end to Rachel's minutes of peace and solitude.

"Little girl, have you lost your mind?" Gina shouted at Rachel.

Rachel remained on the couch, relaxed. She turned her head to the side like she was thinking. Finally, she looked back at her mother.

"No. My mind is perfectly clear, Mother. Perhaps yours is the one that's finally clouded over," she simply replied, then shrugged in a childlike manner.

"Don't play with me." Gina contorted her face and pointed her finger at Rachel. "I have spent the last thirty minutes cleaning up your mess in the ballroom. I have convinced all the attendees that you reacted badly to the food. That, combined with your pregnancy, caused your episode. So, instead of them thinking that you're crazy, you now have everyone's sympathy. Hell, Peter wants to give you an award."

Gina stood before Rachel, her gaze expectant, waiting for an apology or, at the very least, an explanation from her favorite daughter. Rachel, however, remained silent, her attention seemingly captivated by the Art Deco painting hanging on the wall.

"Looks like Twila broke her ankle," Gina said, breaking the silence. "Caleb and Eli are escorting her to the emergency room."

The small smile returned to Rachel's face. "A broken ankle. Good. But I'm sure she will be fine. Since her legs can still open, she can perform the only thing she's good for."

Gina stepped forward, grabbed her daughter by the wrist, and jerked her to her feet. Now, Gina stared Rachel directly in the face.

"You think this is some kind of game? You embarrassed Caleb tonight. You made me look like a fool in front of a lot of important people, and I will not have it. I will not have it!"

Rachel squared her shoulders and held her head high, the defiance in her eyes burning for the first time in her life. "I don't care."

Gina's face twisted. "What did you say?"

"I said I don't care about you looking like a fool. It's about time everyone found out about the real you anyway. Hell, I'm sure half the men in the room already know you very, very well," Rachel smugly responded.

Gina released Rachel's wrists, then subtly shifted her right foot back. Without warning, she drove her knee forcefully into Rachel's unguarded abdomen. The air was violently expelled from Rachel's lungs, a sharp wince contorting her features as she crumpled onto the sofa, clutched her aching stomach, and gasped for breath.

Gina swiftly moved, settling beside Rachel on the sofa. She leaned over her prone daughter, her voice a low, menacing whisper in Rachel's ear.

"You listen to me," she hissed. "I've worked too damn hard to get where I am. I've sacrificed more than you could ever imagine to get us both into rooms like that— rooms filled with powerful people. I'll be damned if I let you, or anyone else, ruin that."

Tears began to stream down Rachel's face, her voice now a fragile whisper, stripped of its earlier defiance.

"You hit me. I'm pregnant, and you hit me," she repeated, the words laced with a child's wounded disbelief.

Gina snarled, still laying her weight on Rachel. "I

know you're pregnant, at least for now. Don't ever defy me again. Never! Ever! Tonight, you will apologize to Caleb and tell him you're very sorry for everything. And I don't want to hear that shit about him cheating on you, either. Boo hoo. Hope has been filling your head with that mess. She knows nothing about keeping a man happy. Powerful men like Caleb need extra attention. More attention than just one wife can provide. Understand that."

Gina rose. With the pressure of her mother's weight now relieved, Rachel could breathe more freely. However, her stomach continued to spasm from the blow it had received.

"Now, I'm going back into the lobby. Fix your face and come out when you have it together. Since Caleb left, I will drive you home. Don't have me waiting all night," Gina commanded, leaving Rachel lying on the sofa.

Rachel sat up and held her stomach. The sharp, searing pain in her abdomen was a physical reminder of her mother's betrayal, a pain that cut deeper than any words. In that moment of raw agony, she understood everything. She understood not only Gina, but also Caleb, Craig, and Hope better. She saw with chilling clarity that Gina's "love" was built on a foundation of control and appearances, just like Caleb's. She finally saw that Hope's warnings, which she had so easily dismissed, were not the ramblings of a troubled woman but the absolute, undeniable truth. And as she clutched her stomach, she felt an overpowering, fierce wave of protectiveness for the life growing inside her. Rachel stood to her feet. She knew she would never be the same.

Chapter 47
30-Day Notice

"Can you appeal the ruling?" Justin asked, masking his newfound desperation.

Ms. Kim, not missing a beat, fired back, "I don't know. Do I look like a lawyer to you? I don't understand all these laws and regulations. I wish I had taken a lawyer down there with me initially."

Sitting on his bench and listening to the exchange, Hank hid his "I told you so" smile. Now was not a time to celebrate. Ms. Kim received word that the zoning committee had rejected her petition for zoning relief. She could no longer rent her renovated garage to Justin. Justin's Repair Shop would likely have to go out of business.

"There has to be something you can do," Justin said, his voice cracking with a desperate edge, trying to convince himself as much as Ms. Kim.

"I don't think so. You'll need to get out of this garage in thirty days. I'll type up a formal notice this afternoon. I just wanted to let you know first."

As he sat, Justin's elbows rested on his desk. The

news weighed on him, and he dropped his head into his hands. Ms. Kim, standing in front of the desk, performed a rare gesture of kindness. Her movements were awkward, unpracticed, as she walked around the desk and patted Justin on his upper back.

"It's going to be all right, son. You're going to figure something out. Mr. Kim would always say how smart and resourceful you were. He would say you were going to be something big one day. I believe that, too. Why do you think I charged you so little rent all these years? I'm no dummy, you know."

Justin looked up at Ms. Kim's smiling face. Her faith in him gave Justin a momentary respite from his worries.

"I'm going to go now. I need to do some research and find out if I can turn my house into a bed and breakfast. A lady has to make a buck one way or another. I'll be back with the thirty-day notice later. Bye." Ms. Kim left through the rear exit that led to her house.

The room fell silent. The only sounds were the distant hum of the city and the soft click of Hank's wrench against the motor he was working on. Justin returned his head to his hands, and Hank kept working on a motor that may or may not be needed one day.

Justin lifted his head. "I guess you heard that. I think it's all over for my shop."

"I heard it."

"Aren't you worried? I mean, I saw CJ working Joe's Janitorial. Neither of us wants to be doing that."

"I never worry. If I must work for Joe's Janitorial, so be it. It all works out for my good in the end."

Hank's unwavering composure was pushing Justin to his breaking point. Justin felt the weight of his world collapsing. He was facing the immediate crisis of unpaid salaries and the daunting task of finding a new workspace—a space he knew he couldn't afford. As Justin's carefully constructed world crumbled around him, his most trusted employee remained disturbingly calm.

"I guess you don't care if I go out of business?" inquired a frustrated Justin.

Hank placed the motor he was tinkering with on the table. "As I said, it all works out for our good." Hank switched to counselor mode. "Do you know how drugs are made? I'm talking about pharmaceuticals, not illegal ones. These big companies start mixing chemicals that, by themselves, are deadly. They keep mixing one deadly chemical with another. Then, in the end, the chemicals come together to make a life-saving pill. The pills cure all kinds of stuff. It's like that in life. All these bad things that happen individually might hurt, but together, they'll work for your and my good. The zoning issue, the lost contracts, even my daughter's school—they might seem like poisons on their own, but together, they're the ingredients for something bigger."

Usually, Justin loved hearing Hank's sound advice. Today, though, money problems blocked all of Justin's receptors for advice.

"Man, I don't need a philosophy lesson. Next, you'll tell me I need to accept the things that I cannot change and have the courage to change the things that I can."

"And the wisdom to know the difference," Hank finished for Justin.

"Hank, I need a loan more than your wise old advice. I'm at my wits' end. Can you help me out? I need fifty grand to get me to the next set of contract renewals in six months. I'll be able to increase my fees to market rates. I'll also be able to take on new contracts and hire some more people. I'm tapped out with all the local banks. Even my running buddy, Brandon, over at Federal Bank, can't help. Are you interested in being my short-term bank?"

Justin was selling, but Hank was not buying.

"I don't have that kind of money lying around. You know my daughter is a freshman at State. Every dollar I make and/or have somehow funds her school. Sorry, boss man. You'll have to find funding somewhere else," Hank explained.

He had asked Hank, but the answer was already etched in his mind. When drowning, one clutches at any passing debris, even if it offers no salvation. The throbbing in his head and the knot in his stomach demanded appeasement, a temporary reprieve from his suffering. But the only solace he could envision was a poison disguised as a cure, the very root of his downfall.

Chapter 48
Misleading Photograph

Sea of Galilee Daycare boasted a room for every age group. In the four-year-old room, Deuce had found many new friends to explore the infinite number of toys and games. Deuce had just finished stacking blocks as high as his chin and was looking for a new adventure. Then, a handsome man knelt and offered him a puzzle box.

Caleb glanced at the photographer, who gave a slight nod, signaling he was ready, before turning his practiced smile on the boy.

"Have you tried these? They're really fun," Pastor Caleb said.

Deuce's eyes lit up, and he grabbed the box. "Thank you, sir."

"You are so welcome. Let me show you how to use it."

Caleb, with a fluid, deliberate motion that pressed his expensive suit, settled onto the floor. He showed the boy the mysteries of the box, much to Deuce's delight.

"I saw your dad drop you off today. Does he bring you every day?"

"No, Bibi drives, too," Deuce answered, but his attention never left his newfound toy.

"Hey, little man, look up and smile," Caleb said, directing Deuce to look at the photographer, who had been capturing the moment digitally. This moment would be the first of the "spontaneous" pictures.

"What's that?" Deuce asked, pointing at the traditional-looking camera. He had only seen phones take pictures.

Caleb reached for the camera and took it from the photographer.

"This is a camera. It takes pictures like the ones on the wall," Caleb explained while pointing at the different pictures of flowers, animals, and himself that lined the walls.

"Okay," said Deuce, then turned his attention back to the mysteries of the now-neglected puzzle box.

Caleb's tone shifted, becoming brisk and business-like as he directed the photoshoot. "Let's get a few more shots of me in action. Then, let's spend time with a group of kids and me. Oh, and one more with me and little man here."

Caleb reached down and picked up Deuce. He held the boy up like a trophy for the camera. Caleb thought about the social media caption he would write. He smiled to himself, certain everyone would love a picture of him with young Justin.

Chapter 49
The Balloon Payment

"**W**hat's up, man!" an athletically built young business executive exclaimed while giving Justin the familiar "brotha-man" grip hug.

Justin was a few inches taller than the junior executive but bent over to embrace a lifelong friend.

"Man, Brandon, I'm good. And look at you, I know you're doing well," Justin said as he stepped back and looked at his old basketball teammate.

Brandon wore a suit that had all the markings of a bank manager. A dark grey button-down jacket, a matching tie with just a hint of color, and comfortable shoes allowed a manager to often walk from his office to the teller booths. The bank Brandon managed was in the same building as one of Justin's warranty clients. Today marked the first time the two had run into each other in the building hallway.

"Thanks, man. We haven't seen you at the 'Y' in a while. You know, Harold and Tyrone started coming. We were running those young bucks off the court. If you join us, we can have four of the five starters from our city title team on the court. Well, that is if you still got your jump shot." Brandon mimed shooting an imaginary basketball with his hand.

Justin gave a sly grin. "You know I still got my shot. I may not be able to run all day like I used to, but I still can shoot the lights out. Is there any chance you're going to start passing the ball, or are you still a shoot-first point guard?"

"You know I still shoot first. Why waste everyone's time passing the ball around? I'm doing the team a favor by letting my perfect jumpers rain down on the defense!"

The two old friends laughed.

"I've been busy trying to get my business off the ground," Justin said after composing himself. "So, I've been working day and night. I have no time for basketball right now."

"Cool, man. Keep grinding. Maybe someday I'll be brave enough to do my own thing." Brandon nodded and encouraged his old friend. "By the way, can you have your mother call me or stop by the branch? I want to make sure she understands all of her options regarding the mortgage balloon payment due next month."

Mortgage balloon payment? What is he talking about? Justin thought to himself. A cold knot tightened in his stomach, but his poker instincts took over. He forced a nonchalant expression onto his face and kept his voice even.

"Okay, thanks. I'll do just that. So that I can help explain it to my mom, what are some of her options?"

"Well, when she refinanced the house, she took most

of the equity out of the home. She got a fifteen-year adjustable-rate mortgage with a balloon payment due after thirty-six months. Basically, it was a great rate, but the whole loan comes due at once after three years. The way the stock market has been going up, cashing in home equity to invest in the market made a lot of sense. She's probably made a killing. I wonder what she invested in?"

She didn't make a killing in the market. She invested in me! Justin thought to himself.

The blood rushed to his ears. It wasn't life insurance money; it was the house. The house his father had bought, the one his mother had risked for him. He remembered his father saying the house would stand forever, a legacy to their family. Despite the painful idea that his mother had risked their home for him, he masked his feelings. When Justin started his repair shop, his mother gave him over a hundred thousand dollars to cover many startup costs, such as repair equipment, tools, a down payment on his truck, licenses, insurance, and miscellaneous nickel-and-dime items that added up to thousands of dollars. She told him it was money left from his dad's life insurance policy. She said loaning him the money would make his dad look down from Heaven with pride. Justin remembered taking the money because he always wanted to make his dad proud.

"She can refinance the balloon payment with no problem," Brandon continued. "The rate won't be as good as before, but I'll get her the best I can. The tricky part is that she must put down an additional twenty-five percent payment this time. Home values in the neighborhood fell through the floor after some houses flooded during the storm. I know my mom's and your mom's houses didn't flood, but they're now considered in a flood zone."

"Twenty-five percent? How much is that?" Justin asked with a concerned voice.

Brandon paused. For the first time, he realized Justin didn't know about the loan. Brandon was giving out personal banking information to an unauthorized person. He trained new bank tellers every month that divulging such private information could and would get them fired.

His demeanor changed instantly, his tone becoming clipped and formal. "Hey, man, I can't discuss this with you. This is confidential information. I don't have all the specifics off the top of my head. Why don't you have your mom set up an appointment with me?"

"Brandon, come on, man. I need to know. How much?"

"Twenty-five thousand dollars. Twenty-five thousand dollars within thirty days, or the bank will start foreclosure proceedings on the house. As I said, I don't think that will be a problem if she invested it," Brandon said bluntly.

"Much appreciated. I'll catch you later," Justin said, his voice flat, and without a word of goodbye, he turned on his heel and marched toward the exit, his jaw tight and his face a mask of stone.

Chapter 50
Rough Day

*J*ustin entered the S.O.G. Daycare and stopped at the checkpoint. He had picked up his son enough times that he no longer needed to show identification, but formalities still required him to stop at the front desk.

As usual, Justin was greeted by Bonnie, who gave him a warm, single-dimpled smile. Her deep mocha face was perfectly framed by silver hair, the ideal crown for a queen. Bonnie, married to the church's head deacon, was twenty-five years Justin's senior, a mother of four, and a grandmother of six. Though her family was perfect, it didn't stop her playful flirtation with Justin each time he picked up his son. Their exchanges always made Justin beam. However, today was different. Justin had just learned that, in addition to losing his business, he and his family could soon be homeless.

"Good afternoon. How are you today, young man?" Bonnie, sitting behind the counter, asked with expectant eyes.

"Just okay today, Mrs. Bonnie. It's been a rough one."

Justin exhaled and lowered his already-dropping shoulders.

"Oh, baby, I'm sorry to hear that. Well, you go on in the back and pick up Justin. I know he'll make you feel better. He makes us all laugh all day long. Today, he grabbed Ms. Young's hand and said he was taking her on a date to Applebee's. He then started walking around the playground with her. We've been howling ever since." Bonnie related the story with a look of joy and disbelief.

On any other day, this story would bring Justin a broad smile. But now, the image of his little boy's playful innocence was immediately soured by the thought of his impending homelessness.

"Okay," was the only word Justin could muster for Bonnie.

Justin headed back to the playroom. Immediately upon seeing his father, Deuce dropped his toy and ran to him with arms extended.

"Daddy!"

Justin grabbed him and headed out of the playroom into the lobby. Deuce's eyes lit, and he pointed at the wall.

"Look, Daddy, it's me! It's me!"

Justin looked over at the lobby wall that Deuce was pointing towards. The wall hosted photos of children playing in various places of the daycare. The pictures demonstrated the variety of activities available to the children, and the kids were all smiling and having fun, playing games. The room was an excellent first impression for potential new students and parents.

Justin surveyed the wall and stopped at the picture his son was gleefully pointing out. The photo, however, did not give the boy's father the same feeling of happiness. In fact, he felt a rage building inside him—a rage that would be difficult to control.

The photo had two subjects. Deuce was smiling into the camera, holding a puzzle box. Holding Deuce was a man with a charming smile and dressed in a two-thousand-dollar suit. He had charisma and a look of charity in his eye.

The rage surged from Justin's gut, and his vision clouded, turning the bright room a hazy red. He could not believe what he was seeing. Pastor Caleb's smile was a sucker punch to Justin's heart. Then Justin's eyes fell upon the photo's caption. If the picture was a sucker punch, the caption was the knockout blow to Justin's soul.

The caption read: *Standing in the gap for underprivileged children.*

Chapter 51
Justin Falls Off the Wagon

Justin settled onto a wooden barstool, his hands flat against the chill of the counter. He closed his eyes, drawing in long, deep breaths. He'd just walked in and taken his usual spot at the corner of the U-shaped bar, a fixture against the pub's central wall. For years, this stool had been his nightly ritual. Nothing had changed, though he hadn't returned in over two years. His seat welcomed him like an old friend, and the years seemed to melt away.

Ray, the pub's owner and bartender, emerged from the back room carrying fresh supplies. A man of considerable size, he bore the build of a former football lineman, a result of his days playing at Justin's high school and state college. After a brief journeyman's career in professional football, his knees forced him to retire. He then opened this bar in his old neighborhood, and his football fame made him a local legend. As Tyrone's older brother, he'd known Justin his entire life. Yet, upon seeing Justin at the bar, Ray's expression was far from welcoming.

"Hey, Justin, what's up?" Ray said calmly.

The pub had only three other patrons, who were watching the game on the flat-screen TV above the bar.

"Not much. Can I get Jim Beam on ice?"

Ray paused. "Are you sure now? Wouldn't you rather have a Coke and a smile?"

Ray was trying to redirect a former patron and a man he viewed as a little brother down a road less traveled.

"Just the bourbon, Ray. Thanks," Justin retorted. His hands remained pressed on the bar in a subconscious attempt not to slap some sense into himself.

Ray did not give ground. He took another run at talking a man off a ledge.

"Hey, you talk to Tyrone lately? He got a new gig, and I think he's also found someone who can put up with his silly ass."

Determined to get the comfort he needed, Justin demanded, "Just pour the drink, Ray, or I'll take my money somewhere that will."

Though conflicted, Ray consoled himself, thinking it was better that Justin got drunk in this bar, close to home, amongst friends. That way, Ray could minimize any damage Justin might do to himself or others. Ray hesitated, his hand gripping the whiskey bottle for a moment before he set the glass down in front of Justin.

Ray poured the glass and set it in front of his customer.

"Leave the bottle," Justin demanded, staring at Ray.

Ray did not follow Justin's command and did not put the bottle down.

"No, let's take these one at a time."

Justin struggled to steady his breathing, his mind a battlefield of unwanted thoughts. The liquid fire reached his core, chasing the memory of Caleb's smirk and the photograph of Deuce on his lap. The bar's ceiling tilted, but the hazy red that replaced his vision was a welcome darkness. For a moment, he didn't have to see his son's innocent face next to a fool nor his mother's lifeless eyes.

He grabbed the glass and poured the drink down his throat. To his surprise, he wasn't struck by lightning, nor was there an earthquake or some other sign from God showing His extreme displeasure. Instead, a warm sensation spread through his stomach. His problems hadn't disappeared, but a welcoming silence momentarily muted them. That was enough for Justin; he wanted the silence to last.

He beckoned Ray over. "Make it a double this time."

Chapter 52
The Dream Book

After parking her SUV beside the curb, Hope walked up the driveway toward Casa de Castillo. Well, that's what her dad always called his home once he stopped living with Gina. Craig's house fit perfectly into the surrounding blue-collar neighborhood. The house was a 30-year-old three-bedroom ranch with a detached garage at the end of the driveway. The front facade of the house was made of dark red brick, and the remaining three sides were covered in pale tan aluminum siding. The driveway and the yard were filled with footballs, soccer balls, frisbees, and other toys of active 10-year-old boys.

Hope could hear children playing in the distance as she passed the secondhand basketball hoop in the driveway. Even though she could not see them, she thought she could decipher the laughter of her twin half-brothers. The late sunny afternoon temperature was in the low 80s, and the wind was light—a perfect day for Pedro and Antonio to play in a neighbor's backyard.

Her dad's wife, Alejandra, met Hope at the iron-rod

screen door. "Hi, Hope. Come on in."

Alejandra was a classic Mexican beauty. She had long black hair, thick eyebrows, brown eyes, and soft, round cheeks. She was much shorter than Hope but carried herself with the confidence of a tall woman. Whether because of or despite her Mexican heritage, Alejandra spoke fluent Spanish without an English accent and fluent English without a Spanish accent. Being bilingual and having an MBA from the University of Texas made Alejandra a coveted commodity in the business community.

"Thanks. How are you doing?" Hope asked as she entered the living room through the door.

Per Hope's norm, she did not call Alejandra by name. Referring to Alejandra as stepmom never felt right to Hope. Calling her Alejandra or Ali, as Craig did, felt way too informal. So, Hope avoided calling out to her altogether.

"I'm fine. I'll get your father. Do you need anything? Some water, maybe?" Alejandra asked Hope and moved quickly toward the back hallway.

She was always cordial to Hope but never warm. When Alejandra met Craig, he was an emotionally battered and bruised shell of a human. Despite their first meeting being three years after his divorce, Gina's impact was still being felt. Alejandra couldn't help but associate Hope with the woman who had done so much damage to the man she now loved.

"No, thank you. I'm good," Hope responded and took a seat in one of the armchairs.

Craig entered the room almost instantaneously after Alejandra exited.

"Hey, there you are. You look good. How are you feeling? You know I could have come to you instead of you driving all the way down here."

"I told you on the phone, I'm feeling much better," Hope replied like a teenager being told to wear a hat because it was cold outside. "I slept in today and needed a reason to get some fresh air."

"Oh, you didn't go to God's Palace today for church?" Craig asked more sarcastically than he usually would with his beloved daughter.

"No, not today. I wasn't ready for all the people and the loud music," Hope explained.

"I understand. Well, thanks for coming down here. Like I said on the phone this morning, I have something to tell you."

More often than not, when a person hears those words, bad news follows. In Hope's life, this was the rule with no exceptions. Hope breathed and braced herself for what she was about to hear.

"Okay, let me have it."

Craig sat in the armchair close to Hope. They were separated by a small coffee table adorned with family pictures, including a portrait of Craig, Alejandra, and the twins, Pedro and Antonio. Hope had seen the portrait before and had noted there was no room for her in this family picture.

Craig began rubbing his hands, and he felt the dryness in his throat. "First, I want to apologize to you. I owe you a big apology."

Taken aback, Hope was confused. "Apologies for what?"

Clearing his throat, Craig continued.

"I need to apologize for all of our lost years. I shouldn't have left you the way I did. But Gina and I argued to end all arguments. I couldn't take one more day with that woman, not another second. I had no choice but to go before something happened that we both would regret. But looking back, I stormed out on your ninth birthday right before your party started in front of a room full of kids and parents. What kind of father does that?"

Craig stopped and remembered Gina the Cruel's evil glare and the terror in his daughter's eyes.

"I know. I know. You don't have to apologize. I know how evil she..." Hope consoled but was cut off.

Craig's anger and disappointment with himself grew before Hope's very eyes.

"No, that's the point. Because that woman is so evil, I should never have left you with her. Then what, I would visit you once or twice a month? That wasn't enough." He shook his head, his hands clasped to slow their trembling.

Hope swallowed a lump in her throat. She thought to herself, *Actually, your visits were more like once or twice per year for the next half-decade.* Hope knew exactly how often he visited because she kept a diary of Craig's every visit. She called it her Dream Book. Hope would read it repeatedly, especially when Gina was in her fury. She would dream of King Craig coming to slay her fire-breathing dragon or her evil queen. The malevolent Gina played both roles. Hope would pray for rescue from the living hell she endured. Her prayers went unanswered.

Hope was speechless. Her dad was right. He was not there for them when she and Rachel needed him most.

Hope took the brunt of Gina's berating. But even Gina's favorite child, Rachel, like all children, needed a father.

Hope thought she would try to alleviate some of Craig's pain.

"Past is past," she said, her voice thin, and offered a forced smile. "You made up for it when I got to college, especially grad school. The money you sent me kept me from starving."

"I didn't send you all that much. And besides, nothing can make up for all those years lost. To be honest, Ali was the real hero. I couldn't afford to send you any money, and she would insist we send you what we could from her paycheck. She is something else," Craig said with pride when referring to the kind woman he now called his wife.

Hope was stunned to learn about her previously unknown benefactor. Although she had a partial college scholarship, Craig and Ali's money allowed her to live without eating Ramen noodles all day, every day. Hope decided she needed to reevaluate her relationship with Alejandra, just not today.

Hope gathered her thoughts and remembered why she had come to Casa de Castillo.

"Is that what you wanted to tell me?"

"No." Craig, still reeling from internal shame, had to deliver what he knew was going to be another blow to his daughter. "Ali got a job offer in Austin. It's a promotion. She'll have eight direct reports, and her salary will almost double. It's an opportunity she can't pass up. It will mean a better house and better schools for the boys."

Hope's heart sank—a familiar, hollow ache spreading

through her chest. Pop was leaving her again. Even though they didn't meet up often, knowing he was only thirty minutes away was comforting. He would now be almost three hours away.

"I was able to get a transfer. Delivering packages in Austin is the same as here," Craig said, followed by a closed-mouth smile. He hoped his new family's good news was not too harmful to the remnants of his old family.

"That's great. I'm happy for all of you," Hope lied with a smile that covered the heart-wrenching pain she was feeling. "When are you all going to move?"

"Tuesday. The school year just started, and the sooner we enroll the boys, the better. This whole thing is happening so fast. I was going to tell you sooner, but you got sick," Craig whispered in a grim, matter-of-fact manner.

Hope had heard enough for one day. Her head began to throb mercilessly, and the room and everything in it appeared to be shrinking. Whether Craig had told her everything he wanted to or not, she knew it was time to go. She popped up.

"I've got to go," she said, her voice strained. "I...I forgot there's something I have to do."

She didn't have a good lie. Therefore, only a flimsy excuse came out. Hope turned and quickly marched out the door.

Craig knew Hope needed to leave. He did not resist her exit.

"Text me when you get back home. Let me know you made it safely. Oh, and one more thing, can you tell Rachel about our move to Austin?" Craig said as he stood at the door, watching Hope walk to her car.

Hope did not respond. Her mind briefly rested on why Craig couldn't let Rachel know himself.

Hope pulled her SUV away from the curb and headed to her condo. She needed to get home because it was time to make one final entry in her Dream Book. The dream was finally over.

Chapter 53
Truth Soaked in Whiskey

*J*ustin sat on the park bench, his gaze fixed on the ducks gliding across the water. He envied their carefree existence, their apparent lack of worries. At that moment, the thought of being reincarnated as a mallard seemed like a blissful escape.

Justin's thermos, a mix of Coke and whiskey, sat on the park bench like an old friend. His morning coffee had received the same treatment, a secret he thought he'd kept from his mother. This pattern of hidden drinking was familiar. He had done the same during his marriage, believing he was fooling Chaka. She, however, had seen through him from the start, convinced her love could be his salvation. She was wrong.

Justin poured another measure from his thermos into a cup. It was midday, and he struggled to find the motivation to finish his workday. Usually, he would devour his lunch and rush to the next job site. But today, the park bench and the ducks held a strange allure. His whiskey-laced drink could accompany him to work, but the whiskey itself whispered persuasively for him to remain exactly where he was.

Just as Justin had decided to take the whiskey's advice, he felt a gentle hand on his shoulder.

"Hey, handsome. Imagine running into you here," Hope said with a smile.

Startled by her presence, Justin attempted to regain his composure. However, his mind and reflexes were slower than usual.

"Hey, Doc. What are you doing here at lunchtime?"

"My appointment for this afternoon canceled. I decided to go home and let Nelson have a potty break since I had some time. I recognized your truck, so I stopped. I hope you don't mind."

Justin wanted to be alone. Hope represented just one of many of his problems. However, her double-dimpled smile caught him off guard.

The only answer that could come from his dulled mind was, "No, I don't mind. I was taking a break. I have a lot going on, causing me to be very stressed. So, I came here to clear my head."

Justin surprised himself with his admission. He had forgotten how the alcohol made his tongue loose and his words uninhibited. He was no longer sure what he would say next. Brutal honesty and deceitful lies were both commonplace utterances when Justin was buzzed.

"Oh, I'm sorry to hear that," Hope said, gently stroking Justin's tight-faded head.

She moved the thermos over, sitting between it and Justin. Justin was now separated from his favorite frenemy. Hope had one arm around Justin's shoulder and one hand on his knee.

"I have some free time. Nelson can wait. Tell me what's going on."

Justin didn't want to tell Hope anything. His brain attempted to think of a good lie through the whiskey-induced haze, but he couldn't come up with one. Hope's arm was acting like some comic book lasso of truth. He was compelled to be honest.

"I told you about my landlord's zoning case. Well, she lost it. I have to move the repair shop within a month. I've scouted two other possible places to move, but the rent for the new properties is twice what I was paying. Also, I must cover the first and last month's rent deposits and moving expenses. It adds up to a lot of money I don't have."

Justin stopped there. While he was compelled to tell the truth, he could withhold some of it. He didn't need to or want to bring up the house's foreclosure. The potential of being jobless and homeless was too much bad news for any woman to hear from her man.

"I'm sorry to hear that. How much do you need to keep the doors of Justin's Repair Shop open?" Hope innocuously asked Justin for the information as if he were one of her clients.

Just like her clients, Justin answered, not realizing the weight of what he is saying. "Fifty thousand dollars."

Hope smiled, watching the ducks glide across the tranquil pond. She looked back at Justin and rubbed his head.

"Oh, that's not too much. I can give you that," she said.

Justin quickly jerked his head toward Hope and stared at her. "What?"

"One of my professors advised me to invest some of my first earnings in a small AI company's stock. It did well. That, plus my savings, is just about what you need," Hope responded, oblivious to the fact that she had crossed the male pride line. "It's not that much money. I can give you fifty thousand, no problem. Call it a loan or whatever. I can cover you." She waved her hand, demonstrating that his request was trivial.

Justin jumped to his feet with a slight stagger, turned back toward the bench, and reached down to grab his thermos.

"What makes you think I need your charity? Why do you women always think you can fix me? I'm gonna be fine. I don't need nobody's help." Justin fired his words at Hope.

Stunned by his anger, Hope stood and assumed the "I mean you no harm" pose with hands extended and palms up. "Hey, hey, I was trying to—"

"To help! I know that. You were trying to help. But like I said, I don't want your help. In fact, why don't you go home and handle your own problems? You got enough of them, right? Leave mine alone," Justin, with the help of his whiskey, retorted.

Hope looked at him like she was looking at a stranger—a stranger she didn't want to be around. Without another word, Hope turned and walked toward her SUV.

Justin wanted to call out to her and say he was sorry, but he then realized he was starting to feel some discomfort. He needed a dose of painkiller. Justin quickly opened the thermos and took a swig from the top. The taste was soothing to his palate and his mind, so he took another gulp, then another.

As Justin screwed the cap back on the thermos, he asked himself, "What was I thinking about again?"

He shrugged his shoulders and sat back on the bench. His afternoon work projects could wait. Justin had ignored his fowl friends for too long and needed to get back to some meaningful duck-watching.

Chapter 54
I'm Bleeding

A tense silence hung in the air of Caleb's home office, a stillness broken only by the faint hum of the central air. The scent of leather and old paper was heavy, and a closed Bible rested on his desk, its gold-leaf inscription glinting in the soft light. It was a preacher's tool, filled with commentaries and cross-references designed to aid in crafting powerful sermons. But first, a preacher needed direction, a clear understanding of what he wanted to convey, or, more importantly, what God wanted him to impart to His flock.

It was Friday, and Caleb had yet to formulate a sermon for Sunday service, lacking even a scripture text or a subject. He'd been praying for divine revelation, for inspiration, but his prayers had yielded nothing. It was as if the conduit between Heaven and him had been severed. Of course, he had a contingency plan. The internet was a vast repository of excellent sermons readily downloadable. In moments like these, he'd rationalize, *You can't copyright the Word of God.* However,

Rachel's shocking entrance had derailed all thoughts of sermon preparation.

She stood framed in the doorway, her shoulders slumped, one hand clutching the fabric of her dress at her stomach, the other gripping the doorframe for support.

"I'm bleeding." Rachel's trembling voice broke the stillness.

Caleb froze, the words echoing in the sudden cavern of his mind. The Bible on his desk, the sermon, the entire edifice of his public life—it all vanished. All that remained was a stark, primal fear. He pushed himself to his feet, knocking his chair backward with a clatter.

"Bleeding? What… how much? Is it… is it the baby?"

His voice was a strangled whisper, the usual smooth cadence replaced by raw terror. His eyes, usually so composed, darted to her hand pressed against her stomach.

"I've been bleeding for hours, and it won't stop," Rachel said, her voice filled with helplessness, a fragile sound that twisted something inside Caleb. "I looked it up online. I think I might be miscarrying."

Caleb was across the room in two strides, his hands reaching for her—not to guide, but to steady, to understand. His fingers trembled as he gently touched her arm, then moved to her pale face.

"Miscarrying? No, no, no. That can't be right." He looked at her, truly seeing her for the first time in weeks—the pallor, the way her eyes seemed too wide, too lost. "We need a doctor. Now."

"I called the doctor's office," she replied, her voice shaky. "They said to come in tomorrow if the bleeding continues."

"No." Caleb's voice was a low, firm growl, leaving no room for argument.

The spiritual crisis of his sermon was entirely forgotten, replaced by a fierce, protective instinct he hadn't known he possessed.

"We're going to the doctor right now. They're going to see you right now!"

He gently, but firmly, began to guide her toward the front door, his hand a solid anchor at her back. His mind raced, calculating routes, recalling the fastest way to the hospital, every thought now consumed by the fragile life within her.

Chapter 55
The Bed Rest Prescription

*D*r. Patricia Nguyen stepped into the patient examination room. She held the unofficial title of the city's top OB/GYN, often appearing on local news segments to promote women's health. She had even been featured performing a live birth on a national morning show. Just two hours prior, she had been excitedly discussing wedding gowns with her daughter. Now, she stood beside Rachel Moore, holding her examination results. Rachel's well-known husband, Caleb, stood beside the examination table where she sat in a hospital gown. He held Rachel's hand, their anxious eyes fixed on the doctor as they waited in anticipation.

Dr. Nguyen offered a reassuring yet measured smile. "Rachel, you did not miscarry. The ultrasound showed the baby is fine. However, there are a couple of concerning findings."

Her pace slowed, and her serious tone sent a shiver of anxiety through Caleb and Rachel.

"You have internal bleeding in your uterus. Given the bruise on your abdomen, I can assume it's from the resulting trauma. You said you fell and hit a table?" Dr. Nguyen posed the question, her skepticism evident.

Rachel gave a hesitant nod. "Yes, I was at an event a couple of days ago. I felt sick and went to the ladies' room. I briefly blacked out and fell, hitting my stomach on a countertop. Luckily, my mother was there to take care of me."

Rachel hated the lie. Repeating it, as she had to Caleb after the charity banquet, did nothing to ease her discomfort.

Dr. Nguyen shifted her gaze from Rachel to Caleb, scrutinizing him carefully. Her eyes probed, attempting to discern if she was in the presence of a potential abuser. Her quick assessment yielded no definitive conclusions, so she continued with her prognosis.

"Okay. Also, your blood pressure is elevated. You're showing signs that could lead to preeclampsia. We're not there yet, but I believe we should err on the side of caution."

Caleb's face paled, his composure crumbling, and he gripped Rachel's hand tighter, a genuine tremor in his fingers.

"Doctor, what does that mean? What do we do? Tell me what she needs." His voice was no longer smooth, but raw with genuine concern.

"The main thing is she needs to stay off her feet for a while. I'm ordering a week of bed rest. Is there someone who can stay with her?"

"I can," Caleb exclaimed, his voice urgent. "I've got it. And if I can't be there, her mother can come by."

"No!" Rachel interjected, the word sharp and immediate. Her forceful response startled both the doctor and Caleb.

"Just you, Caleb. We don't need her help right now. Okay?"

"Whatever you want, baby," Caleb said, his voice soft with understanding as he gently ran his hand over her back, a gesture of pure comfort.

"I'm going to hold off on prescribing any medications. How about you rest all weekend and come in and see me on Monday or Tuesday? Unless the flow of bleeding increases. If the flow increases, go to the emergency room immediately. Okay?"

"Yes. Thank you, Doctor," Rachel said.

"Yes, thank you so much, Doctor. We appreciate you seeing us on such short notice," Caleb said.

"No problem. Based on the costs my daughter's wedding is incurring, I need the business," Dr. Nguyen said with a wink. "Rachel, you can get dressed and make an appointment on your way out. Bye, you two. See you next week."

Dr. Nguyen headed out the door.

Caleb's hand, which had been soothingly rubbing Rachel's back, now cradled her head. He pulled her gently towards him, pressing the side of her face against his chest. His other hand rested on her stomach.

"I've got you," he murmured, his voice a promise. "I've got both of you."

He wasn't talking to the room or an audience. He was talking to them, his family.

Rachel listened to Caleb's steady heartbeat, imagining her unborn child's tiny heart beating in unison.

Chapter 56
The Lonely One

The words tumbled out of Nurse Michael, unfiltered. "Girl, another Uber home? Just like last year, after your fibroid procedure? Don't you have any friends?"

Twila's gaze, sharp as a laser, focused on Michael's annoying face. The nurse, busy with his paperwork, flushed under her intense focus. At the hospital, Twila and the other nurses avoided him. His constant gossiping and eagerness to be "one of the girls" made him unbearable. Her death stare after his last comment landed.

"I'm so sorry, honey." He patted Twila's leg. "Sometimes my mouth talks faster than my brain can think. We're all done here. Your ankle is healing fine. You take your time. You know you can fill your prescription downstairs. Bye-bye." Michael hurried out of the room.

Twila slid off the examining table, the walking boot a now familiar weight on her broken ankle. She left the room, her steps measured as she walked down the hallway. Nurse Michael's words echoed in her mind, yet she was suffering from a deeper ache than any physical pain. She was alone.

As if to amplify Twila's loneliness, the scene outside the lobby window was a stark contrast to her own situation. A man she knew too well, his face filled with love, carefully helped his wife into their car. The way Caleb's hand lingered on Rachel's back as he guided her into the seat, the way his smile was soft and genuine—it was a private moment, a tenderness Twila had only ever seen fragments of. Watching them drive away together, Twila knew, with a pang of certainty, that her relationship with Caleb was over.

Twila paused and steadied herself on a railing usually reserved for the elderly or the handicapped. The cold metal bit into her palm, a physical reminder of her solitude. The weight of past disappointments weighed her down. This loneliness was a constant companion. After her endometrial ablation, she'd walked this hall alone last year, then taken an Uber home. She had walked these same floors as a high school senior, leaving the boy she still loved and the baby she would never meet. The drive home was a blur of physical pain and a silent, raw heartbreak that had never fully healed. The boy who'd abandoned her then had taken a piece of her with him.

Chapter 57
The Final Breath

*J*ustin stood before the numbered keypad on his garage, his gaze fixed but unfocused. Clouded by bourbon, his mind struggled to recall the pin code that would open the garage door. He repeatedly ran his thumb across the empty spot on his ring finger—a nervous tick he couldn't control. He knew the code was tied to a birthday, but whose? Frustration surged, and he thumped his leg, the jingle of his keys a sudden, jarring reminder.

"Oh yeah, I have a key," he whispered loudly, the sound echoing in the 2:30 a.m. stillness and startling him.

He fumbled for the keys in his pocket, staggered to the front door, and disappeared inside.

Justin had chosen to walk home from Ray's Bar. He knew that if he'd driven, Ray would have cut him off long before he reached his desired state of oblivion. And utter intoxication was precisely what Justin sought. He craved a night of complete detachment, a state where feeling and thought ceased to exist. Numbness was the prescription he desperately needed to be filled.

Justin navigated the darkened family room and

entered the kitchen. He noticed the sink was filled with dirty dishes, an unusual sight. A single, half-empty coffee mug sat on the countertop, a misplaced book lay spine-up on the floor, and a glass of milk had a thin, congealed layer on its surface, as if left for hours. Lorraine never went to bed with a messy kitchen; it disturbed her sleep. He didn't dwell on it, as his hunger overtook any other thoughts. He grabbed a container of leftover fried chicken from the fridge and devoured a cold chicken breast without bothering to heat it.

Before collapsing into bed, Justin paused to check on his son. Deuce was sound asleep, one arm and part of a leg dangling precariously off the edge of the mattress. As always, he looked like he was about to tumble out. Following his usual routine, Justin gently shifted his son closer to the wall. Deuce had never actually fallen out of bed, but this small act always eased Justin's mind.

On Justin's way to his room, he noticed his mother's light on. Because of his inebriated condition, he would like to avoid her, so he hoped she had just fallen asleep and left the light on.

As he passed his mother's door, he froze, his heart seizing. Lorraine, dressed in her familiar housecoat and slippers, lay flat on her back and motionless on the floor. In his drunken haze, her figure seemed unreal—like a strange, forgotten doll. He stumbled toward her. Her eyes were open, staring blankly, seeing nothing. He touched her cheek; it was frigid as an ice cube. The cold was a shock—a brutal, instant sobriety. The room's silence wasn't just quiet; it was an absolute absence of sound, the final, empty stillness of a life ended. Her presence, her warmth, and her life were gone. Justin knew that stillness intimately.

Chapter 58
Explaining Death

Justin sat beside Deuce on the twin bed, watching his son manipulate the action figure, transforming it from a human form to a fighter jet and back again. Deuce played with complete, unburdened joy. Justin knew his son's world had irrevocably shifted, though the boy remained blissfully unaware. He wrestled with the impossible task of explaining to his son that the woman who had nurtured them both was gone.

"Hey, Deuce, you remember that I told you your mommy lives in Heaven with God and that Heaven is a wonderful place where everyone is happy and nobody gets sick? Well, God decided it was time for Bibi to go to Heaven and live with him, Mommy, and my dad. So, she left for Heaven last night."

"When is she coming back?" Deuce asked, continuing to play with his toy.

"She's not. When you go to Heaven, you stay there. She and your mommy are waiting for us to join them, but first, you have to grow up and get old before going there."

Deuce's fingers fumbled with the toy, unable to get it to click into place. He slowed his play, his small brow furrowed in concentration. He didn't look up, but his voice was a quiet, direct statement.

"Are you going to Heaven?"

Justin's voice was filled with a promise, not just a hope. "Yes, I am, but not for a very, very long time. I want to see everybody again and have fun with them. But don't worry, I plan on being here with you for a long, long time."

"I don't like God," Deuce said, the words a raw, factual statement without a hint of emotion. "He won't let Mommy and Bibi come home."

Justin felt a wave of bitter agreement wash over him, a shared anger that was both lonely and strangely comforting. He wanted to scream in frustration, but instead, he fell back on the familiar, hollow words he'd heard his mother speak countless times.

"Son, it's going to be okay. God has a plan, and we win in the end," Justin said, his voice strained and unfamiliar while gently rubbing his son's hair,

Deuce didn't cry. He didn't understand death or just how impactful the end of his Bibi's life would be for him or his dad.

Justin sat watching his son play with his convertible jet/man. He reached out and gently touched his son's shoulder—a desperate, silent vow. Keeping his son safe and happy was the only thing that made sense to Justin right now.

Chapter 59
Hannah Is Missing

"Hello, Dr. Castillo. Have you heard from Hannah today?" a frantic, weary female voice asked.

"No, I haven't. Is something wrong?" a concerned Hope replied.

"Wrong? My baby is missing! Her best friend, that...that monster's daughter, Abigail, freaked out on her. She said it's all Hannah's fault that her sick, perverted father is dead! And now, I can't find her. Not since yesterday. She's gone, Dr. Castillo. My baby is gone!" Ariella's voice cracked, and a raw, guttural cry of fear escaped her lips. "You know about her suicidal thoughts, right? The police don't care. They told me to wait another day. Wait? How can I wait? What if...what if I'm too late?"

Hope pushed aside her personal problems, the noise of Justin's actions and Craig's departure fading into a distant hum. A cold dread settled in her stomach—a familiar feeling from her own past, a fear she had worked hard to bury. She quickly accessed Hannah's file, searching for any possible location—a place where a scared, guilt-ridden girl might go. Hope's thoughts raced back to her own past, the deep-seated fear of abandonment from her father's departure. She understood the desperate need for a father figure and how easily that need could be exploited. She had been fortunate; Hannah was not. She had to find Hannah. She had to, before it was too late.

Hope's own turmoil, her father's past, and her complicated relationship with Gina faded into the background, momentarily silenced. Her focus sharpened, centering on Hannah's well-being. She knew Hannah carried a heavy burden of guilt, blaming herself for the imprisonment of the man who had abused her. A grown man who had preyed on a vulnerable child, a girl starved for paternal attention, taking advantage of her innocence.

Hope's thoughts drifted to her own past, to Craig's absence during her teenage years, and how Big Preach had, in many ways, filled that paternal void. She counted herself fortunate that Big Preach's influence had been free of any predatory intent; she could have easily become another victim like Hannah.

Snapping back to the present, Hope turned to her computer, intending to review her notes on Hannah and search for any clue to her whereabouts. Fear gripped Hope's heart as she typed frantically.

Chapter 60
Gina's Cruel Confession

Hope recognized the familiar three sharp raps on the door—Gina's signature knock. A knot of dread instantly tightened in her stomach, a knot that would take hours to unravel. For a fleeting moment, she considered ignoring the summons, pretending she wasn't home. But, with a sense of resigned inevitability, she walked to the door like a lamb being led to slaughter and opened it.

The air seemed to grow colder as Gina swept past her, a wave of coldness washing over Hope before the door had even closed.

"We need to talk, and you need to listen," Gina blurted out as she marched into Hope's living room and abruptly turned to face her foe. She was drawing the first position in this duel.

Hope stood staring at her mother in silence. She would allow her mother to take the first volley.

"Rachel humiliated herself, Caleb, and me the other night, and it's all your fault," Gina declared, her words laden with accusation.

Hope felt the familiar weight of being accused of an unknown crime, a sensation that had become constant under Gina's gaze. She always felt like a convict in her mother's eyes.

"What are you talking about?" Hope retorted.

"You know what I'm talking about. At the awards ceremony the other night in front of the most important people in town. Rachel showed her ass right after Twila introduced Caleb!" shouted Gina.

Hope wrestled with a complex mix of emotions. A surge of pride for her sister warmed her, a silent cheer for Rachel's unexpected defiance. Yet, this feeling was overshadowed by a rising tide of anger towards her mother and her lingering disgust for Rachel's betrayal. Once again, she was unjustly reprimanded by Gina, a victim of her mother's misplaced blame.

"Well, good for Rachel," Hope replied with a clenched-toothed smile. "I didn't tell her to do that. But to be honest, I wish I had. Caleb is a dog. A dog in constant heat. He can't keep his pants up for more than five seconds. Rachel deserves better."

"You don't know anything about keeping a great man like Caleb. You're obviously not over him leaving your weak, sickly ass. You'd better believe he knew he was too good for you and decided to upgrade. That's all. You should be happy for Rachel. Why don't you just run off with your little plumber boy?"

Hope had momentarily pushed Justin to the back of her mind with everything that was going on with Hannah. But now, Gina's relentless accusations and the looming crisis with Justin added another layer of misery to the already turbulent stew of her life. Gina's words landed like punishing body blows from a heavyweight boxer, each accusation driving deeper into her core. The knot of pain that had formed in her stomach at the sound of the knock had intensified, spreading into a full-blown torso muscle spasm. This agonizing pain was a stark contrast to the unsettling numbness that had spread through her hands and feet.

"You are pure evil. What Craig saw in you to marry you and have two children by—"

"I didn't have two children with your father," Gina interrupted.

Hope was stunned and confused. *What is she talking about?*

Gina seemed taken aback by her confession, as if the words had slipped out unexpectedly. Then, a sense of pride settled over her as if she were revealing a well-aged secret, a fine wine finally uncorked. She tilted her head back slightly and began to explain with a distinct air of triumph.

"Craig is your father, but not Rachel's. I did much better with her father than I did with yours."

"Stop lying, you witch," Hope demanded.

"You wish I were lying," Gina sneered. "Rachel's father is a great man, unlike yours. Craig's stupid, broke ass didn't know for years after Rachel was born that he wasn't her daddy. He left when he found out. I told him right before your ninth birthday party. He couldn't stand that a man of such high position and power ever wanted me," Gina said, speaking of her deception with a chilling sense of pride.

Gina's words landed like a series of devastating headshots, each syllable a brutal blow to Hope's soul. A ringing sound filled her ears, a physical manifestation of the agonizing pain.

"He was the kind of man I could've had if I hadn't gotten pregnant with you and married that loser," Gina continued, her voice laced with bitterness. "I could have finished nursing school. I could have lived with Rachel and her dad. I could have been the first lady."

First lady? Hope thought, a wave of confusion washing over her. Then, like a sudden, torrential downpour, the truth crashed over her, every piece falling into place. The ringing in her ears vanished, replaced by an unsettling silence.

"No, no, it can't be true. Not Big Preach," Hope gasped, her voice trembling.

Hope's thoughts went to the man she considered a father figure. The one man she believed in with no guardrails.

With her tone thick with self-satisfaction, she elaborated. "John would meet me when I dropped you off at The Sea of Galilee Church nursery. He'd also be there when I picked you up. At first, I thought it was a coincidence—that he was just a good pastor. Then we started having long talks. Before long, every morning, before I went to work, we were making love in his new Cadillac, the pastor's study, and even sometimes in my bed. I was blessed to be in his presence. When I got pregnant with Rachel, I knew deep in my heart it was John's baby, not your father's."

Hope sank onto the couch, her mind reeling. The two pillars she trusted—her moral father figure and her sister's identity—hadn't just crumbled; they were shattered, leaving her to choke on Gina's venom and the terrifying silence of total betrayal.

Now fully immersed in her confession, Gina continued. "Obviously, we had to end the relationship before people connected the dots and ruined his burgeoning ministry. His guilt led him to always be nice to you while remaining indifferent to Rachel. I remember when he baptized her, she had that swim cap on in the pool, and anyone paying attention could have seen that their faces were identical. Like he'd created her all by himself, without my involvement. I was terrified someone would put two and two together while standing in the water, but thankfully, no one did."

As she spoke, Gina's gaze drifted as if she were addressing the world, proclaiming her past connection to a great man.

"Rachel is living the life I should have had," she declared, her voice hardening. "I want a better life for her than I had. So, I'm telling you, you better stop meddling in her marriage, or I will make you stop. You ruined my life. You will not ruin Rachel's."

Having unburdened herself, Gina turned toward the door but paused, delivering one final, devastating blow.

"I never loved you," she stated coldly. "When you were a toddler, I considered placing a pillow over your face and pressing down. I wanted you gone. Forever. I was pregnant with Rachel at the time, and every time I had those thoughts, she'd kick me. It was as if she could read my mind and was trying to protect you. I regret not having the courage to use that pillow." Gina placed a hand on her stomach. "Your sister saved your life."

Knowing she'd wounded her opponent deeply, Gina pressed her advantage, aiming for the kill.

John Gary Long

"I was so happy when you were diagnosed with lupus. I pray that lupus, a car accident, or even a bolt of lightning takes your miserable life. The sooner God removes you from this planet, the better." With that, Gina slipped out the door.

Hope remained motionless on the couch, her mind a chaotic battlefield of searing thoughts. Each one felt like a scalding brand, too painful to grasp. She felt completely broken. She imagined she could die at that moment, even without the help of her medication. She even thought that if God had any mercy, He would grant Gina's wish and end Hope's life then and there, swiftly and painlessly.

Chapter 61
First Love Revisited

*J*ustin answered the knock with a sigh that felt like a thick cloud of dust in his throat. The day had begun with the hollow chill of the funeral home, viewing his mother's body beside his aunt Maxine, and had dissolved into a relentless torrent of condolences. Each whispered "I'm sorry" was a prickling needle, leaving him raw and thoroughly spent. He craved the kind of silence that hums with nothing but its own emptiness.

The thought of Hope was a fleeting, soft breeze, but a dark, magnetic pull led him to the glint of a whiskey bottle instead. The heavy glass felt cool and smooth in his hand. Whiskey, he knew, demanded nothing—no explanations, no gentle words. He didn't have the emotional currency to explain his drinking, especially not with the fresh, gaping wound of his mother's death. He would face Hope tomorrow, after the liquor's dulling fog had lifted.

An hour ago, he'd silenced his phone, the buzzing against the wooden table a small, frantic sound he could no longer bear. But his front door offered no such surrender. With a low groan of heavy reluctance, Justin dragged his leaden feet across the floorboards, each step a testament to his exhaustion.

When he finally opened the door, a wave of dazzling emerald light hit him. Twila Gooden, his high school sweetheart, stood framed in the fading afternoon sun. Her smile, a perfect line of sparkling, white teeth, was a beacon of the past—unchanged, just like her face. The very sight of her was a jolt, a punch of memory that sent him tumbling back to a simpler time. A decade fell away, and he was a teenager again, consumed by his first great love, a girl whose presence had filled his world since fourth grade.

"Hi Justin," she said, her voice a gentle, familiar balm. "I heard about your mother, and I wanted to come and see how you're doing."

"Hey," Justin replied, the word escaping him with a warmth he hadn't known he still possessed. "Come on in."

She moved past him, her scent—a light, fresh, dewy aroma, like fresh-cut stems—filling the air. Her eyes scanned the living room, settling on the large, plush sofa.

"This couch looks new," she observed.

"Yeah, it's fairly new. Just a few years old. You remember that old, brown one, don't you?" he said with a wry smile. "We finally got rid of that thing. It was older than I am."

"Oh, I remember that couch," she replied knowingly, the words hanging in the air like a secret.

That couch was where they had truly become "us," where their shared history was written in whispers and tender touches. It was where they had lost their virginity together. A comfortable, heavy silence descended, thick with shared memory.

"So, how are you doing?" she asked again, her tone softer now.

"Okay, I guess. I'm just trying to be strong for Deuce," he said, the name of his son a weight on his tongue. "I don't think he understands all that's going on. He just wants his Bibi to come back."

"That's tough," she murmured, a genuine sadness clouding her eyes. "I remember when my mom died. It was rough. I appreciate you being there for me."

"It was the least I could do. Your mom was always so good to me," Justin replied.

Twila's face lit up with a small, fond laugh. "Good to you? Boy, you know my mother loved you. She had her eye on you since we were in fifth grade. She would ask about you and wonder why I wasn't paying you more attention. When we finally started hanging out, she was happier than I was."

"She was cool," Justin said, a faint smile touching his lips. "She always made me laugh. I miss her."

"Me too," Twila said, her voice dropping to a raw whisper. "After my mom died, I had nobody. My sister and I hadn't spoken since she left when she was sixteen. And who the hell knows who my father is? I surely don't. I don't know how I survived after we broke up. I've been so alone for so very long."

Justin paused, the air growing still and heavy around them. A truth that had weighed on him for over a decade suddenly felt like it was suffocating him. He had to say it.

"I'm sorry," he said, the words a low rumble in his chest.

"Sorry? About what?" she asked, a frown of confusion creasing her brow.

"I'm so sorry I pressured you into the abortion," Justin said, the regret a sharp, metallic taste on his tongue. "If I hadn't, you wouldn't be alone now. You'd have a teenager who loved you."

For years, she carried the ache of his silence and longed for a single apology. The abortion left a deep physical scar and an even deeper emotional wound. When she told him about the pregnancy, he had become a closed-off stranger, his face a mask of cold distance. It was the summer before their senior year, a time that should have been full of joy. She had considered keeping the baby, a child to love and be loved by, but his frigid influence had prevailed. She walked into the clinic alone that Saturday, the day before their senior year started, feeling completely abandoned.

"Thank you for saying that," she replied solemnly, the words barely a breath. "I think about it often. I haven't been able to conceive since. The doctors aren't sure why, but I feel like it's God's punishment for harming my babies."

Justin was about to offer his usual empty platitudes, telling her not to blame herself, as if his guilt wasn't the very poison he was drinking tonight. But then he heard the plural—*babies*. The word hit him with the gut-wrenching force of a wrecking ball. His hands clenched, his breath caught, and his eyes involuntarily darted to her stomach, a hollow ache in his chest.

"Babies?" he asked, his voice thin and strained, as if it weren't his own.

She looked at him, her emerald eyes brimming with

a pain so intense it took his breath away. She hadn't intended to burden him with this tonight, but the words had spilled out—a truth too heavy to hold back.

"I was carrying twins."

He gripped the armrest, his knuckles white. Two babies. Two lives. The word echoed like a judge's hammer in the emptiness left by his mother. He leaned his head against the cool wall, allowing the cold to seep into the exhaustion behind his eyes, needing a moment to find his anchor before speaking again.

The news was a cruel, devastating punch to his heart—shattering his already fragile emotional state. He felt the phantom weight of a loss he had never experienced before. But his mother's death had left him emotionally bankrupt. There was nothing left to feel, only a deep, numb ache.

Seeing the raw anguish on her face, he found a reserve of strength. She had carried this burden alone for so long, a burden he had created. He moved closer, the cool denim of his jeans brushing against her leg. His arm went around her, pulling her into a tight, comforting embrace.

"I'm so, so sorry," he whispered, the words a desperate plea.

She looked up at him, the man she had loved since she was a girl, and her lips found his. He responded instinctively, the decade of separation dissolving in the familiar warmth. They were teenagers again, their bodies molding together on the worn couch, on the very edge of recreating the night that had given them twins.

Then, Hope's image surfaced in the whiskey-fueled fog of his mind—a sharp, unyielding clarity that would not be dismissed. He broke the kiss, slowly pulling away.

"We should stop," he said, his voice husky.

"Justin, I know the timing is terrible," she pleaded, her voice a soft, frantic whisper. "But my relationship just ended. I thought it was a sign that I should be here for you during the funeral. Maybe it was a sign we should get back together. I want to be with you again. I'm so lonely."

Her face, so familiar and breathtaking, was a roadmap of longing. Justin still loved her, a different kind of love than he had for Hope—a love rooted in shared history, care, and concern. He wanted her happiness above all else.

"Sweetheart, I can't," he explained gently, the words burning like coal. "I'm sorry. I'm in love with Hope. She's my future, and she's my lifeline."

She pulled away, a familiar disappointment shadowing her face. Her time with Justin was the only true love she had ever known. For twelve years, she had dreamed of this reunion. When he married, she had stood silently in the church's audio room, an uninvited spectator watching her dream lover marry someone else. Her obsession with Justin had never faded; all other men had been a series of disappointments. She always thought she could try again in another decade or two. This moment was just another heavy consequence of her decision that fateful Saturday before senior year.

She looked up, a brave, fragile mask on her face. "Don't be sorry. Just be happy. I truly hope she makes you happy." She paused, her eyes meeting his. "I should go. Call me anytime if you need anything. We're closer than friends, always will be."

She walked to the door, and Justin held it open for

her. As she stepped onto the porch, he grabbed her by the hand, the warmth of her palm a fleeting comfort. He pulled her close—his hug an embrace of deep caring, his heart mournful with unspoken loss. Despite the years, Justin knew that when he let her go, she would be returning to a world of loneliness without him.

Eventually, the two former lovers separated, their last lingering touches fading. But not before Twila reached up, her fingers brushing the stubble on his cheek, and gave him one final, desperate kiss. Justin, with a heart too broken to resist, did not pull away. Then she turned and limped away, her ankle still encased in a walking boot.

Justin watched her get into her car and pull away from the curb, her taillights like a pair of angry red eyes in the twilight. The car passed a luxury SUV parked a short distance away. Hope was in the driver's seat, her knuckles white on the steering wheel, her breath catching in her throat. She had seen it all—the lingering hug, the kisses. Her blood ran cold with a fury that consumed her. It wasn't the simple comfort of old friends she had witnessed; it was a deep betrayal.

She threw open the door and stepped out, her heels tapping sharply and firmly against the pavement. She had to confront him before he could retreat back into the house and the comfort of his lies.

Chapter 62
Girl Loses Boy

"**What** in the hell was she doing here?" Hope's voice was a low growl, the fury in it a physical presence that stopped Justin dead in his tracks.

He squinted, his whiskey-soaked mind struggling to focus on her silhouette against the streetlights.

"Hope? What are you doing here?" he slurred, a confused half-smile on his face. "I thought you were—"

"I'm having the day from Hell and thought I would reach out to you," she snapped, the words lashing out like a whip. "I called you, I texted you, and when you didn't answer, I drove over here to check on you. And what do I find? You're on the porch, hugging and kissing that…that *woman!*"

The word *"woman"* was laced with such venom that it cut through his drunken haze.

"Whoa, easy," Justin mumbled, his hand raising in a weak gesture of defense. "That was just Twila. An old friend."

Hope's laugh was a harsh, bitter sound.

"An old friend? You didn't bother to tell me at the gala that you knew her. Did it just slip your mind? Don't lie to me, Justin. I saw the way you were holding her. I saw that kiss." Her voice trembled with a rage that felt cold and brittle. "Don't even try to give me some lame-ass lie."

"Lie? I'm not going to lie. I just needed someone," Justin stammered, the words getting caught in his throat. He wanted to tell her about his mother, about the twins, about the crushing weight on his shoulders. But the words wouldn't form.

Hope's eyes, usually warm and full of light, were now twin points of fire. The betrayal she felt was not just Justin's; it echoed a deeper wound. She was living a new, horrific nightmare. Justin was playing Caleb's role, breaking her overly trusting heart. It all clicked into place—a sick, twisted pattern. Justin was a liar and cheat, just like Caleb. They were all the same. She felt foolish for being played twice.

"You needed someone?" she spat, her voice rising. "I'm your girlfriend, Justin! Why didn't you call me? But no, you run into that skank's arms."

Justin tensed up, feeling the need to defend his old love, whom he had hurt, "Hey, no need to call her that. She's been through a lot. And—"

"Stop! Just stop right there!" Hope's shout pierced the air. "*She* has been through a lot. You have no idea what I'm going through. But you know what?" Hope asked the question without giving Justin time to answer. "Caleb is cheating on my sister with *that* woman. But I expect nothing less from his cheating ass. Hell, he cheated on me with Rachel when we were engaged."

Justin's mind, slow and fuzzy from the whiskey, reeled. *Caleb? Rachel? What is she even talking about?*

He had no context, no information, just her rage and the sting of her accusation. The thought hit him with a vicious clarity, a hateful pretense. Hope had been lying to him, hiding her sister's pain and her own secrets.

His exhausted, half-drunk brain couldn't process the nuance. It only saw a new betrayal, a fresh layer of deception. He felt the cold rage swell, a reaction to her hidden cruelty. He was emotionally spent, raw, and when he spoke, his words were packed with pure venom.

"I don't know what the hell you're talking about," he snarled, his voice low and dangerous. "I don't know anything about Caleb or Rachel or Twila and affairs. And I definitely don't know about you having been engaged to Caleb. When were you going to tell me that? Did that slip *your* mind? But you know what? After tonight, I guess I understand now why Caleb would leave your deceiving ass."

Utilizing a skill Hope learned from Gina, when words are weapons, cut your opponent deep.

"And what kind of father are you? Bringing your other woman to your home. You're going to teach that boy to grow up to be just like you. Worthless."

The air was pushed out of his lungs. Shooting Justin with a 12-gauge shotgun would've hurt him less than the woman he loved calling him worthless. The words hung in the air—a final, devastating shot. Hope's face went pale. The fury was gone, replaced by a deep, shattering emptiness. Her hands dropped to her sides, trembling with emotion. Justin's eyes were wide with painful shock that even his whiskey couldn't dull.

John Gary Long

The words were out and neither could take them back. The silence that fell between them was a thick, suffocating thing—a silence that could not be repaired. Hope turned and walked back to her car, thinking this would be the last time she would ever be this way again.

Chapter 63
Dark Night of the Soul

The door slammed shut with a violence that rattled the frames of every picture on the wall. The sound was a raw, percussive echo of the fury raging inside Hope. The image was burned into her mind's eye—a constant, looping horror show: Justin and Twila. The lingering hug, the way her hand had touched his face, the final, desperate kiss. It was an insult, a betrayal that cut deeper than any she had ever known. Of all the people in the world, it had to be Twila. The she demon that was defiling Rachel's marriage was now corrupting her relationship with Justin, as well.

The excuses—old friends, a shared history, a momentary comfort—were nothing but worthless lies. The cold reality was that she had lost him. He was gone, a part of her life that was as shattered as the lampshade she now swiped off the end table. It crashed to the floor, the ceramic shards a sharp, physical release. Her rage turned from Justin to the world, to the relentless, unbearable weight of her own life. She kicked the wall, a hollow thud followed by a tearing sound, and the drywall gave way. The hole in the wall was a gaping, ugly scar—a mirror of the one in her soul. Nelson cowered in the spare room, instinctively knowing to stay away from the brewing storm.

Her fury eventually burned itself out, leaving behind a cold, desolate emptiness. The raw, guttural rage gave way to a pain so extreme it felt like a physical weight on her chest. She crumpled to the floor, her body trembling with a soul-crushing grief. The betrayal of Justin was a fresh wound, but it was nothing compared to the slow-acting poison that had been running through her veins for a lifetime: the knowledge that her own mother, Gina, was pure evil.

The memory of their conversation was a constant loop of torment. The chilling, unapologetic confession that Gina had considered smothering her in her crib. The bitter, hateful wish for her death. This was the woman who had given birth to her, the woman whose face she saw every day in the mirror. And worse, the man she had always idealized as a paternal figure, a moral compass, was a liar and a hypocrite. The man she had known as Big Preach, a pillar of the community, had a child with her mother—her sister, Rachel.

Rachel. The recurrent thought of her sister's betrayal was a constant wave of agony. She had once loved Rachel more than anyone, but the betrayal was so great, so complete, that the love had turned to a gnawing emptiness. She missed what they once had—a simple, carefree bond of two sisters against the world. But that bond was a lie, built on a foundation of deceit, secrets, and a father she never knew.

Hope dragged herself to the kitchen and grabbed a

bottle of vodka. She drank it straight from the bottle, the acrid taste a perfect reflection of her soul. As the liquid fire burned its way down her throat, she felt a profound, utter defeat. She was a woman with a man who had lied to her, a family that had betrayed her, and a body that was failing her. Her entire life, all her problems felt like a sadistic joke. She had tried to be a good person, a good daughter, a good sister. And for what?

Her eyes drifted to the medicine cabinet—the pills a quiet, tempting solution to all her pain. They were more powerful now than before, a more permanent option. She stared at them, the bottles a silent promise of peace. But she didn't move. She just stared, her mind a blank, empty canvas.

And then the tears came. Not the angry, frustrated tears of rage, but deep, soul-shattering sobs that ripped from her chest as if from a different person. She cried for the man she had lost, for the family she never had, and for the life that had been stolen from her. She cried for the little girl who just wanted to be loved.

As she knelt on the cold tile floor, a single question burned in her mind, a question she could not, would not, stop asking. *Why? Why is this all happening to me?*

Chapter 64
Hannah Reaches Out

The cold light of dawn filtered through the blinds, casting stripes on the living room floor. Hope lay on the couch, wrapped in a blanket, a half-empty bottle of vodka on the floor beside her. Her eyes were swollen, and her body ached from a night of all-consuming misery. She felt as though she had been to the depths of the earth and back, her soul scoured raw. In the hazy, semi-conscious state between sleep and wakefulness, a soft chime from her phone pierced the silence.

She fumbled for it, her movements slow and clumsy. The screen's glare was harsh, and her eyes struggled to focus on the unread message. Her heart sank, anticipating another cruel message from Gina or an unwanted text from Justin. But the name that appeared was Hannah. Hope's body went instantly rigid.

Dr. Hope, I'm so sorry for disappearing. I'm okay, but I can't tell my mom where I am. Can you meet me at your office at 7:00? Please don't tell my mom. I promise I'll explain everything. Please come alone.

The words were a bucket of ice water, snapping her out of the fog of her pain and grief. Hannah. Hannah was alive. The wave of relief that washed over her was so powerful that it brought tears to her eyes. The anguish of the night before—the betrayal, the lies, the loneliness—vanished in an instant. Hope felt a surge of pure, unadulterated happiness. Hannah was safe.

A pang of guilt immediately followed. She hadn't contacted Ariella, Hannah's mother. The poor woman must be frantic. Hope quickly justified her decision. If Hannah knew her mother was involved, she might run again. It was a risk Hope couldn't take. She would meet Hannah, confirm her safety, and then get permission to call Ariella herself. It was the only way.

Her own problems—Justin, Gina, Big Preach, her broken past—were now just distant, muffled noises in the background of her mind. A singular focus took over. She had a purpose. She had a patient who needed her, a young woman who had placed her trust in her.

Hope hopped off the couch. She went to her bathroom, splashed water on her face, and quickly threw on a pair of jeans and a sweater. Her hands moved with a swift, purposeful energy she hadn't felt in days. She looked at Nelson, her beloved dog, who was curled up on his bed, watching her with sleepy, concerned eyes.

"I'll be back soon, buddy," she whispered, her voice a promise.

She was out the door and in her car in a flash, her mind clear and sharp, her heart hammering with a renewed sense of purpose. The mess on her living room floor, the broken lampshade, the bottle of vodka—all of it could wait. Her purpose was waiting for her.

* * *

The office was still and silent, a stark contrast to the chaotic night Hope had just endured. The early morning light cut through the blinds, illuminating dust motes dancing in the air.

Hope sat down, a wave of weariness washing over her. She felt like a vessel that had been emptied and then refilled with a new, stronger resolve. The anger and pain from the night before, while not gone, had been pushed to the periphery, a muted hum beneath the surface of her focused mind.

She looked at Hannah, who sat opposite her, a fragile but determined young woman.

"Hey, how's it going?" Hope asked, her voice soft.

"Not great."

"I assume you know about Abigail and her dad, right?"

"Yes, I do."

Hope considered the situation with a judicial detachment. She knew that to her, the man was a monster who deserved whatever happened to him in prison, but to Abigail, he was a father. She pushed her personal feelings aside, a small victory in her own emotional battle.

"Tell me how you are feeling."

Hannah reached into the small purse slung over her shoulder and pulled out a packet of razor blades, placing them deliberately on the coffee table between herself and Hope. It took a moment for Hope's mind to register what they were and the chilling symbolism they represented.

"Those things are expensive," Hannah said casually. The statement was in sharp contrast to the weighty matter of potential suicide they represented.

"I didn't know that. You know, I don't think I've ever purchased razor blades before," Hope said, searching her memories for any time she may have purchased them.

"Well, they cost more than I expected, at least. So, I bought those yesterday to, you know, slit my wrists. I googled the best way to do it. You know, cut this way along the vein instead of across the wrist. That way, you're sure to bleed out." Hannah mimicked the different movements along and across the vein.

She spoke freely, and Hope did not want the free dialogue to end.

"I've heard that was the case."

"You know, I know what you want to know, so I might as well explain it all. I drove to the reservoir and parked. I thought about walking into the water, cutting open my veins, and drifting into nothingness. It sounded perfect. You know, every time I tried to get out of the car, I, you know, couldn't move. I kept hearing your voice and recalling what we talked about last time. I mean, you were sick in the hospital, maybe dying, and your fiancé and sister hooked up and got married. That's messed up. Really messed up. You attempted suicide. But later in the hospital, you remembered you were valuable, whether you had anyone or not. You enrolled in graduate school the next month and went on to become a doctor. I kept thinking about that—how I am valuable. What great things can I do? Just like you. And why should I kill someone who is valuable? So, I didn't use the razor blades."

"I'm glad you didn't."

"Dr. Hope, you saved my life." Hannah shifted her tone from casual to deeply emotional. "Not just last night, but every day since we talked about suicide. Our last session changed my life. It's the reason I am alive today."

Hope felt a pang of heartfelt humility and a rush of purpose.

"You're here because of you and the decisions you made. You decided to acknowledge your worth. I can't make you do that."

Hannah smiled—a genuine, relieved smile that made her face radiant. Hope's phone buzzed with a text from an unknown number.

"Hannah," Hope said gently, "I need to ask you something. You're safe now, and I have to call your mom. She's worried sick."

"I know," Hannah said, her smile fading. "But can I call her myself? And can you promise not to tell her about the last two nights? She would just get more upset."

Hope nodded, understanding the fragile bond between mother and daughter. "Of course. And yes, I promise. Now, call her."

Hannah picked up her phone and dialed. Her face, a mask of shame and defiance, softened as she spoke.

"Mom? It's me. I'm okay."

Hope watched her as she told her mother she was at her boyfriend's house.

"Yes, I have a boyfriend. He's a really good guy. He's a student at U of H, and I'll bring him home for dinner one night this week."

As Hope listened to the exchange, a single thought settled in her mind, as quiet and sincere as the morning light on the floor. Her life, a chaotic knot of betrayals and emotional pain, was not a curse. It was simply the journey she had to take. Her suffering hadn't defined her; it had carved out a space inside her—a space for a young woman like Hannah and for every lost soul who needed to know they weren't alone.

She had survived her own darkness, and in doing so, she had learned the path out. She had walked through her own personal hell and had emerged with a map. Her purpose wasn't about saving the world or becoming a beacon. It was simply about helping the next person who came looking for the same way out. She was not a hero. She was a guide, and for the first time in a long time, she felt truly at peace.

Chapter 65
The Confession

Psalm 51 New King James Version (NKJV)

³ For I acknowledge my transgressions,
And my sin is always before me.
⁴ Against You, You only, have I sinned,
And done this evil in Your sight—
That You may be found just when You speak,
And blameless when You judge.

¹⁰ Create in me a clean heart, O God,
And renew a steadfast spirit within me.
¹¹ Do not cast me away from Your presence,
And do not take Your Holy Spirit from me.

"You may be seated," Reverend Caleb Moore announced from the pulpit, addressing a packed sanctuary at the Sea of Galilee Church. Big Preach sat behind him, to his right.

"We are all born inclined towards wrongdoing," Revered Moore began. "Every parent knows this truth:

we must teach our children how to do what's right. It's as if doing wrong is instinctive. Just as a duckling instinctively swims the moment it enters the water, toddlers instinctively gravitate towards the one dangerous or fragile object you don't want them to touch.

"As we age and continue engaging in harmful behaviors, those actions have a wider impact. They don't just affect our own well-being—our minds, bodies, and spirits. They create a ripple effect that harms innocent people. And sadly, those we hold dearest, who love us unconditionally, often suffer the most.

"Today's scripture brings us to King David, a man who, until this point, had achieved remarkable feats. He triumphed over Goliath with a simple slingshot, led countless successful military campaigns, and was a gifted musician and poet. From humble beginnings as a shepherd, he ascended to the throne of Israel. Some might say he was at the top of his game. He had it all. The Bible speaks of women singing his praises. He could have had any woman he desired.

"But David's desire settled on Bathsheba, the wife of his loyal friend Uriah. He pursued her, slept with her, and she became pregnant. To conceal his sin, David devised a treacherous plan that ultimately led to Uriah's death. Uriah, David's faithful friend, was dead, betrayed by the very man he served.

"David attempted to conceal his sin, but God sees all, even the deeds we hide in darkness. A prophet, Nathan, publicly confronted David, declaring, 'You are that man!' David was then consumed by guilt. He penned Psalm 51 as a plea for divine forgiveness."

Caleb stepped away from the podium, took off his

ministerial robe, and placed it on a chair near Big Preach. He then removed his jacket and tie, laying them on the same chair. Now, in his white dress shirt with the wireless mic still attached, he walked down to the floor in front of the pulpit.

With a face etched in pain, Caleb continued, "David confessed as a sinner before God, not as a powerful king, a victorious warrior, or even a simple shepherd. He stood as a man who had broken God's law, acknowledging his transgression. He sought God's forgiveness first before seeking reconciliation with others. He needed God's spirit to purify him so he could begin to make amends."

Caleb pointed to himself. "I am that man."

"We have all fallen short of God's glory. We all need cleansing. Please close your eyes and join me in prayer. Lord, we stand before You as sinners. As David said, 'Against You, You only, have I sinned.' Cleanse us, Lord, so that we may truly worship You. Cleanse us so that we may walk in Your spirit. Cleanse us so that we may become more like You. In Jesus' name, we pray. Amen."

"Amen," the congregation echoed.

"The Bible asks, 'If you don't love your brother, whom you have seen, how can you love God, whom you have not seen?' I want each of us to take a moment. Think of someone close to you whom you have wronged—a sibling, a friend, a colleague." Caleb paused, looking directly into the camera. "Perhaps a spouse you have failed. Picture that person and repeat after me:

"I am sorry that my sins have hurt you." (The congregation repeated.)

"With God's help, I will do better." (The congregation repeated.)

"Please find it in your heart to forgive me." (The congregation repeated.)

"Church, I have sinned. I have sinned against God. My sins have caused pain to those I love and who love me. I ask for forgiveness from those I have wronged and from all of you."

Caleb turned to face the cross above the pulpit, then knelt, bowing his head in humble submission.

The congregation sat in stunned silence, deeply moved by Pastor Caleb's heartfelt personal message. They felt convicted and transformed by his words. Eventually, Pastor Emeritus—moved by the confession—reached the microphone.

"Today, we are all David. Thank you, Pastor Caleb, for that deeply moving message. Today, we will forgo our usual announcements and offerings. The Bible calls us to be living sacrifices, so offer your whole self to God instead of a financial tithe. Give him everything. Pour yourself, figuratively, into the offering plate. Go forth and be a living testament to your faith. You are dismissed."

Most of the congregation left the sanctuary in quiet reflection. However, many joined Caleb at the front, kneeling in prayer. They were dedicating themselves to a life of service to God and their fellow humans. Big Preach, deeply moved, also knelt and joined the group.

Miles away, in the master bedroom of a sprawling mansion, Rachel sat in bed, tears streaming down her face as she watched the church service on her tablet. She clung to the hope that Caleb's conversion was genuine, believing their shared journey could flourish, transforming them into a loving couple and, more importantly, devoted parents to their unborn child.

Chapter 66
Bed Rest and Forgiveness

The aroma of basil-tomato soup and grilled cheese filled Rachel's senses, tempting her as she gazed at the bed tray resting across her legs. Oyster crackers, ginger ale, and a single rose completed the meal. Rachel leaned against the headboard of their king-sized poster bed, nestled within their opulent 700-square-foot master suite. While many would admire the room's 100-inch TV or the lavish infinity shower, Rachel's heart belonged to the sumptuously soft pillow-top mattress and 1800-thread-count sheets. But today, she yearned for a reason to be in bed other than medical necessity.

"Does it look all right? Try it and tell me if the soup needs to be warmer or if it needs more seasoning," Caleb said, his eyes filled with anticipation.

He stood beside the bed like a chef awaiting a renowned critic's verdict. While he was no culinary expert, he insisted on preparing Rachel's lunch. With Dr. Nguyen's prescription of bed rest, Caleb was determined to ensure Rachel remained comfortable and received the best possible care, which, in his mind, meant his undivided attention.

After gently blowing on the steaming spoonful of soup, Rachel tasted it and smiled. "It's delicious, thank you."

"So, how are you feeling?" Caleb asked, carefully dabbing a stray drop of soup from the corner of Rachel's mouth with a cloth napkin.

Rachel chuckled. "For the tenth time today, I'm feeling fine."

"I'm sorry. I know I keep asking," Caleb said, his voice smooth and reassuring. "I just want to make sure my girls are doing well."

Rachel's expression turned quizzical. "Your girls? How do you know it's a girl? We won't know for weeks."

"I just know," Caleb said, his voice confident. "Our baby is a girl. And she'll be beautiful, just like me." He grinned and playfully touched his face.

"You're too much," Rachel said, a smile spreading across her face.

Their laughter was a brief return to the joy they once shared.

"But, in all seriousness, I know she'll be beautiful and dazzling, just like you. You still make my heart skip a beat when you walk into a room. We attend all those fancy dinners and receptions with the rich and famous, and I can honestly say, without exaggeration, that you're always the most charming, stunning, and simply captivating woman there."

Rachel's cheeks flushed, a warmth spreading through her body. Over the past year, she'd grown weary of Caleb, his infidelity and lies eroding her affection. She'd seriously considered divorce before her pregnancy, which had placed everything in a state of suspended animation, clouding her judgment.

Caleb's words today caught her completely off guard. Her anger had made her forget how effortlessly charming he could be, the very charm that drew women like Twila to him. The conflicting emotions—burning anger and deep affection—left her mind and heart in turmoil. She sat silently, struggling to reconcile the two opposing forces within her.

"What should we name her?" Caleb asked.

"I have a short list of girl and boy names. I'll stick with the girl names because you're so sure," Rachel conceded.

"I'm very sure it's a girl. So, let's hear the list," Caleb said confidently.

Rachel began, "I wanted a family name. A name with meaning. You admired your mother, so I thought we could name the baby after her."

"Whoa, I appreciate the thought and loved my mother more than you can imagine. The sacrifices she made for Eli and me. The extra jobs she worked to pay for Eli's special living requirements. I can't say enough about how much I loved her. But Renetha? My mom didn't even like her name."

"I was thinking of Renee. That way, we honor your mother," Rachel revealed.

Caleb's previously racing thoughts came to a sudden, peaceful halt upon hearing the name Renee.

"That's it," he declared with a sense of finality in his voice. That's our baby's name—Renee. There's no need to hear the rest of the list. If you agree, we'll call her Renee from now on."

Rachel nodded and smiled.

"Thank you. If my mom were still alive, she would love little Renee as much as we do. Too bad she's gone, and the deserter of a father of mine is still alive." Caleb spoke of an old wound that always stung afresh.

Perry, Caleb's father, abandoned Renetha when Caleb and Eli were both toddlers. Renetha faced a relentless struggle to provide for her sons, battling to put food on the table, clothes on their backs, and cover Eli's substantial medical expenses. Caleb deeply resented watching his mother sacrifice herself to keep their family afloat.

For fourteen years, Perry remained absent until Caleb's press conference announcing his full football scholarship to a prestigious college. Caleb's remarkable performance of scoring six touchdowns in a single game had garnered national attention, attracting scholarship offers from universities across the country. This news had evidently reached Perry. He approached the podium with an air of authority as if he'd been present all along. Later that day, after the cameras were off and the reporters had left, Caleb punched his absentee father in the face. It was the first of two times he'd struck Perry. Caleb often wished he had hit him more.

"I wish I could have met her," Rachel responded. "She sounds like an amazing woman."

"She was, and so are you. Hey, go ahead and finish your lunch. I'll be back up in about thirty minutes. If you need anything—"

"Call you. I know, I know. Thank you. Now go! Please." Rachel pointed to the door.

"Okay, I'm gone."

Caleb left the bedroom, and Rachel exhaled as she

looked at her lunch. She tried to recall if Caleb had ever made her a meal and served it to her in their bed. *Oh yeah,* she thought, *last night he served me dinner in bed, and before that...never.*

Caleb descended the stairs and entered his home office. A sense of fear and dread quickly replaced Rachel and Renee's joyful thoughts. Rachel's near miscarriage had deeply impacted him. He couldn't bear the thought of his family ending before it truly began. He reflected on his past actions, the misdeeds that seemed so glaring in light of his abundant blessings. He recognized the urgent need for change. He needed to strive to be a better pastor, a more devoted husband, a more reliable friend, and a more virtuous man if he ever hoped to be a worthy father. He was determined to break the cycle, to be nothing like the absent and disappointing Perry. He prayed that his sermon on redemption would come true in his own life.

While Caleb lay face down on the floor, praying earnestly, he ignored multiple calls from Twila Gooden, whose name appeared on his caller ID.

Chapter 67
The Bartender's Tale

*H*ope decided she couldn't bear the thought of the last words she said to Justin being a condemnation. Her own pain, her own betrayal, had blinded her. She had called him worthless. She needed to see him, to find out if anything was salvageable between them, or at the very least, bring some measure of closure to their relationship.

Hank locked the door to Justin's Repair Shop, the clatter of the bolt a final note on a hectic Monday afternoon. His workday was done, and he planned to head home for a brief rest before turning on his Uber app.

A sleek, sporty SUV pulled up to the curb, its engine purring. Hank's gaze was drawn to the woman who stepped out. She was well-dressed in slacks and a loose blouse, and she approached him with a warm, dimpled smile that he instantly recognized. *This must be Hope.* Justin's description had not done her justice.

"Excuse me," she said, her voice a soft bell in the late-day quiet. "I'm looking for the shop's owner, Justin."

"He's not in today. You could try texting him," Hank

replied, a hint of sadness in his tone.

"No, I wanted to see him face-to-face."

"He hasn't gotten back to me either. It's understandable, though. He's probably busy making funeral arrangements," Hank explained, his expression somber.

The smile vanished from Hope's face as if wiped away by an invisible hand. Her posture straightened, and a flicker of genuine concern crossed her features.

"Funeral? What funeral?" she asked, her voice tight with worry.

Hank's back stiffened. He hadn't realized she didn't know.

"I'm sorry," he said, speaking with a quiet solemnity. "I thought you knew. His mother, Lorraine. Justin found her a couple of nights ago. She's gone."

A horrified gasp escaped Hope's lips.

"Oh God, no," she whispered, her hands flying to her face, forming a stunned barrier.

Her mind reeled, a torrent of flashbacks and sickening realizations. The last time she saw Justin, he was standing in the darkness, looking so tired and defeated. Twila was actually providing him the comfort of an old friend. He wasn't avoiding her or trying to hide something sinister. He was a son who had just lost his mother. He was in a grief-stricken haze, and her words had been a relentless torrent of accusations—cruel, callous, and undeserved. He hadn't been lying or putting on a show; he was devastated.

Her breath hitched. She hadn't just called him worthless; she had done it while he was standing in the ruins of his world, mourning the woman who gave birth to him. Her self-pity and anger had blinded her, and she had driven a knife into an open wound.

"I have to go," she said abruptly, the words a raw exhale. "I'll try to catch Justin at his house."

She didn't wait for a response, turning on her heel and heading back to her car with a new, frantic urgency. The hope she had felt moments before was gone, replaced by crushing regret. All she wanted now was to get to *her* Justin.

* * *

Hope knocked on Justin's front door. She heard moving inside, and when the door opened, a familiar face greeted her. Reverend LaTavious Turner from the Church of the Open Sky waved her in.

"Hey, Miss Hope. Come on in, darling."

"Hi, LaTavious. I just found out about Lorraine. How's Justin doing?" she asked, her voice filled with a desperate concern.

Reverend T.'s broad, toothy smile transformed into a tight-lipped grimace. He looked away for a moment, the cheerful facade dropping entirely. He turned back to Hope, pushing his glasses up his face.

"You just found out? He told me this morning that he would spend some time with you. In fact, he told me the reason he didn't answer my calls last night was because you were consoling him."

Hope looked at him, confused. "But...I wasn't with him last night. I was at home."

A flicker of understanding crossed Reverend T.'s face, then faded into a deep, pained sorrow. He realized the truth, the hard truth. He didn't just assume she knew; he now understood Justin had lied to him, too.

"I found out about his mother's passing from Brandon, and I called Justin last night as soon as I heard. I offered to come over and sit with him, but he said you were with him. In stressful moments like these, alcoholics like Justin and I need someone to be with us at all times. Justin was lying about where he was last night, and today is not a good sign. Not at all."

The words landed with the weight of a sudden, brutal truth. Her face turned pale, and she felt a cold pit form in her stomach. A thousand fragments of the past few days clicked into place: his glassy eyes, his avoiding drinks when they were on dates, his recent emotional distance. It all created a terrible, sickening realization.

"Justin is an alcoholic?" she asked, the question barely a whisper, a half-statement of disbelief.

Reverend T. realized his assumption that Hope knew about Justin's condition was wrong. But for him, talking about alcoholism was not a secret that anyone should keep. He felt perfectly fine with telling Hope about Justin's disease.

"Yes, Justin is an alcoholic. He joined AA after his wife died a couple of years ago. I am his sponsor. He had been doing very well but has missed all his meetings in the last two months. He told me he was busy at work. Now, he's lying about his whereabouts. That is not a good sign. I came over to do what I could, but only his aunt and son are here."

Hope's psychologist's mind could absorb all the information Reverend T. had just provided and put each tidbit in the appropriate compartment in her brain. But her heart was in turmoil. Her anger from the other night was gone, replaced by an acute guilt and a new, terrible fear. She hadn't been arguing with an unfeeling man; she had been fighting with a man battling a demon—a man grieving and alone.

She had only one question for Justin's sponsor: "Do you have any idea where Justin could be right now?"

* * *

Justin had been steadily drinking beer for hours. The lower alcohol content, compared to his usual whiskey, gave a flimsy sense of moral justification, a feeling that he wasn't being "as bad." However, the cumulative effect of the beer had eroded his self-imposed restraint, and he was ready for a proper, destructive binge. He was a son who had just lost his mother, a man whose pain had been cruelly misjudged, and an addict on the verge of a precipitous fall. The memory of Hope's sharp and cold word—*worthless*—flashed in his mind like a broken strobe light. He craved an escape, a vacation from the wreckage of his life.

"Hey, Ray, Jim Beam on the rocks?" he asked, his voice a little too loud.

Ray looked up at his longtime friend, a conflict raging within him. He wanted to refuse service to avoid contributing to Justin's self-destructive spiral, but his deep desire to keep Justin under his watchful eye ultimately won out. His hands, usually so steady, trembled as he poured the whiskey.

"Take it easy, my friend," Ray said, his voice filled with gentle concern, like a counselor offering quiet support.

"I'm good. No need to worry, big guy," Justin replied, the lie slipping out easily.

He reached for his drink, ready to embark on his voyage, when a hand settled on his shoulder. A gentle weight, a beautiful head, rested on his other. The scent of her perfume cut through the stale smell of the bar—a clean, fresh scent that was both startling and familiar.

His frantic breathing slowed. A soft, gentle hand nudged the glass away. Justin's hand, cold and trembling from hours of drinking, was suddenly enveloped in Hope's warmth.

He craved the drink's oblivion, but Hope's presence offered a different kind of solace: the warmth and safety of human connection. The chaotic noise of the bar and the demons in his head seemed to quiet to an immediate and unnatural stillness.

"Hey, friend, what's the damage?" Hope asked the visibly relieved bartender.

"It's on the house," Ray exhaled.

Hope's hands moved to one of Justin's, slightly tugging it. Like a toddler holding the steadying fingers of his mother, Justin arose and followed Hope's guiding hand out of the bar and away from another precipitous fall.

Chapter 68
The Accident

"All right, that's enough. I'm driving us both home, big boy," Chaka declared, wiping whiskey and ice from her husband's shirt. Enjoying the house party a little too enthusiastically, Justin had spilled his drink.

"Oh, baby, you don't have to drive," Justin slurred, his words laced with drunken honesty. "We both know you hate driving, and honestly, you're a terrible driver."

The party's host, Tyrone, interjected, "Yes, she does need to drive. Someone's gotta get your sloppy drunk ass home."

"You drank just as much as me," Justin mumbled, his defense weak and unconvincing.

"Man, first, I can handle my shit better than you! Second, this is my house; I don't have to drive home, blockhead. Please, Chaka, take this man home before he does something stupid like he did back in my dad's basement. Ray, Brandon, me, and your husband started drinking some of my dad's Jack Daniels. Justin was so drunk that he got up to pee and—"

"Hey, hey, that's enough," Justin interrupted, frantically waving his hands, attempting to shield his wife from the impending onslaught of embarrassing teenage tales.

He vividly recalled the story's climax: he was standing on a table, urinating in a corner. The subsequent punishment from his father, Ike, was etched in his memory—Ike, despite being shorter, lifted him and threw him against a wall, leaving a permanent mark.

"She doesn't need to hear all that," Justin stammered, his words slurring. "Mrs. Thompson, would you please drive me home?"

Chaka wrapped her arm around Justin's waist, providing steady support. Justin leaned on her, using her as a human cane to steady himself. They waved a wobbly goodbye to the remaining six guests, remnants of Tyrone's sweltering house party.

In the car, Chaka meticulously adjusted her seat and the mirrors while Justin settled in for a nap during the drive home.

With eyes closed, a drowsy Justin said, "I love you, Mrs. Thompson."

"I love you, too, Mr. Thompson," Chaka smiled, then meticulously adjusted the car's mirrors again.

Driving was a rare occurrence for her, as anxiety would typically overwhelm her behind the wheel. Right now, she could feel her mouth becoming dry, and her hands, though warm moments ago, were growing cold and clammy. A steady rain had begun to fall, and the windows were rapidly fogging. The thick clouds overhead obscured any trace of moonlight, and the car's defrost offered little relief from the condensation.

Chaka briefly contemplated returning to the party and waiting out the storm. However, her decision was swayed by the short twenty-minute drive home, coupled with her desire to relieve the babysitter and hold Deuce. This was the first time they'd left their nearly two-year-old son with a babysitter outside the family, and she was eager to be reunited with him. With Big Justin's snoring growing steadily louder in the passenger seat, Chaka cautiously pulled away from the curb.

* * *

Agony! Justin's entire face throbbed with excruciating pain. He awoke from a sleep that felt like a deep-sea ascent, struggling to surface. He tried to scan the room, but his vision was blurred, as if he were peering through a narrow slit in blinds. Everything was out of focus.

Pain! A relentless pounding joined the facial agony, making his head feel impossibly heavy and muffling all sound. Instinctively, Justin raised his right hand, rubbing his throbbing head and then his face. His fingers encountered something foreign: a plastic layer over his nose. He tried to move his left hand, but it remained unresponsive.

He lifted his head slightly and saw his left hand encased in a white bandage. He had to crane his neck to get a clear view. Then, he realized he could only see from his right eye. His right hand returned to his face, and he discovered his left eye was covered with tape, similar to that on his nose.

"Son, son," a very familiar voice called out.

Justin turned his head, his vision clear enough to see

his mother standing beside his hospital bed.

"Huh? What?" he managed to croak out.

Lorraine grasped his right hand tightly. "Son, you and Chaka were in a car accident last night. You hit a construction barrier. You've broken your left arm, and your nose is broken, too, probably from the airbag. The doctors suspect a concussion, but they needed you to wake up to be sure."

Justin's mind struggled to process the information, the combined effects of head trauma and alcohol making it challenging to comprehend. He couldn't recall the accident or even getting into the car. As his thoughts slowly coalesced, a single, urgent question pushed through the fog.

"Chaka... what about Chaka?" he rasped.

Lorraine knew there was no gentle way to deliver the news.

"Chaka is badly injured. Broken ribs, a punctured lung, and significant internal damage causing bleeding. They operated all night, but they're not sure..."

Her voice trembled, the rock of the family finally cracking. Tears welled in her eyes, preventing her from finishing. She couldn't bring herself to say that her cherished daughter-in-law, the woman who helped Justin find his way and the mother of her only grandchild, was likely going to die.

"Can I see her?" Justin asked quietly.

* * *

Chaka was a fragile figure in the hospital bed, her body connected to a maze of medical equipment. A nasal cannula delivered vital oxygen. When Justin was wheeled to her bedside, her eyes opened, and a weak smile graced her face. Justin looked at his wife, the image of her vibrant spirit now so vulnerable and weak, a sight that threatened to break him. No nightmare had ever been this terrifying. No pain had ever been this sharp. He reached out, his right hand finding hers.

"I'm so sorry," he said, his voice thick with guilt.

Chaka smiled. "My man. My good man."

"I love you."

"I love you, too," Chaka whispered. Her eyes fluttered rapidly, and with a small gasp, she said, "Deuce, I..." Her words trailed off, her eyes rolling upward, fixed on the ceiling. "Love, love, love..." Then, her eyes closed.

The monitors began to emit a cacophony of alarms, and a flurry of nurses and attendants rushed into the room.

Justin was wheeled just outside the door. He prayed fervently, begging God to take him instead of Chaka. He pleaded that Deuce needed his mother, not his flawed, alcoholic father. He continued his prayers as Chaka was rushed into emergency brain surgery to stop undiagnosed bleeding. He prayed for divine guidance for the surgeons and for Chaka to be returned to her family.

God answered Justin's prayers that day. His answer was *no*.

* * *

"That's how I killed my wife and left my son without a mother. It's all my fault." Justin concluded his story, his voice heavy with guilt. "The thing is, I can't even tell you what caused the crash. Knowing Chaka, she probably swerved to avoid hitting someone or something—a person, a child, a dog, a deer, or even a squirrel. She was so gentle that she couldn't hurt a fly. She was the kindest person I've ever known. When I lost my mom, all the guilt just came back, the same feelings I had when I lost my wife. It's all my fault."

Hope sat across from him on the couch, the woman who cared deeply for him wanting to reach out and pull him into her arms. The psychologist in her wanted to analyze his trauma and offer a path forward. But both women inside her knew that neither therapy nor a simple hug would fix this. This was a man drowning in a grief so overpowering it had become a part of him. Her own body ached with a familiar grief, a pain that echoed her own.

Adrift in a sea of guilt and despair, Justin could only see the wreckage he had caused. He looked at her, his rescuer, and in his eyes was a silent plea for help.

"Please let me help you," she said, her voice a soft, steady anchor in his storm.

"Yes," he replied, conveying surrender and hope with a single word.

Chapter 69
The Promise of a New Beginning

*I*t was 3:15 a.m., and Justin sat at the kitchen table. An unopened bottle of bourbon and a large, empty glass sat before him. He had been staring at the bottle for over an hour, his mind filled with painful memories. He knew the liquor could numb his thoughts, but something inside him resisted.

His mind was a maelstrom of regret: the sight of his son alone with his lifeless grandmother, the ghost of twins he had never known, Chaka's life cut short because of a drunk husband. He reached for the bottle, his fingers fumbling with the seal.

"Why?" a soft voice asked from behind him.

Justin didn't turn around, gripping the bottle tightly. His breathing quickened.

"Because it hurts. It just hurts too much."

"Why?" the voice repeated, gentle but unwavering.

"Because I deserve it. God is punishing me for all the things I've done wrong."

A warm, steady hand settled on his shoulder.

"That's not how it works," Hope said, her voice a calm

anchor in his storm.

Justin's grip on the bottle tightened. "Yes, it is. God punishes those who hurt His children. I hurt His children. I hurt my wife. I hurt my son. I deserve everything that's happened."

"You think God is punishing you," Hope said, walking around the table to face him, "but you're punishing yourself."

She reached for the bottle, and with a quiet authority that left no room for argument, she took it from his hand. She held his hands in hers, her warmth a stark contrast to the cold bottle.

"God forgives. Even when we don't deserve it. Especially then. Your guilt is killing you. It led to depression, depression led to alcohol, and alcohol led to a tragic accident. It wasn't God's punishment; it was the result of a sickness. You have to believe that. You have to believe in His grace."

Despite his closed eyes, Justin experienced a deep sense of clarity. His frantic thoughts quieted, and his breathing slowed. The weight of a decade of guilt began to lift, replaced by a warm, internal light. He realized he didn't have to carry this burden alone anymore. He had to walk in faith and believe in forgiveness.

He opened his eyes and saw Hope. She wasn't a beacon of some distant, abstract love. She was right there, in the fragile glow of the kitchen light, holding his hands. She was the simple, beautiful, and tangible embodiment of the grace he so desperately needed.

Chapter 70
The Funeral Home

ope had never been to a funeral home and had no idea what to expect. Her mind conjured images of embalmed bodies in open caskets lining dark, musty rooms illuminated by dim, flickering lights. She imagined the air thick with the sickly-sweet scent of formaldehyde and the cold presence of death, a sinister mortician in a black suit and white gloves eagerly awaiting his next client.

The reality of Stewart's Funeral Home was far different. It was a sanctuary of gentle light and hushed warmth, designed to disarm grief. The air was filled with the delicate scent of lilac, not death. The reception area resembled a welcoming apartment complex lobby, with a receptionist desk, tables, comfortable chairs, and two plush couches. To the left, Hope could see a large, sunlit room, casket models on display through its double French doors.

A silver-haired receptionist greeted Hope and Justin, informing them that Mr. Stewart would be with them shortly. Hope couldn't fathom what Justin was experiencing.

Stewart's establishment was the same funeral home that had handled both Chaka's and his father, Ike's, funerals, neither of which was a distant memory.

When he looked at her, he offered a strained, reassuring smile—a transparent façade. He stood with his shoulders hunched, his eyes unfocused, a body language that screamed of a man barely holding himself together. Justin, ever the stoic, didn't want her to worry.

Hope thought, *"Your mother just died. It's okay to be sad. Hell, cry if you need to! It's normal. You're human! I'll never fully understand the male ego. But I'll be here for him as long as he needs me."*

Before Justin and Hope could sit, Mr. Stewart emerged from the office on the right, his arms outstretched in a welcoming gesture. He ushered them into his office. Hope had known of Stewart's Funeral Home her entire life; it was one of the area's top three African American funeral homes. The founder, Armon Stewart, stood before them, a man likely in his late seventies or early eighties, yet moving with a remarkable youthful energy.

"Please come in and have a seat," he said warmly.

They settled into two of the four chairs arranged around a circular table. Mr. Stewart joined them, placing a black portfolio in his hand.

"First, I want to express my sincere condolences. I had the privilege of knowing Lorraine over the years. You might not be aware, but she taught two of my grandchildren at Charleston Elementary. When I informed my eldest son of her passing, he spoke highly of her dedication and caring nature. He also mentioned her firm but fair approach in the classroom."

For the first time that day, Justin offered a genuine

smile. "Thank you. She ran a tight ship at home, too," he added.

"Secondly, thank you for entrusting Stewart's with these arrangements. We will do our utmost to serve you and your family carefully."

Justin simply nodded in acknowledgment.

Mr. Stewart opened the portfolio and began reviewing the documents. "Well, there's not much we need to cover today. Your mother's prearrangements were quite detailed. She came in about six weeks ago and updated all her wishes."

"Six weeks ago?" Justin asked, a flicker of surprise in his voice.

Mr. Stewart laid down the forms and looked at Justin. "Son, you know, it happens more often than people realize. People often 'put their affairs in order' just before they're called home. It's like they have an intuition."

Hope couldn't decipher Justin's expression. She could only imagine the whirlwind in his mind—the confusion, the hurt, the guilt of not seeing the signs. He remained silent, lost in thought.

Hope stepped in, placing a gentle hand on Justin's knee as a silent signal of her support.

"So what remains to be decided?" she asked Mr. Stewart.

Mr. Stewart glanced back at his portfolio. "Well, she'll rest next to her husband, Ike. Same casket style and color. She requested a graveside service, saying she didn't want 'too much muss or fuss.' I just need a few details: how many death certificates, the flower arrangements, and the tombstone inscription."

Justin remained silent, so Hope asked, "How many

death certificates are typically needed?"

"At least two."

"Let's get four, just to be safe," she decided.

"That will be a small additional cost," Mr. Stewart informed them.

"No problem," Hope replied.

Justin started to object but then remained silent.

Without prompting, he muttered, "Daisies."

Hope took over. "Do you have daisy arrangements?"

"Of course."

Hope selected two arrangements from the pre-purchased package and added three more, covering the extra costs herself. Justin, who usually protested such things, remained quiet, perhaps because it was for his mother.

Justin then provided the epitaph. "Beloved wife, mother, Bibi, sister, teacher, and friend. Can that fit on the stone?"

"Yes, no problem."

Mr. Stewart, patient and composed, concluded their meeting. "One last thing: please schedule a time to view Lorraine tomorrow. Janice, our receptionist, can assist you. Feel free to bring close friends or family."

As they left and walked to the car, Hope took Justin's hand. She felt his skin—cold and unresponsive—and noticed his fingers were limp, incapable of returning her grip. He lacked the strength to do anything, even hold her hand.

Chapter 71
Big Preach Explains Himself

"I always thought Gina would tell Rachel first before you," Big Preach said, seated behind his desk in his church office.

His hands gripped the edge of the wood, a subconscious shield against her. He was terrified.

"I'm pretty sure Mom had no intention of telling me when she did," Hope replied. "She was on a rampage, and it just slipped out."

She sat in one of the armchairs, her fists clenched but hidden beneath her arms, a tight knot of contained fury.

"Are you angry with me?" Big Preach asked, his voice barely above a whisper.

"Yes," came the sharp reply. "I'm outraged. Deeply disappointed. I never thought you were capable of such deception, such betrayal. I held you in the highest regard. How could I have been so blind for so many years?"

Big Preach paused, his gaze dropping to his hands. "It was a mistake."

"No, let's be clear," Hope retorted, her voice rising. "It

wasn't a mistake. There were hundreds of mistakes. How many times have you lied to me in the last thirty years? How could you let Rachel believe Craig was her father? Did your wife know? The church? You've made and are still making countless mistakes."

"You're right. I have no excuse. What can an old man say? I can't say I wish it hadn't happened or that Gina and I had never been together. Rachel is a blessing. If I have to pay for bringing her into this world, so be it."

Hope stood abruptly, slamming her hands on his desk.

"No, no!" she exclaimed. "You don't get to use my sister to absolve yourself! She's the biggest victim here, and you have to atone for your lies."

Big Preach remained silent. Over the years, every time he saw Rachel, he was confronted with his original sin. He'd tried to pay for his mistakes, giving Gina money for Rachel's dance, singing, and other lessons, supporting her pageant aspirations.

"It was a clumsy, desperate attempt to be a father to her, to show her I loved her," he confessed, the words heavy with shame.

"Can you answer me one thing?" Hope demanded. "You were married to Ms. Dora. She was the kindest, sweetest person I've ever known. So why? Why would you cheat on her with my mother?"

"Please, sit down," Big Preach said, gesturing toward the armchair.

Hope reluctantly complied, wanting answers more than anything.

"I was the smallest, weakest kid in my class growing up. 'Geek' or 'bookworm' would have been compliments. I went to college and then seminary, and women showed no interest in me for all those years except for Dora. I loved her, and I still do. She was beautiful, perfect. My affair had nothing to do with her. The church was experiencing explosive growth. I'd been the pastor for almost ten years, and as my status grew, so did the attention of women. I was under tremendous pressure, and that insecure, unwanted kid was still there, terrified of not being enough."

Big Preach looked to Hope for sympathy, but her eyes remained cold.

"I wish I could say Gina was my first and only affair, but that wouldn't be true."

He paused, looking at Hope. She stared back, her expression unwavering, refusing to offer any hint of forgiveness.

"But why Gina, if you had so many women to choose from? Why Gina?" Hope had to know.

"She was a drug," he confessed, his voice a low, raspy whisper. "Say what you will about your mother, but she is a stunning, beautiful creature. When I saw her dropping you off at daycare, I was captivated. When she showed interest in me, I had to have her. She became an obsession. I'd lie, cheat, and risk everything to be with her. She was my escape, and I couldn't get enough of her."

"I think I'm going to be sick," Hope said, her hand rising to cover her mouth.

Hope rose from her chair, backing away from the desk. His words—Gina was a drug, a lie, an obsession—left a film of filth across her soul. She braced her hands against the cool stone of the wall, letting the shock pass through her like an electrical current, taking several ragged breaths before she could face him again.

She realized his defense of Caleb now made terrible sense.

"I will tell Rachel. She will be devastated beyond words. I'll let you know when the time is right for the two of you to talk."

"Of course. I'll wait until we agree the time is right," he conceded.

She looked down at her hands, which had been clenched for so long that they were grey. She realized the hate she carried for him and Gina was heavier than her illness. She stood, not in anger, but with quiet exhaustion.

"I forgive you," she said, the words falling onto the plush carpet with a heavy, almost tangible weight.

"Thank you. That means—" Big Preach began, but Hope cut him off.

"Stop. I don't care what it means to you. It's about what it means to me. I will no longer be collateral damage in your and Mom's mistakes. Goodbye."

Hope walked out, leaving the ruins of his deception and choosing not to look back.

Chapter 72
Rachel's Emotional Reaction

The knock on the door was hesitant, a soft punctuation in the quiet of the afternoon. Rachel opened it to see Hope standing there, her expression unreadable. An awkward silence hung between them, a silent acknowledgment of the chasm that had formed. Rachel was surprised Hope had reached out to meet, let alone at her house.

"Come in," Rachel said, stepping back to let her sister pass.

They took their seats in the living room, the space feeling vast and unfamiliar. Rachel started to apologize.

"Hope, about everything—"

Hope raised a hand, stopping her. "No. Not today, Rachel. There's time for that, but that's not why I'm here."

A knot of dread tightened in Rachel's stomach. Hope took a deep breath, and the air seemed to thicken with the unspoken weight of her words. Hope's hands were clasped so tightly in her lap that her knuckles had lost their color.

"Rachel," Hope said, her voice low and steady, "Big

Preach...Reverend John Rice is your biological father."

Rachel's lips parted to form the word "What?" but only a shuddering exhale escaped. The quiet that followed was deafening, a silence so intense it could make a brave person tremble. For a fleeting moment, Rachel's face was a mask of confusion. Then, a horrifying clarity settled over her. She knew instantly that what she had heard was the truth.

Her eyes lost their focus, her lips began to tremble, and her hands clenched into fists. Her breath grew shallow and rapid, her mouth open in a soundless gasp. A deep, bone-chilling cold spread through her veins, and a violent tremble began to shake her. Every despicable, loathsome, self-hating, and fearful emotion swarmed her mind, body, and soul. Her life, to this point, made perfect sense and no sense at all. So many lies, she thought, what was real anymore?

Hope moved over and placed an arm around her. At the touch, Rachel's face contorted into an unrecognizable grimace of horror, and a raw, guttural shriek tore from her–a sound that seemed to claw its way up from the very core of her being.

Rachel slid from the couch, her body a dead weight, and Hope's hands shot out, catching her just before her head slammed into the floor. Rachel was now on her knees, her face buried in her hands, her head bowed to the floor. The tears came then, a torrent of them, a release so violent it was a storm unto itself. Hope, on her knees next to her, wrapped her arms around her sister like a protective blanket, feeling the cold of her body, the violent tremors of her sobs, and the weight of her pain.

Hope had no words. No creative insight. No textbook

answers to fix this. Her deepest desire was to take her sister's pain away, a pain she knew all too well. But all she had to offer was her presence. Hope would stay right here, on her knees on the floor, for as long as her sister needed. She rested her head against Rachel's, a silent promise to stay and share the deep feeling of exhaustion and pain.

Chapter 73
Sins of the Father

Sins of the Father. The phrase echoed in Rachel's mind, an unrelenting loop, even as Hope knelt beside her.

As unbelievable as Hope's words were, they resonated with an undeniable truth. Rev. Dr. M. John Rice, Big Preach, was her biological father. This revelation made sense of so many previously inexplicable aspects of her life. Ever since Craig abandoned the family on Hope's ninth birthday, he had treated Rachel with cold indifference, as if she were contagious.

Big Preach's behavior towards her was perplexing, almost schizophrenic. He would generously fund her pageants and events, yet he consistently avoided her presence, always finding a swift excuse to leave. His inconsistent, indifferent behavior left Rachel confused and hurt.

Rachel looked down at her stomach, consumed by a chilling dread. Her deepest fear—that she was cursed by the lies of her birth—was being confirmed.

Sins of the father curse subsequent generations. Rachel reflected on the parallel between her father's desire for another man's wife and her own desire for her sister's fiancé. While Hope believed Caleb initiated their relationship, Rachel's motives were rooted in deep-seated envy. She envied Hope's effortless connection with Craig and Big Preach, a connection she herself yearned for. This envy propelled her to pursue Caleb, Hope's most cherished possession. During Hope's hospitalization, Rachel enticed Caleb into an adjacent empty room.

After resisting her advances for months, he yielded to her desires. They engaged in an intimate act in one room while Hope struggled for survival in the next.

Hope leaned forward, her voice a soft anchor. "I'm sorry to lay this all on you, but I thought it better to hear from me than anyone else."

"You're sorry?" Rachel thought, a wave of guilt washing over her. *"I'm the reason you lost Caleb. I'm the reason you tried to take your own life that night. I'm the reason Mom has treated you so cruelly. I'm the one who should be sorry. I'm the coward who did her sister wrong."*

These thoughts swirled in her mind, creating a mask of sorrow that Hope misinterpreted as grief over the Big Preach revelation.

Rachel and Hope sat on the large, comfortable sectional couch in Rachel's spacious family room. The room was quiet, punctuated only by the steady rhythm of the grandfather clock's pendulum. Hope moved closer to Rachel and gently placed her hand over Rachel's.

"Rachel," Hope began, her voice filled with emotion, "there's something else I need to say. I apologize for my part in all of this. I failed to be the big sister you needed all these years. I'm no longer blaming Mom for the distance between us. At this point, who our parents are doesn't matter. What matters is that we reclaim our sisterhood. I want us to love and support each other through every challenge and every joy for whatever time we have left on this earth."

Rachel placed her other hand atop Hope's, creating a comforting three-layer stack.

"I love that idea," she said, squeezing Hope's hand. "It's the only real thing we've had in years. I'm done living a lie, Hope. All I want now is to live for truth and for her." Tears of love and guilt flowed freely, and her breathing became labored, accompanied by a stream of mucus. Hope, witnessing her sister's emotional release, swiftly retrieved facial tissues.

"It's all right," Hope comforted her, gently stroking Rachel's head. "You are, without a doubt, a beautiful woman. However, I must confess, you possess the most spectacularly ugly crying face I have ever seen!"

Rachel's laughter mingled with her tears and mucus. "Hope, I love you," she managed to say.

"I love you too, my dear sister," Hope replied. "I'm genuinely happy that you're having a baby."

Hope's approval was a moment Rachel had secretly longed for. She knew what she and Caleb had done to Hope was unforgivable, and they would have to find a way to make amends.

Rachel felt compelled to make things right with Hope, hoping to break the cycle of generational sin that threatened the child growing within her. She looked at Hope, a silent vow passing between them. They had both been victims of the same lies, and this was the moment they decided to heal together. A new, stronger bond was forming in the quiet aftermath of the storm.

Chapter 74
The Mentor's Warning

Akil was nearing completion of his routine maintenance on the McReynolds building's HVAC system. He stood beside the outside air conditioning unit, adding thirty pounds of freon to bring it back to optimal performance. While watching the pressure gauge, his thoughts drifted to Andrielle and her pregnancy.

"Hey, Akil." Justin's voice broke his concentration.

"Hi, Justin. What are you doing here? I mean, with your mom's funeral coming up and everything. I thought..." Akil stammered, caught off guard by the unexpected visit.

Justin smiled reassuringly. "It's all right. First, thank you for your kind voicemails. I really appreciate it."

"No problem. Your mom was always good to me."

"Second, thank you for taking the extra work. You and Hank are helping me out by stepping up."

"Again, no problem. I actually could use the extra work. Money is tight, and I have a situation I need to handle."

"Akil, your situation is the reason I'm here. Let me

tell you why. I couldn't sleep for much of last night. A million things were going through my head. My life is crazy, and it's so much more than the funeral and the business, but no need to go into all that."

Justin motioned for them both to sit on an old wooden bench along the side of the building.

"As I said, a million things were racing through my mind until I thought about you and Andrielle. Then, my mind slowed. I thought about y'all's situation and what I did in a similar situation."

"Similar situation?" Akil did not understand Justin's words.

"Yeah, pretty similar. Last night, something spoke to my spirit and said I must tell you what I learned from my experience. Deep down, I said I would tell you in the morning. Once I said that to myself, I fell instantly into a deep sleep. I woke up this morning thinking of talking to you directly despite everything else going on in my life."

"Wow, I don't know what to say. Thanks." Akil shook his head.

"Don't thank me yet," Justin continued. "I have something I need to tell you. In high school, I got a girl pregnant. I was terrified of being a father and of the responsibilities. I convinced her to have an abortion—not for her, but for my own convenience. I acted out of fear. The impact on her and the baby never occurred to me until it was too late. For years, I was consumed by guilt and shame. It created a void filled with pain. I turned to alcohol to numb it, which led to alcoholism, which cost me so much. So, my advice to you is this: never make decisions out of fear, especially fear of failure. Life will work out if you choose to do what's right, not what's easy. You're a strong man, Akil. Act like it. And whatever you decide, be ready to face the consequences. You create them."

Justin's words resonated deeply with Akil. He realized he had been viewing his situation through the lens of fear, a prism that distorted his perceptions and actions.

Akil straightened his back and looked Justin in the eye. "I hear you. I hear you," he repeated.

Justin stood up, placed his hand on Akil's shoulder, and gave his shoulder a slight pat. Then, he turned and walked away, praying that Akil could benefit from his hard-learned life lessons.

Chapter 75
The Funeral Service

The heavy rain of the night before had given way to a perfectly clear day. The sky was a vast, cloudless blue, the sun shining brightly above the cemetery. The weather was so ideal that Mr. Stewart chose not to erect the graveside tent. A closed casket rested above the open grave, prepared for its final resting place. Daisy floral arrangements were thoughtfully placed around the site, their white petals seeming to glow in the brilliant sunlight.

Thirty folding chairs were arranged in orderly rows and filled with Lorraine Thompson's immediate family and close friends. An additional fifty people stood respectfully around the perimeter, a gathering of former students, teaching colleagues, and Justin's childhood friends—Tyrone, Ray, and Brandon—who were serving as pallbearers. Their broad shoulders and somber expressions formed a solid, unwavering line of support behind the casket.

In the center of the front row, Justin sat, with Deuce resting his head on his leg. Deuce was awake, his eyes heavy with a sleepy confusion he couldn't quite name. To Justin's left, Hope sat, her hand resting on his unoccupied leg. She had offered her seat to Aunt Maxine, but Maxine had insisted, placing Hope next to Justin.

Reverend T., dressed in black, began the service with the traditional greeting for a celebration of life. He outlined the order of the brief ceremony and then passed the microphone to Lorraine's younger sister, Maxine.

"My dear sister asked me a couple of months ago, when the time came, if I could sing at her funeral. I said, of course, if I am able. I thought she was talking about something that would happen way down the line. Little did I know it would be so soon. Too soon if you ask me, but God didn't ask me. Her favorite song was 'I Need Thee Every Hour,' so pray with me as I attempt to do my best."

Justin smiled, anticipating the power of his aunt's voice. He knew she had the ability to stir the most heartfelt emotions. He also knew she wouldn't limit herself to one song. He was right. Her heartfelt rendition of "I Need Thee Every Hour" transitioned into "His Eye Is on the Sparrow" and culminated in "Yes, Jesus Loves Me."

Reverend T. reclaimed the microphone, wiping away tears and audibly blowing his nose. Maxine's singing had touched everyone deeply, leaving no one unmoved. Even the experienced staff from Stewart's Funeral Home, accustomed to witnessing countless services, could not suppress their emotional response.

A lone figure, positioned to hear and observe without being noticed, also wiped tears from her emerald green eyes. While a part of her felt a pang of envy for Hope's place beside Justin, Twila was weighed down by a more acute sense of loss. Mrs. Thompson's passing extinguished any hope of the motherly relationship Twila had always secretly craved.

Reverend T. invited those who wished to share their memories of Lorraine. A representative from Lorraine's teaching colleagues spoke about her dedication to her students and her transformative impact on her fellow educators, demonstrating that a disciplined classroom could be a place of love, learning, and even joy.

A former student, now a local judge, validated the colleague's words, sharing how Lorraine's unwavering belief in her potential had pushed her to achieve greatness, instilling the belief that "ordinary" was simply unacceptable.

The third speaker approaching the microphone surprised Justin. It was Henry D. Roccia, or Hank.

"Over the past few years, I've been fortunate to converse with Mrs. Thompson," Hank began. "Each time, I felt like I gained some valuable insight. Her words were always filled with wisdom. She stopped by the shop a few weeks ago to see Justin, but he was at a job site. We talked about life. She said the worries of this world are temporary. I agree. Interestingly, she added that she wore this life like loose clothes. She took her responsibilities seriously, but not herself. She loved life, but she knew it wouldn't last forever. During that conversation, as in all others, Mrs. Thompson spoke of her joy in watching her son and grandson grow. She was incredibly proud of Justin, repeating that he was a good man. She thanked God for her husband and son. I thank God for her gift to the world, Justin."

Hank returned the microphone to Reverend T., then walked over to Justin and extended his hand. Without hesitation, Justin rose and embraced Hank, an uncharacteristic gesture.

Reverend T. closed with a brief eulogy. He reminded everyone that the book of Psalms says, "Life is but a vapor." We should not waste our time on Earth because we will not be here long. He said, "That is how Mrs. Thompson lived her life, and let that be the final lesson from a great teacher for all of us today."

Hope was always a good student. Today's lesson, on a life well lived, she took and hid it in her heart.

* * *

Aunt Maxine expressed her gratitude to the final visitors, a couple from the neighborhood who, like so many before them, had brought food. The kitchen and dining room tables were laden with a remarkable variety of dishes, a testament to the community's support. The fried chicken was the most popular, enough to make Colonel Sanders envious.

Deuce's eyes were bright and focused as he played on the tablet, the screen illuminating with each correct answer. Hope, seated beside him, provided gentle guidance. She had loaded the tablet with preschool educational applications earlier in the day. Deuce was mastering the games with ease, consistently achieving near-perfect scores. Hope recognized that she would need to seek out more advanced games to pique the intellectual curiosity of the remarkably bright four-year-old.

"You're doing great, Justin. You know your numbers

and your ABCs. That's very good," Hope said with a congratulatory smile.

"I know my ABCs two ways. I show you," Deuce announced and began reciting the alphabet song.

Hope smiled, intrigued by what he meant by "two ways." After finishing the traditional recitation, he started again, this time backward: "ZYXW...CBA." Hope's jaw dropped in genuine amazement. This was more than just a party trick; it was a testament to his Bibi's patience and dedication.

"My mom taught him that," Justin chimed in from the hallway entryway.

Hope was surprised to hear his voice, as he had been unusually quiet since their return from the funeral.

"She said the exercise would help keep his mind flexible. She was always in educator mode."

Hope, rubbing Deuce's head, said, "I see. Your Bibi taught you a lot. You are brilliant."

"That is what Bibi said," Deuce added and immediately returned to his exciting work on Hope's tablet.

Aunt Maxine returned from the front porch to the living room. "Justin, my favorite nephew, you know me and your Uncle Preston will be going back to Tyler in the morning. Are you sure you and Little Man are going to be all right?"

"We're going to have to be. I'll sign up for before and aftercare at the preschool until I can figure something else out. But you go on back to work. Don't worry about us."

"Now you know I'm going to worry. That's what Lorraine would want me to do, and that's what I will do. I would stay if I could, but I have work, and your uncle has his dialysis treatments."

"I'm going to help, too," Hope chimed in.

Both Justin and Aunt Maxine stopped and looked at the unexpected volunteer.

"Hope, that won't be necessary. I can—"

"Boy, hush!" Aunt Maxine said, abruptly interrupting him. "Don't be that way. I'll tell you. Black men always turn down help on the front end, and we sisters have to sneak and give you help on the back end. Just take the help. Please!"

"Yes, please," Hope said much more gently than Aunt Maxine's command.

Cornered between two strong women, Justin relented. "Okay, okay. We will accept any help you can provide, Ms. Hope. Now, are you two satisfied?"

Hope and Aunt Maxine looked at each other and nodded in unison.

Then Aunt Maxine told Hope, "If he gives you trouble, you call me. I will drive down here and smack him upside the head. Okay?"

"Okay," Hope replied.

"Now, I'm going to clean up the kitchen and try to put away some of this food," Aunt Maxine said and marched into the kitchen.

"Hope, I insist you sleep in my bed. I'll be fine out here on the couch. Any other arrangement will make Aunt Maxine ask questions that I have no energy to answer. I have fallen asleep on this couch more times than I can count."

Justin's request was sincere. Aunt Maxine was his favorite aunt, but she believed men should always act like gentlemen. No exceptions.

"It's kind of weird for me to sleep in your bed, in your

house, and you out here on the couch. But for tranquility's sake, I will do as requested. See you in the morning."

"Goodnight, and don't look under my bed," Justin said.

He had nothing to hide, but the thought of Hope resisting the urge to investigate brought a small, tired smile to his face.

Chapter 76
Pre-Arranged Funeral

*B*ig Justin and Deuce sat patiently at the kitchen table. Hope turned from the counter, placing breakfast plates in front of each of them.

"All right, so," she began, her shoulders tight with a mix of apology and pride, "I know it's not quite Mrs. Thompson's standard. The biscuits are from a can, the bacon was microwaved, and the eggs are a little overdone. But the grits turned out great. I just followed the recipe. I did my best, really."

Hope smiled. A touch of humility mingled with genuine pride in her first attempt at cooking for someone other than herself.

"It looks great," Justin piped in. "And I think you can see my little man's vote all over his face."

Deuce had a fist full of eggs in one hand and a piece of bacon in the other. The only thing slowing him down was his mouth filled with grits. The sight of Deuce enjoying his breakfast started a small joy machine inside Hope. Her smile grew larger when Big Justin tasted his breakfast, and like a ball rolling downhill, he ate faster and faster with each moment.

"Are you going to eat? Or are you returning to your bad habit of not eating breakfast?" Justin inquired of the chef.

"I'll have some bacon and a biscuit. Is that satisfactory, Mr. Thompson?"

"That is acceptable, Dr. Castillo," Justin formally stated.

Hope sat down at the table with her plate of bacon and a biscuit. Justin reached over to his son's plate and pretended to take a piece of bacon.

Deuce's hands covered the plate, and he commanded, "No, Daddy. No! You eat your bacon."

Justin rubbed his son's head, and they both laughed. Hope watched the interaction, feeling a deep sense of peace in the moment.

"Tell Ms. Hope thank you for breakfast," Big Justin directed his son.

"Thank you. Can I have some more after school?"

"Boy, you aren't even done with that plate yet and are working on your next meal. You act more like me every day," Big Justin added.

"And that's a good thing," Hope chimed in. "But tonight, before dinner, we must remember to say grace. Okay, my friend?"

Deuce nodded. Big Justin smiled as Hope taught Deuce a lesson that was reminiscent of his mother.

"So, I'll drop him off and pick him up from daycare," Justin said.

Hope's eyes widened, and she took a deep breath of dread.

"Don't worry if I run into Pastor Superstar," Justin continued. "That's a tiny issue—like a gnat—a very irritating but small gnat. Deuce has enough changes going on right now. I'm not going to have him change schools, too."

Hope exhaled with only partial relief, her shoulders relaxing but still not fully settled. The Caleb/Justin bridge would take time to build before it could be crossed.

"Okay. I have a few appointments today. Anna has Nelson. I have a couple of errands to run, but I should be here by the time you both get home tonight. Don't expect a banquet, but I'll have something for you boys to eat."

"Can you cook for four? Reverend T. is stopping by tonight. He plans to pitch for me to return to our Monday meetings," Justin said in a bit of code, not wanting his son asking questions about AA. "I'll say yes. Going back is the right thing to do. I want to go back."

Hope rose from her seat and kissed Justin on the forehead. "I'll buy pizza for four."

"After he leaves this evening, I'll sort through my mom's stuff. It shouldn't take too long. She started throwing out old clothes and boxing stuff for the Goodwill a few months ago. I tell you, for an unexpected stroke, she sure did prepare like she knew she was moving on from here."

Hope conceded, "As Mr. Stewart told us at his funeral home, sometimes people just know."

A flicker of a new idea sparked in her eyes, a chilling realization that settled into a quiet, unwavering resolve.

* * *

Mr. Stewart smiled, inviting Hope to sit at his office table. The room remained exactly as it had been in recent days.

"Good morning, Dr. Castillo. Good to see you again. How can we help you today?" Mr. Stewart said with a quiet, steady tone.

Hope leaned forward, her posture firm and professional, a stark contrast to her grief-stricken posture she had days before.

"I would like to review your funeral prearrangement packages."

"Sure. Preplanning is a brilliant idea. Is this for you or a loved one?"

"It's for me. Also, would it be possible for me to choose a package and pay for it today?"

"Of course, no problem. Let me show you what we have."

Chapter 77
Amira Rebellion

*H*ope sat at her office desk catching up on paperwork from the week. She finished drafting a counseling plan for Hannah's family. Alexander Domnhall's death was not a resolution but the beginning of a process. Significant trauma remained, requiring attention before genuine healing could occur.

She had rescheduled most of her appointments for the week, making time to support Justin and assist with Deuce at his house.

A gentle knock sounded at her door. With no appointments scheduled and April off for the afternoon, Hope was puzzled about who could be there.

"Come in," she called out.

The door opened, and a petite young face peeked inside.

"Hi, Hope."

"Amira, what are you doing here?" Hope asked, surprised.

Amira had never visited her office uninvited. Hope had taken her on a couple of tours, but those were the only times Amira had been there.

"Can we talk?" Amira inquired.

"Sure. Come in and sit down," Hope said, then, remembering Amira's age, added, "Do your parents know you're here?"

"No, and that's what I want to talk to you about," Amira stated, sitting down with a huff.

She crossed her arms and glared at Hope, a look of pure teenage fury radiating from her. Hope had never seen this side of her before. While they'd had some serious talks, this one would be different.

"Go ahead," Hope said.

"I hate my mom so much," Amira blurted out, her voice raw and filled with a bitterness that startled Hope.

"What makes you say that?" Hope asked, her professional calm beginning to slip.

"She grounded me," Amira ranted. "Can you believe that? Grounded me! No phone, no computer, no electronics for a month. I also have to come right home after school. No band or theater. I can't stand her."

"There must be a reason. Amira, what did you do?" Hope said, her tone firm, siding with parental control.

"Nothing. I mean, well. Okay. The school called my mom because I got caught kissing Jackson in the black box. The school has a no-kissing-or-holding-hands rule, so they called Mom. She freaked out and put me on punishment."

"Whoa, wait. Who's Jackson?" Big Sister Hope was realizing she was out of the loop.

"Oh. Jackson is this boy that I kinda like. We aren't doing anything—just kissing and sitting by each other in class. But Mom didn't believe that. She also thinks twelve is too young to have a boyfriend. I wish she would leave me alone," Amira said, slumping in the chair with her head down.

"She cares about you," Hope stated firmly. "You need to stop saying you hate her."

"But I do hate her," Amira said, her voice now filled with a deep sadness, the anger cracking to reveal the genuine pain beneath. "It's not just about Jackson. Why can't I have a mother who can hear me? Someone who understands my perspective, who can actually hear me sing? She always claps at the wrong times during my performances and makes these weird noises when she cheers. It's so embarrassing. I want to be a singer; she'll never truly hear me. I just want a normal mother like yours."

The thought of Gina as a typical mother would have made Hope laugh if this situation had not been so serious. Hope knew Amira had no idea how blessed she was to have such a wonderful parent as Esther.

Hope took a slow, deliberate breath, choosing her words carefully. "Amira, you know what greatness is?"

Amira stared at Hope, not responding.

"Greatness is when challenges arise; a person not only meets that challenge but also uses it for the greater good. Your mom was born without the ability to hear. You and I cannot imagine how difficult it is for her to be deaf in a hearing world. Yet, I have never seen her without a smile on her face. She works full-time, has a husband who is also hearing impaired, and is raising a strong-willed, smart young lady. Esther's only mistake might be that she has spoiled her daughter. Her daughter doesn't know a good thing when she sees it."

Hope paused, letting the silence fill the space and her words settle.

"But I just want to have a normal family," Amira weakly retorted.

Hope smiled. "Little girl, a family with challenges is normal. We can only hope and pray for the strength and love to overcome those challenges together. Your mother and father love you so much."

"I guess you're right," Amira conceded.

"There's no need to guess," Hope said. "I am right. We need to work through our challenges together as a family. You and I are family, too, so I hope you'll let me help."

"I will," Amira replied. "You know, you're pretty good at this advice thing."

"I better be. It's how I pay the bills," Hope replied. She then continued, "Okay, two things. First, text your mom to let her know you're here and you're sorry. Second, you need to tell me about Jackson. Tell me all about him. Then we'll talk about this 'kissing and touching' business. And while we're at it, we will also talk about the appropriate way to and not to hug a grown man."

Amira nodded in compliance, even though she didn't know the discussion would be about her jumping into Reverend Caleb's arms for a hug.

Hope watched as Amira and Esther exchanged texts. She was always in awe of Esther, Hector, and Amira's nuclear family, and of something she felt was only a dream for her. Hope's professional advice had helped Amira, but in a way, Amira's simple, loving family had healed a part of Hope, too. She smiled, a deep sense of gratitude settling over her. This moment was a gift.

Chapter 78
A Race Against Time

*J*ustin and Hank said little to each other. Hank worked on yet another rebuild of an old motor, while Justin sat at his desk, trying to figure out the next steps for his business.

Justin's phone lit up, indicating an incoming call.

"Hey, B. What's up?" Justin asked his old friend Brandon.

"Hey, man. A couple of things. First, you've always known how to pick 'em. Now that Hope is fine—I mean, finaaaah. You know what I'm saying. And she got just the right amount of junk in the trunk that makes a brotha wanna holla! If she weren't with you at the funeral, I would've made a move on her."

Justin chuckled. Amid trying times, a friend you have known your entire life can make you smile.

"Dude, you stupid. Is that really why you called, to tell me my woman is fine? Tell me something I don't know."

"Okay, I'll tell you something you don't know. You need to come down to my office and complete some paperwork."

Justin's tone shifted. "Why? You're gonna foreclose on me today?"

Upbeat, Brandon, replied, "Not at all, my friend. Quite the opposite. I'm sitting here looking at a certified check for twenty-five thousand dollars made out to the order of Justin Thompson and Springfield National Bank."

"What? What are you talking about? Are you high?" Justin asked in a half-serious manner.

"Funny. Real funny. You know I don't do that anymore. Seriously. I have a check here. A fine young lady with dimples came in this morning and wrote a check for twenty-five thousand dollars to pay off your balloon payment. And because I'm such a great mortgage broker, I set the terms so that your next mortgage payment won't be for ninety-five days. Now, who's da man?" Brandon exclaimed with particular joy.

"But how? But..." Justin fumbled, completely at a loss for words.

"Well, Hope and I had a long conversation at the repast after the funeral. I probably said a little too much after she found out I wasn't just your friend but your banker. Hope called me yesterday, and she just left. By the way, she was wearing these jeans. Nice! I could watch her leave all day."

"Okay, enough with the Hope lust. I cannot believe this." Justin shook his head in disbelief.

"All right. You need to come down and sign the check. You also need to bring a copy of your mom's death certificate for the file."

"Okay, I'll get back to you. Peace," Justin said, putting the phone down.

He sat back in his chair in total disbelief, his mind replaying every word.

Having heard only one side of the conversation, Hank asked, "Hey, Justin, what's going on?"

Still shaking his head, Justin replied, "It's Hope. She just gave me a check to pay for my house balloon payment."

"Praise God. That's great!"

"Yes, but I can't accept any money I don't deserve," Justin answered back.

Hank's demeanor changed. His words began to channel Justin's mother, Lorraine.

"Justin, do you have enough money to pay the mortgage this month?"

"No, but—"

Hank interrupted, "What happens if you don't pay the mortgage?"

"The bank forecloses on the house."

"Then what happens?"

"Deuce and I will live with my aunt or in my truck."

"Is that what you want?"

"Of course not, but—"

"You know what you need to do. The only thing keeping you from being homeless is your pride. Don't let your pride be why your son has to leave his home."

Justin looked at Hank. Yes, it was his pride—the little pride he had left after it seemed that life was doing all it could to chip it away.

"I know you always think God is punishing you for things you've done. But when God sends you a life preserver, you'd rather drown than use it. God will send you provisions from friends and enemies in times of need. It is not a coincidence that you and Hope are together now. Helping you now is part of the reason she's in your life, and there's a reason you are in hers. Don't push the check—or Hope—away from you. In fact, you need to run to both before either is no longer there for you."

Hank's words struck a chord within Justin. He recognized the truth in them. Hank was right. He had been so blind.

Justin grabbed his tool bag, but then stopped, turning on his heel. He didn't just want to save his house—he wanted his future. He wanted Hope.

* * *

Justin's heart pounded in his chest. The loud beats drowned out the music on the truck's Dolby stereo.

He stopped at his house after signing Hope's check at Springfield National Bank. Aunt Maxine, who had returned to help over the weekend, was watching Deuce. He wanted her opinion on his plan. He intended to propose to Hope and give her Lorraine's wedding ring. Aunt Maxine's reaction was one of pure joy. She cheered as if witnessing a game-winning shot in a championship game.

"Lorraine would be honored to have Hope wear her ring," she said. "It meant so much to her. It was her most prized possession, cherished from the moment your dad gave it to her."

He approached Hope's condo, his heart filled with anticipation for the proposal. His mother's wedding ring, encased in a small jewelry box, rested securely in his front pocket. He maintained a firm grip through his pants, ensuring its safety. He parked the truck and paused, taking slow, deliberate breaths to compose himself. A wave of warmth washed over him as he thought of Chaka, feeling her loving approval. With a gentle and thoughtful gesture, Justin removed his own wedding ring and placed it carefully in the glove compartment.

He mentally rehearsed the proposal. He knew he'd kneel. He pictured Hope's joyous tears as she accepted. He'd explain the ring's significance, then place it on her finger. She'd cry, and he'd gently wipe her tears, promising, I hope never to make you cry again. It would be the perfect moment.

Justin leaped from his car and hurried into Hope's building. He bounded up the stairs, skipping steps in his eagerness. He paused at her door, a wide grin on his face, knowing that with a single knock, their lives—his, Deuce's, and Hope's—would be forever changed.

Justin knocked, but there was no reply. He knocked again, harder, and still got no response. A strange quiet settled over the hall. Looking out the window, Justin saw Hope's SUV parked below. He dialed Hope's number, hearing her phone ring inside. Fear tightened its hold.

He began banging on the door, shouting, "Hope, are you in there? It's Justin!"

Just as Justin was about to knock again, Anna and Nelson appeared in the hallway. Nelson immediately rushed past Justin and began barking wildly at the door, his barks escalating into frantic howls.

"Hey, what's going on?" Anna shouted over the dog's deafening barks.

"Hope isn't answering, and I'm pretty sure she's inside," Justin explained.

Anna acted immediately, using her spare key to gain entry. As the door opened slightly, Nelson, driven by instinct, surged through and sprinted toward Hope's bedroom.

Anna and Justin followed with haste.

"Oh, God!" Anna exclaimed, her hands covering her face.

Justin stood in stunned silence, a wave of distressing déjà vu engulfing him. He was confronted with an identical scene to the one he had witnessed only a short time ago, but the agonizing difference was that it was Hope lying motionless on the floor, not his mother.

Chapter 79
The Diagnosis

*J*ustin stood at the window with his gaze fixed on the clouds rambling across the blue canvas. The sight of them soothed his troubled mind. He envied the clouds. While they experienced no love, the clouds also experienced no guilt, worry, or loss of loved ones. The clouds could remain above Earth, far from street-level crime and heartache.

Is it better to have loved and lost than never to have loved at all? Justin thought about one of the few quotes from his high school English class that, inexplicably, had stayed with him all these years. He wished the author had answered that question.

Anna sat in a chair behind Justin, her legs crossed and her elbow resting on the chair's arm. Her head lay in her hand. She kept her eyes closed, praying this was all a nightmare. She prayed that she would open her eyes and see Hope miraculously walk through the door. However, unlike her mother, Anna did not believe in miracles. She hoped her mother was right about the supernatural power of God—that somehow, God would intervene on Hope's behalf.

The door opened, and for a micro-moment, Anna thought miracles could happen. But Hope did not walk through the door. It was Dr. Bamenda, returning to his office.

"Hi. Please have a seat," Dr. Bamenda said, addressing Justin.

Justin sat in the armchair next to Anna, while Dr. Bamenda took his seat behind his office desk. The doctor's office walls displayed degrees in Chemistry and Medicine from Nigerian and Ivy League colleges.

"First, I concur with the diagnosis the emergency room doctor provided you last night. Hope suffered acute kidney failure, which led to her grand mal seizure."

Dr. Bamenda paused and looked down at his charts again. Anna's and Justin's eyes never left Dr. Bamenda as they waited to hear the whole story.

"I'm not exactly sure what caused the kidney failure. I hypothesize that it was the new medication we prescribed Hope. We changed medication after her last seizure, and the new meds must have caused this adverse reaction. Sometimes it takes a few weeks for side effects to manifest. Unfortunately, we didn't see this coming sooner."

The reason for Hope's seizure generated anger inside Anna, who trusted doctors to do no harm. She took a slow, deep breath, her hands clenching into fists. She kept her composure, but the question she wanted to ask, the accusation she wanted to make, was a hot coal in her throat.

Justin, on the other hand, always expected terrible news in hospitals. From the moment he saw Hope lying on her floor unconscious, he assumed the worst. His shoulders were tense, and his breathing was shallow, a conscious effort to maintain his composure. The doctor's words confirmed his deepest fears, and he was prepared for the blow.

"How is she? What happens now?" Justin asked.

"She's still unconscious but resting comfortably. I expect her to sleep most, if not all, of today. But we are going to have to discuss long-term care."

"Long-term care?" Anna interjected.

"Yes. Hope's kidneys will never work again. She will require dialysis for the rest of her life," Dr. Bamenda informed them.

Dr. Bamenda, known for his gentle approach and clear communication, struggled to deliver the news. The words felt too heavy to say.

"There's more," he finally said. "Hope's lupus, combined with the strain of dialysis, will significantly shorten her life expectancy. I can't say by how much."

Anna, usually a pillar of strength in times of crisis, felt her resolve crumble under the weight of the news about Hope. She bowed her head, hugging herself tightly as if trying to hold herself together. Her skin grew cold, and tears streamed down her face, pooling on her cheeks.

In stark contrast, the doctor's diagnosis ignited a fire in Justin. The news solidified his determination. Dr. Bamenda's answers were unacceptable. Justin was determined to find another solution for Hope.

He leaned forward, his eyes burning with a sudden, fierce resolve. "Come on, Doc. There has to be another option," Justin demanded.

"We could try a kidney transplant. We would need to find a compatible donor."

A flicker of light appeared in Justin's eyes. "Okay, let's do that," Justin said.

"Well, immediate family is the best place to start. Can the two of you reach out to her mother and father? Also, I believe she has a sister," Dr. Bamenda stated.

Anna wiped her tears and looked at Justin. Just as quickly as the tears had formed, her eyes turned off the faucet, and she shifted into action mode.

"We can contact them. I'll call them right now."

"Great. Have them come in, and we can test for compatibility today," Dr. Bamenda told them. "If we take the tests today, we should have results back tomorrow. The sooner we move forward, the better."

Justin and Anna had their marching orders. Each was determined to do whatever it took to help Hope.

Chapter 80
The Offer and the Lie

"Ms. Georgina, I have good news," Dr. Bamenda said as he entered his office.

Gina was sitting patiently, waiting for the kidney compatibility results. Her eyes lit up as the doctor took a seat behind his desk.

"What is it, Doctor? I knew a man of your obvious talents would figure something out," Gina responded with a playful girlish voice.

"Well, actually, I have two pieces of good news. First, your kidney is compatible with Hope. On almost every key indicator, you're exact matches. It's almost like you made Hope out of your DNA alone." Dr. Bamenda smiled.

Gina turned her 75-watt smile up to a full 100 watts. "That's wonderful."

"You are a much closer match than even her sister Rachel. I guess it's for the best anyway. We wouldn't have attempted a transplant now because of Rachel's high-risk pregnancy."

"No, we wouldn't risk any harm to the baby. It's too bad her dad is visiting his family in South America. He won't be back for days to even get tested. By the way, what's the second piece of good news?"

"Sorry, Ms. Georgina, I almost forgot. Hope is waking up. You can go and see her now."

Gina maintained her smile. "Thank you, Doctor. While I could stay here and talk to you all day and night, I would like to see my daughter now and discuss the next steps."

Dr. Bamenda stood and escorted Gina to the door. "Of course. I'll be down to check on Hope later this afternoon.

Gina turned and softly placed her hand on his cheek. "Thank you again, Doctor. You are a Godsend."

She walked away, knowing the doctor couldn't help but watch her curvy form as she strolled down the hallway.

* * *

Gina slipped into Hope's room, silent as a cat. She stood over her daughter, watching her semi-conscious state. An IV dripped into Hope's arm, and oxygen flowed through a tube in her nose. Her lips were cracked and dry. Seeing her helpless daughter stirred something deep within Gina.

She set her bag down and, reaching inside, retrieved a tube of lip balm. Gently, Gina began applying the balm to Hope's lower lip. Hope involuntarily smiled and opened her eyes. But when she realized it was Gina, her eyes widened in shock, and she jerked her head away.

Hope raised her hand and wiped her lip. "What? Are you trying to poison me? Are the pillows in here not strong enough to smother me?"

Gina gritted her teeth and nodded her head. "I deserved that. I deserved that."

"Why are you here? Where's the nurse?"

Hope started searching for the call button, feeling vulnerable as she lay there. She was weak and had tubes running into and out of several parts of her body. At her full strength, Hope would lose a fight against Gina, so she knew she would definitely lose in her current state.

"Wow, I guess I am that bad of a mother. I come here to get tested to see if I can give you my kidney, and all you can think about is that I'm here to hurt you." Gina took a step back and lowered her head.

Hope stopped looking for the call button as she tried to decipher what Gina had just said.

"You came here to do what?"

"I came because you need a new kidney. You suffered acute kidney failure, and your kidneys will never work again."

"Where is Dr. Bamenda? Where is…?"

Through the fog of sickness and medications, Hope struggled to remember her loved ones' names.

"Anna, Rachel, and that boyfriend of yours are down the hall in the waiting area. After you and I discuss the kidney surgery, I'll get them," Gina said softly, her tone a calculated performance of a motherly tenderness.

Hope looked around the room, and the pieces of her current situation started to fit together. The fog was lifting, and Gina's offer to give Hope a kidney finally became a reality.

"You would give me a kidney?" Hope asked with a dry throat.

"Hope, I haven't been a good mother. In fact, I've

been a terrible mother, especially to you. I have made some poor decisions. But I'm not going to ask for forgiveness. The mistakes I've made are my mistakes. I've done what I had to do to survive. All things considered, you and Rachel have had it simple. I have fought and scratched for everything that I have in my life. Growing up in foster care was no picnic." Gina paused and turned away from Hope. "While I've done some degrading and humiliating things, I know I am not all bad. Look at you and Rachel. You two would not be who you are if I were all bad."

Hope had never seen her mother show an ounce of self-doubt or contrition. Could there be redemption even for a person like Gina?

"Mom, I don't know what to say," Hope admitted.

Gina was now at the side of Hope's bed, her hands gripping the safety railing.

"I know what you should say. It's what I want you to ask. Dr. Bamenda told me that my kidney is a perfect match for you. Please just ask me for my kidney. If not for you, do it for me. Please ask," Gina pleaded.

As much as Hope despised Gina, the little girl inside her always wanted to be loved by her mother. She was a little girl who pushed for straight A's throughout high school and eventually graduated summa cum laude from college to earn her mother's approval. The mother who always withheld her love was about to save that little girl's life.

Hope laid her hand on top of one of Gina's hands on the bed railing.

"Mom..."

Hope paused. Emotion swelled in her throat. She had

no energy to cry, but her entire body vibrated with sentimental electricity.

"Mom, can you help me live a normal life? Can you give me one of your kidneys?"

Gina placed her other hand on top of Hope's. Her smile was not warm, but predatory, and her eyes held a cold, unwavering gleam.

"No, you stupid bitch. I would rather die than help you."

Shock enveloped Hope's body. A severe pain seized her heart. Gina now had Hope's hand crushed between her two hands as she quietly cackled.

"I can't believe you were stupid enough even to ask me that. But thanks for asking. Being able to tell you 'no' is the highlight of my year. It's the only reason I came down here to be tested in this smelly shithole of a hospital. I hoped we would be compatible. I wanted to rip any possibility of happiness away from you personally. Whoa, this feels so, so good. Thank you, little girl," Gina said, tossing Hope's now throbbing hand back to her daughter.

Hope was speechless.

"Oh, and by the way, Craig is out of town. It wouldn't matter anyway. His blood type is A positive. You and I are B positive. So, there's little chance he's compatible. And Rachel is too much like her daddy, John. Her kidney won't work for you either. You are so screwed. Ha!"

Gina paraded around the room as if she had won a prize fight.

"Mom, I forgive you," Hope stated flatly.

"What? Come again," a confused Gina responded, stopping in her tracks.

"I said I forgive you," Hope repeated.

"Really? You little soft trick. You forgive me for being mean to you today. You are so sweet," Gina mockingly stated.

"No, not just for today, but for everything. I forgive you for how you have treated me my entire life. I cannot and will no longer carry the burden of hating you. Whatever little time I have left, I will live it free of hate. The hate I held onto will no longer have a hold on me. I choose to live free."

"You weak little piece of shit. Please die soon. Please," Gina snorted and waited to see the pain on Hope's face.

"Nice try, Mom. Your words no longer affect me. You might as well leave and find someone else to torture. You can no longer hurt me."

Hope leaned over, found the nurse's call button on the side of the bed, and pressed it.

Feeling stripped of her power, Gina glanced at Hope one final time, tossed her purse over her shoulder, and walked briskly towards the door. As she exited, she collided with the nurse entering the room. The nurse, holding her shoulder, was taken aback by the rudeness of someone who bumped into her and didn't even turn to apologize.

* * *

Just as Gina approached the waiting area at the end of the hospital hallway, Anna, Rachel, and Justin rushed toward her.

"Dr. Bamenda told us the great news that your kidney is compatible," Rachel began. "He said they could have you both prepped and in surgery first thing in the morning."

Gina stopped and glared at her daughter. "Listen. I am going to give that person nothing. You hear me. Nothing!"

Rachel was surprised, but Gina could no longer shock her. Rachel had held out hope that her mother had a shred of decency, but she now knew that shred did not exist.

Anna growled and bared her teeth. "You are a horrible person."

Gina turned and balled her fists as if to strike Anna, but after watching Hope's friend transform into a protective werewolf, she paused.

"Please hit me," Anna taunted. "Go ahead. If you do, you will not leave this hospital for a long time." Anna's movements were those of a jungle cat.

Justin stepped between them and turned to Gina. "Please, Mrs. Castillo. Hope needs you. This is a matter of life or death."

Gina scowled at Justin and considered not responding. Then, Gina simply said, "I guess it's death then."

Justin's lower jaw dropped at hearing a mother sign her own daughter's death warrant. Gina turned and momentarily glanced at Rachel. She then walked away with her head up and a smile on her face.

Justin, Anna, and Rachel stood mute and motionless in a circle. Anna and Rachel then turned toward Hope's room and started down the hallway. Justin turned towards the stairwell and headed to Dr. Bamenda's office.

Chapter 81
What Is Mine Is Yours

"Baby, I can't let you do that for me. Thank you, but no." Hope's mind was racing, a whirlwind of calculations. "The recovery time for a kidney donor is six to twelve weeks. You'll lose your repair business during that time. You've worked so hard for that. I can't ask you to give up your dream."

"You are my dream," Justin's deep voice resonated, captivating Hope.

Anna and Rachel felt a shiver of warmth, the power of his words raising goosebumps on their skin.

"Listen," Justin continued. "There's a good chance I was going to lose the business anyway. But thanks to you, I won't be in fear of losing the house for another three months. That gives me time to find some other job. I can drive for Uber or dig a ditch. But whatever happens, I want you there by my side. I want to face life's challenges with you and no one else."

Hope couldn't help but notice that Justin's eyes sparkled more than usual. It was as if his eyes were putting on a small laser light show.

"You know, if I had fifty thousand more, I would give it to you," Hope explained.

"I know, but let's not talk about that now. Let's focus on the fact that I love you and want to give you life. Please, Hope. Don't make a brotha' beg, but I will if I have to. I love you so much it hurts."

Hope squeezed Justin's hand.

"I love you, too," she said.

It was the first time she'd said those words to a man since her breakup with Caleb.

"I love you so much that I've been scared to say it," she admitted. "I've been scared that if I let myself love you, the world would see it and might snatch you away from me like a thief in the night."

Anna and Rachel exchanged a knowing glance, silently agreeing it was time to leave. They quietly exited the room.

"You will never lose me because I'll be there wherever you are. My job is to care for and protect you. I'll never hurt you." Justin's words were like song lyrics.

"Justin, you don't have to do this. I can go on the waitlist." Hope wanted to give Justin every opportunity to change his mind.

"Hope, sweetheart, we don't have time to waste on any waitlist."

He looked down at her, his expression serious but full of quiet certainty. He remembered the night she found him drunk, drowning in his despair. She hadn't judged him or tried to fix him. She had simply been there—a silent, steady presence that pulled him back from the brink. It was the most intimate gift he had ever received, a demonstration of selfless love. Now, he saw his chance to return that gift, to give her life, to give her a future.

"Justin, I love you, and yes, let's go through with the surgery tomorrow." Hope smiled.

Justin leaned down and kissed Hope's forehead, then her cheek. Hope reached up, cupping his cheek, and drew him closer. Their lips met in a series of trembling kisses. As they kissed, they felt a connection transcending physical intimacy, a bond too deep for words.

Chapter 82
The Hospital Chapel

For the past four hours, Rachel, Caleb, and Big Preach had occupied the hospital chapel. Earlier, a woman entered, lit a candle, prayed for fifteen minutes, and then left. The chapel, typical of a Catholic hospital, had wooden pews, crucifixes, a Madonna, and portraits of saints. The air was still and heavy, weighed down by unspoken sins.

Big Preach sat near the back on one of the four benches. He was absorbed in reading his Bible, which displayed Greek scripture alongside its English translation. He also jotted notes on a legal pad, seemingly preparing for a future sermon. He and Rachel had previously decided to postpone their discussion about their relationship.

Rachel and Caleb sat silently on the front pew, their minds consumed by Hope and Justin's surgery. They were also burdened by the weight of the pain they had caused Hope over the years.

"I feel helpless. I wish there were something we could do for Hope," Caleb whispered to Rachel.

"You must've read my mind. And I do believe there

is something we can do for Hope. Let's discuss it when we get home," Rachel quietly replied.

"'There has never been a night so dark that there was not a sunrise hitched to it.' That's one of my favorite Gardner C. Taylor quotes," Big Preach interjected from the back pew. "Hope's life seems to be one situation after another, and it always worsens. I have to believe God has a sunrise for her someday. But alas, maybe not in this world."

Rachel and Caleb both prayed silently that they would get an opportunity to make things right with Hope on this side of Heaven.

Unexpectedly, Twila Gooden, dressed in hospital surgical scrubs, stepped into the chapel. Her scrubs were a stark, bright green against the somber tones of the room. Rachel's eyes squinted to a steely stare. Both Big Preach and Caleb rose to their feet. Twila's eyes were puffy and red, as if she had been crying.

"Pastor, Pastor, and Rachel. The surgery ran long because there were complications," she reported.

Rachel's stare morphed into one of concern. "Is it serious?"

Twila lowered her head and replied, "Yes. Very serious."

A single tear slipped down her cheek as she spoke, a silent confirmation of the tragedy.

Chapter 83
Sunrise

ope's gaze was fixed on the still form of Justin, lying motionless on the hospital bed. Her heart and mind struggled to grasp the magnitude of his sacrifice. The kidney donation procedure—meant to be a simple, routine operation—had transformed into a harrowing ordeal for the man she loved. Shortly after the kidney was removed, Justin's vital signs dropped dangerously low. He had suffered severe oxygen deprivation due to a life-threatening allergic reaction to the anesthesia, which caused his throat to constrict and block his airway. Hope shuddered at the visceral image of Justin gasping and choking, his body seemingly turning against him. Justin endured so much suffering for her sake. She felt deeply unworthy of such an extreme act of love.

Hope's mind was filled with thoughts of Deuce. He was so cute and clever. Hope became angry at Big Justin for taking such a risk when he should have considered his son. Hope wanted to be part of Deuce's life more than ever. She wanted to raise him as her son, help him grow up and be a good, strong man like his father and his father's father before him.

Hope wanted to yell at Justin, *You should not love me! I'm not worth such a sacrifice!* But it was too late now. The deed had been done, and everyone would have to live with the consequences.

Hope learned of the heroics of Dr. Bamenda, who personally assisted Dr. Daniels, the transplant specialist, who had performed in the operating room. The doctor did all that he could to save Justin. Now Justin lay there motionless, and Hope could do nothing but pray.

"Please help Justin," she cried out to God. "Please have him wake up and be okay. Please, God. I beg you."

The rhythmic beeping of Justin's heart monitor provided Hope with some comfort as she sat by his bedside. The sun peeked through the window, casting light into the room. The white curtains, recently drawn around the bed, were pushed aside, opening the space to the outside world.

Justin's slight squeeze of Hope's hand was the precursor to his eyes opening. His gaze fell on Hope's face framed by the glory of the sunlight.

Laying her second hand on their two hands already connected, Hope stated, "Hi there, you."

The heart monitor's beeping picked up to a slow jog.

"Hi," Justin croaked out, pushing the words through his dry throat.

Hope settled back into her wheelchair, which Justin now noticed. She placed a hand on her side, where the stitches from her surgery were, and her eyes filled with tears.

"You nearly died on the operating table," she said

softly. "I never thought anyone would make such a selfless sacrifice for me... to donate a kidney... to put their own life on the line." Her words faded, choked with emotion. "I just want to... I need to say thank you."

Justin smiled, feeling as happy as the day Deuce was born. "There's no need to thank me. It's the least I can do for someone I love as much as you."

The water that had been filling Hope's eyes began to spill over. Justin's emotions took over, and waterworks also began to flow from his eyes.

Justin pointed to the nightstand next to the bed and asked, "Can you get that box out of the drawer for me?"

Hope, uncertain why Justin made the request, reached into the drawer. She pulled out a small box and handed it to him.

"I don't want to waste another second, and tomorrow is not promised to any man or woman."

Justin's voice was still dry and weak, but he was determined to say what he must. He opened the box, revealing Lorraine's diamond wedding ring inside.

"Sorry I can't get on one knee and do this right."

Hope stared at the sparkles in the ring and how they matched Justin's eyes. Her body trembled in anticipation of his next words.

"Dr. Hope Camille Castillo, will you do me the honor of being my wife?"

Once again, Hope placed a trembling hand on her side near the incision site. "I am flesh of your flesh. I want nothing more than to be your wife and Deuce's mother."

Justin placed the ring on Hope's finger.

As the tears continued to flow down her face, Hope said, "I wish I could jump into your arms."

"I wish you could, too, but we'll have a lifetime to be in each other's arms."

"I love the sound of that."

Hope rose slowly to her feet and lay next to her future husband. Side by side, they watched the dawn through the window together. The sun's rays illuminated the room. Justin had found Hope, and for the first time, Hope cherished the beauty of the sunrise.

Epilogue

Akil and CJ exited the service entrance of the Sea of Galilee Church. Both carried toolboxes and were surprised to see Hank, who had just pulled up in a new pickup truck with a fresh 'Justin's Warranty and Repair' logo on the side. Hank jumped out of the truck and met his colleagues at the curb.

"Justin told me you guys might need some help. He was worried the HVAC wouldn't be running in time to cool down the sanctuary before tonight's revival."

"We took care of it. No problem," Akil said with a confident smile. "Ever since we got the warranty contract for the church, Justin wants to handle every issue here with kid gloves. But we got it covered."

"I ain't complaining. This contract and Justin raising his rates about six months ago opened the door for him to rehire me. I'm glad to be back in the warranty repair game," CJ said with pride.

"Yeah, and Justin gave me a raise. I almost make as much per hour as you two old men," Akil said with a laugh. "And raising twins isn't cheap. We're spending a fortune on diapers and formula."

Hank moved into mentor mode as usual. "Akil, you keep grinding. God will make a way somehow. Look at Justin. Less than a month after his mother passed and that kidney transplant, a money order for seventy-five thousand dollars made out to Justin showed up at the shop. That money was a lifeline for Justin and us."

CJ shook his head. "That's still hard to believe, and you're telling me no one knows where the money came from or who gave it?"

"Nope. From what I know of Justin, that's a good thing. He probably would have given the money back if he'd known who gave it to him. On the other hand, I take money from whoever wants to give it to me. Hank, you wanna donate to my twin's college fund?" Akil replied.

"No, not today. But you never know what may come your way. Remember, God is good all the time," Hank said.

"And all the time, God is good. You never know when He will move or who He may use to fulfill his purposes," added Reverend Caleb Moore to the guys.

He had listened to the end of the conversation as he walked to his car. Caleb couldn't help but smile, thinking about what God could do through some less-than-perfect people like himself.

The End

www.ingramcontent.com/pod-product-compliance
Lightning Source LLC
Chambersburg PA
CBHW071725150726
47998CB00005B/1514